Joyce Mandeville was born in California and now lives in Sussex.

Praise for *Careful Mistakes*

'A witty and satisfying debut novel' – *Home & Country*

Praise for *A Twist of Light*

'This fascinating, subtle novel is informed throughout by a gritty, black humour' – *Woman & Home*

'Superb, beautifully written . . . Read it. You will never forget it' – *Sussex Express*

'Sensitively done' – *The Times*

GLORY
DAYS

Joyce Mandeville

WARNER BOOKS

A *Warner* Book

First published in Great Britain in 1999
by Warner Books

Copyright © Joyce Mandeville 1999

A CIP catalogue record for this book is
available from the British Library.

ISBN 0 7515 2244 9

Typeset in Bembo by M Rules
Printed and bound in Great Britain by
Clays Ltd, St Ives plc

Warner Books
A Division of
Little, Brown and Company (UK)
Brettenham House
Lancaster Place
London WC2E 7EN

For my husband John, who has always shown an amazing capacity to believe in me

With special thanks to the following:

To my daughter, Amy Mandeville, for reminding me to look in my old files. I'd like to also thank her for her gathering of Marion lore.

To my son, Benjamin-John Mandeville, for sharing his slightly bizarre insights.

To my agent, Sarah Molloy, who has cheerfully led me through the minefields of publishing for the last two years.

To my editor, Imogen Taylor, whose help has been invaluable for my first three books.

To Jill Foulston, who did a fine job of editing whilst filling in for Rebecca Kerby, who was busy birthing Miss Alice Kerby.

CHAPTER ONE

Slipping behind the kitchen door, she hoped Mama wouldn't notice her. It wasn't as much fun if they knew you were watching.

Glory knew that whenever Mama got real wound up, like she was right now, she started noticing everything. Sometimes she was as lazy as a big cat, but when she was mad she seemed to develop super-senses like some kind of character in those comic books that Pammy's brother Little Beau was always reading. If she was wound up she could practically see through walls and hear dust swirling up the stairs when things weren't going the way she thought they should. The sensible thing would be to slip out to the yard and wait until this blew over, but Glory wanted to hear what Mama had to say this time.

Not only did Mama have extra powers when she was mad, but she would say things a child from a nice home didn't normally get a chance to hear. She would say words that normally required mouth-cleaning with half a bar of Ivory soap and five minutes of extra prayers, at least in most families.

When Glory told her best friend, Pammy Reynolds, some of the words her mama said, Pammy said it was impossible for a grown woman to say those things. Pammy said they just wouldn't fit in a woman's mouth. She said her tongue would get stuck trying to shove those words out. Glory told her she was nothing but a pile of old cat shit and Pammy stayed away for the whole of the next day. Glory had been especially pleased with her ability to upset Miss Pammy 'I wear Mary Jane shoes and take tap lessons' Reynolds, but she'd been even happier when Pammy came back to hear more about what her mama would say.

She watched as her mama's nostrils flared and it reminded her of the times she'd seen her look around the room and start throwing things just because they seemed to be irritating her. She would shove at the furniture, kick the rugs, and once she even threw one of Aunt Flo's little ceramic shepherdesses with the real lace skirts right through the picture window that Uncle Hoyt had worked overtime to pay for.

Aunt Flo had cried like a big blond baby that time and run out to the yard in her nightgown looking for the pieces of her shepherdess. It took about twenty seconds for half the kids in the neighborhood to be out there watching her. She would lean over to pick up some little bit of face or a tiny hand and one of those big things would pop right out like a giant water balloon. She'd shove it back in her nightdress, but the next time she leaned over with a grunt the other one would pop out like it wanted to have a look around like its partner had done.

All that boobie-popping upset Aunt Flo even more until she started yelling almost as loud as Glory's mama. The louder she yelled and cried the more things started jiggling and jumping until Aunt Flo looked like a hundred cats were fighting underneath her thin cotton nightie. The neighborhood kids watched in complete silence, their curiosity about what the woman had moving under her clothes finally satisfied as the cotton clung to her and hiked itself up around her waist. Vast expanses of white, pink, and bluish flesh vibrated in the morning light, smacking against the air with little clapping sounds. Mama had always said the woman would keep moving five minutes after she was dead and Glory now knew that this was probably true.

Many of Aunt Flo's parts did seem to have a mind of their own. She was always slamming her behind into the doorways and then looking surprised like she hadn't known that big thing was following her around. Aunt Flo said she had a glandular condition which was related to her not being able to have children. Her mama said the only glandular problem her sister-in-law had was an inability to stop shoving food into that surprisingly small mouth of hers. She also said her brother probably couldn't figure out where to stick his thing, what with Aunt Flo having so many ripples and creases. This always made Glory laugh, even if she didn't have any idea what kind of thing Uncle Hoyt would want to stick into his three-hundred-and-sixty-pound bride. Whatever the thing was, it had something to do with why Aunt Flo collected ceramics and didn't have kids like the other women.

Not that her mama was a small woman by anybody's reckoning. Mama was so well formed and solid she almost looked like she had sprouted out of the ground itself. She wore her heavy muscles and bone the way some women wear beautiful clothes. She wrapped herself proudly in her thick flesh and stroked herself while others admired her fine-textured skin. Almost without pores, it would gleam and her mama would smile, knowing the picture she presented to the world. She kept her light brown hair combed to the back of her handsome head where she would twist it into a thick braid. She'd tie up the end of the braid with any old piece of string she could find, making it seem like she didn't know she had the most wonderful hair in the world.

Her hair only seemed to be brown, but up close it was as bright with colors as a grain of sand held up to the noonday sun. In its braid it would twist and turn, showing about a hundred different shades from snowy ash to chestnut brown, all stirred up with reflections of red, blue, and every other color. Mixed all up, it almost matched the color of her skin.

Glory knew that Mama's skin was that rich color all over. Proud of her body, she would climb naked out of her bed or bath and walk into the kitchen where Aunt Flo would have to look at all that richly colored flesh and compare it to her own marbled lumpishness. Sometimes she'd pretend to flick a bit of lint off her fine skin and smile while she watched Flo reach for the cookie tin or the jam jar with a trembling frown on her tiny mouth.

Glory had thought that nobody in the whole world could look like her mama until she saw the pictures of Teacher's summer vacation. There was a park somewhere in Norway, or Sweden, or maybe even Holland that was filled with statues that looked like Mama. Big beautiful statues of women with broad faces and wide hips who swung stone children in the air and curled themselves around stone men who looked almost alive with love for those statues. Stone men made alive by wrapping themselves around all that solid beauty. In Teacher's pictures they were only statues, but Glory had seen real men look like that, plenty of times.

Walk down the street with her and you'd see men look just like that. They'd tip their hats and say, 'Morning, Miss Eva, Glory', and then they'd walk right past. They'd walk right past, but Glory knew they'd turn around and watch her mama walk away. They'd smile goofy smiles and sometimes they'd shake their heads, but they always watched.

Sometimes the men would touch her mama too, but she wasn't supposed to have seen that. Late at night she'd hear things coming from her mama's room, but she knew that she had to go to sleep and forget those sounds by the morning. The sounds were always gone by then, but on those mornings Uncle Hoyt was usually really mad. Not that Mama cared. She'd drink her coffee and look at her brother over the top of her souvenir mug from Mount Rushmore.

This was going to be one of those mornings. Glory knew it even last night before she heard the man-sounds coming from behind Mama's door. Things would just build up between the three big people in the house. They'd seem to growl and sniff circles around each other for a day or two before the fighting would start.

'Jealous, Hoyt?' She'd stretched out her long legs and let her robe fall partly away from the brown skin as she smiled at the man. Glory felt her shoulder-blades draw together as she recognised the dark shards of anger in her mother's eyes.

'Eva Gorman, you are a disgrace to this family. We used to be the best family in this town and now look at us. You whoring around and having a bastard under our roof. What do you think Daddy would have said if he could see you right now? What would he say if he saw you sitting there with your robe open halfway?' He reached over in an effort to close his sister's robe, but she kicked him, square across his kneecap.

'Hoyt, are we talking about the same Daddy who screwed his office nurse for twenty years? Are we talking about the same Daddy who my girlfriends wouldn't go see because his internal examinations always felt like something you don't usually get at the doctor's?'

'You're the only one who ever said those things and I think you made them up. Daddy was the best-respected doctor this town ever had.' He rubbed at his knee, refusing to look at his wife or his sister.

'Daddy was the only doctor this town ever had until he died. It's easy to be the best when you're the only one, Hoyt.'

'He'd hate to see you like this, Eva. You were always his favorite.'

'He'd hate to see me like this because even he drew the line at incest. I'm sure he'd be bitterly disappointed that he didn't have the privilege of my bed and body.' She looked down the front of her robe and pulled it tighter across her chest. 'Not that he wouldn't have thought about it.'

'Glory, hon, better get ready for school or you'll be late. Grown-ups say the dumbest things and don't mean a word of it.' Aunt Flo threw her bulk between Glory and the others. 'You get along now and forget their trashy talk.'

She craned her neck to see around her aunt. All she could see was her uncle's red face and the big old veins popping in his neck. 'I didn't hear anything, Aunt Flo. I was busy thinking about what I'm doing after school.' She smiled at the woman and hoped Aunt Flo wouldn't figure out that she was lying. Lying was a terrible sin, at least according to Pammy, but it wasn't so bad to lie if you didn't get caught. At least that's the way it seemed.

'That's my good girl. Since today is the last day of school you've got a whole summer of after school ahead. Don't want to be late, sugar. You hurry up now.' Aunt Flo shooed her out of the room and closed the kitchen door behind her. Glory pulled out her notebook and carefully wrote i-n-s-e-s-t. She wasn't sure if she had it right, but she could check the dictionary in the library during recess. It was terrible to be kicked out before things really got going, but at least she had a new word. She figured every new word brought her a little closer to knowing why they were all so angry. Almost all the time. She hoped that she'd have a better disposition than them when she was a grown-up.

About half the fights with Uncle Hoyt were about men and the other half were about the house. Grandpa Gormon had left the house to his two children. Uncle Hoyt said he'd done that because it was fair, but her mama said it was because the man wanted to look up from Hell and see his children fighting and screaming. She told Glory it was so the old man didn't need to feel too homesick. Aunt Flo said Grandpa Gorman had gone to Heaven the day he died and was an angel these days. She said he wore wings and spent all his time praising God. Her mama had shook her head and laughed when Glory told her what Aunt Flo had said.

Whatever his reason for leaving the house to his children, he'd left them the biggest, finest house in the whole town. It was the only house with two stories and it was set back on a lot that was big enough to hold three or four houses. Grandpa Gorman's own daddy had won the house in a poker game. He'd never lived in it because he'd been shot on the way home from that same poker game.

His young wife had moved herself and her son into the house a few hours after she'd buried her husband. There'd been some grumbling about it at the time because she'd cut short the funeral lunch as she was so anxious to move into the grand house with its ten rooms, wraparound porch, and indoor privy.

The grumbling didn't stop when the young widow started putting on airs. Most of the people in the town remembered when she'd come to town with her late husband. Neither one of them had been too ready to talk about where they were from. When asked about who their people were, the young couple would come up with one or two names that didn't mean anything to anyone who heard them. Some people in the town suspected they were no-accounts and hadn't been afraid to say just that.

For a while the grumbling got pretty loud. The Widow Gorman issued invitations, but they were always politely, if firmly, refused. She joined the Presbyterian Church and even started singing in the choir. This was a cause for concern until Easter morning when she sang 'The Old Rugged Cross' and there was hardly a dry eye in the pews. Most people realised that a woman who could sing like that must be a good Christian and a fine mother. People began to notice what a fine job she was doing with her young son and how nice the yard looked at the big house. The townspeople came to realise that what had appeared to be putting on airs was merely a reflection of the young widow's true nature.

She was a hard worker and her boy was the best-dressed child in school. She saw to that by sitting up late into the night, carefully sewing his smart yet sturdy clothes. Within a few months, what with the late-night sewing, which she did in front of the window that looked onto the street where people would see her doing it, and singing in the choir, which she did better than anyone could ever remember, she became a respected member of the community.

Her invitations were accepted and she found herself sitting in other people's homes and attending lectures on high-minded subjects when the Chautauqua League provided speakers four times a year. She was asked to oversee the cake booth at the town festival and two mothers asked her to give singing lessons to their young daughters.

Singing lessons turned out to be the one thing most mothers wanted their daughters to have. Some of the mothers were surprised because they'd never known how much they wanted their daughters to sing until someone else's daughter started warbling out Stephen Foster or short bursts of Gilbert and Sullivan. Pretty soon it seemed as though the whole town was reverberating with songs about black veils, cockles and mussels, three little Japanese girls, and home on the range.

With this flood of mothers and daughters running through the big house it was only a matter of time before attention was turned toward the young widow's son, Joe. His head of thick hair was noted and his quick smile and ready wit resulted in positive comments. As his mother still spent many hours on his wardrobe, his clothes were a point of admiration. Along with singing tuition, the Widow Gorman taught her pupils the love of Joe.

Even his teacher succumbed to his charms. Though he was not the brightest boy in her charge, she none the less convinced herself that his beauty and wit were combined with great intellect and high purpose. She graded him well and urged him to aim high. This was fine with Joe, but his interests were of a different sort. His inclinations turned him toward the earthier pursuits of the flesh.

Being raised by a high-minded woman with artistic tendencies and surrounded by young women from good homes gave him ample time to observe the female of the species. He studied the walk, the smell, the eye movements, the breast-heaving, and the speech patterns as diligently as an anthropologist in darkest Africa or far-off Fiji studies head-shrinking or missionary-boiling. He quickly understood the pleasure women obtained from the touch of silk and the whisper of lace. He practiced on himself and on his mother's elderly tabby the movements of his fingers that could barely be felt. In anticipation of the real thing, he kissed the inside of his own wrist so often he chapped his lips.

His mother instructed him in dancing, teaching him to waltz and foxtrot without ever so much as brushing against one of her calfskin boots. Even though he was holding his mother in his arms he quickly saw the possibilities inherent in dancing. He became an excellent dancer.

The teacher, a plump spinster in her mid-forties, gave him a slim volume of Tennyson to read. She insisted he read it aloud and Joe noted the look of longing in her short-sighted eyes. He began to memorise short stanzas and allowed his hair to grow into Byronic curls which rested against his collar. His artistic sensitivity was commented on by mothers and daughters alike.

The decision to attend the state college with the intention of studying medicine was greeted with a mixed response. Even women well past the years of longing found themselves thinking about what it would feel like to have young Joseph Gorman palpitate their abdomens or cradle their twisted ankle in his long white hand. The younger women and girls, not averse to medical attention at some point from such a man, grieved when they looked to the months and years ahead with nothing but farm boys and men from the mill stretched out in a rough, strong-smelling line.

College was difficult, but help was usually available from fellow students who hated to see such a fine young man struggle. He joined a fraternity and his fraternity brothers took turns tutoring him and preparing him for his exams. Their kindness and concern was repaid with the assortment of young women who flocked to any party where Joe was present. Never greedy, he graciously handed out the gin-soaked maidens with the largesse of a young lord, always reserving the most deserving of the girls for himself.

After his graduation, medical training was continued at the same school. Although the course work was difficult, Joe quickly realised he'd made the right choice. The velvet touch he'd perfected for the seduction of girls proved invaluable in the practice of medicine. Patients in the charity ward where the student doctors were first allowed to attend to live bodies responded to his gentle ministrations with gratifying speed. His brighter but ham-handed fellows were in awe of his ability to deal with the most frightened and difficult of patients.

His mother, and the other women of the town, eagerly awaited his return. The Widow Gorman, as ever concerned for her son's welfare, had the good sense to die and leave him a small inheritance in addition to the fine house in the same month he graduated from his training. When some alterations had taken place he proudly hung up his shingle outside the house and began his career with gusto and enthusiasm.

Within days, he'd hired a nurse to assist him in his duties. Maggie Jute was the daughter of a local farmer. As the oldest of fifteen children, marriage and motherhood held no charms for her. Maggie saw nursing as her ticket out of endless child-bearing and vegetable-canning. She donned her white starched uniform with the joy of a novitiate nun, happy to forsake the dubious charms of hearth and home for a higher calling.

Her delight was only increased when she discovered that Dr Gorman didn't expect her to forsake the pleasures of the flesh for her career in nursing. On the contrary, Dr Gorman was more than happy to help her enjoy the stress-relieving properties of regular sexual intercourse. Not only did it relieve tension and stress, he told her, but it was excellent for bowel regularity and the enhancement of the complexion. Dr Gorman not only explained about the careful use of condoms to avoid the more obvious complications of healthy living, but he recommended that the treatment be taken every day during her lunch break.

Dr Joe and Nurse Maggie soon fell into a comfortable routine of health-giving daily intercourse at noon, sometimes interspersed with the addition of coffee-break fellatio or tea-time cunnilingus. It was understood by both that health treatments could be given to others as long as medical confidentiality was scrupulously maintained.

Almost ten years of enhanced complexions and regular bowel movements passed before Evangeline Hoyt moved to town to live with her married sister after completing her studies in Boston. Evangeline's sister was married to Judge Faber. Judge Faber was the Circuit Court judge as well as being the only partner in the law firm of Faber, Faber, and Faber, the two previous Fabers having been lost in the Jonestown Flood, or so it was thought. Some thought they'd just taken the Flood as an excuse to start over someplace else. Many had.

Dr Gorman was introduced to Evangeline Hoyt the second day she arrived in town. Her sister and brother-in-law had arranged a musicale to which they invited some of the leading citizens in order to welcome Evangeline to the community and in the hopes that they could marry her off as soon as possible. They were by no means an ungracious couple, but times were not easy and, judging by her clothes and luggage, Evangeline seemed to have grown used to the finer things while studying in Boston.

Joseph thought she looked as though she fed on an exclusive diet of champagne and orchid hearts. She moved as easily as a vapor through the dark rooms of the Faber house. When their hands touched during introductions he was certain that he'd felt a small jolt of electricity in his loins. His head began to buzz in a not unpleasant manner and he was relieved when the guests were urged to sit down for the musical entertainment.

He attended several musicales a month as they were the primary form of entertainment at the time. The evening stumbled along at a predictable pace, altered only by the opportunity to study the back of Evangeline's fine head and the delicate curve of her exquisite neck. Mrs Faulkner was finishing her forgettable, but oft-repeated, rendition of 'Greensleeves' when he found himself drifting off to sleep. A movement caught his half-closed eyes and jolted him upright when he saw Evangeline stand and approach the front of the room.

She sang something. She sang something about fields, or maybe it was stars. She sang so sweetly that he almost cried. Her beautiful breasts rose and fell with the notes and her perfect lips . . . Enough to say he knew they could accommodate anything he might think of. For the first time in his life, he was in love.

Now that he was in love, he felt it imperative that he forsake all others. He gently explained the situation to Nurse Maggie who was surprisingly not all that disappointed. It seemed that she had become interested in Spiritualism. Contacting the dead was a terrific reliever of stress and she could always call on Judge Faber if she suffered from constipation or an unclear complexion. She told Joseph that Judge Faber also subscribed to the health-giving properties of regular sexual intercourse, but had been unable to convince his wife of the inherent benefits. Mrs Faber, the sister of the excellent Evangeline, was convinced that more than twice a month would certainly result in a sharp rise in her female complaints which were already numerous. Nurse Maggie took a moment to remind Joseph that health problems often ran in families and he might consider giving Evangeline a thorough check-up at the soonest possible date.

Anxious as Joseph was to examine Evangeline, she made it clear that her Ideals were of the Highest Order. Love was the emotion that urged her forward and gave her hope for the future. Only through a pure and perfect love could a woman achieve her full potential. Joseph agreed completely before going back to his empty bed where he masturbated four times before he could finally fall asleep.

In the morning he wasn't the least bit surprised to see that his complexion was already slightly sallow. His bowels seemed to be functioning, but he knew it was only a matter of time before he'd have to resort to a strong purgative. As he dressed in his usual careful fashion he resolved to bring matters to a conclusion that very day. Ignoring what he knew to be a full morning of appointments, he walked directly to Judge Faber's office and sought his permission for the hand of Evangeline.

★

Evangeline accepted with a sweet docility that Joseph found enchanting. She even allowed him to kiss her gently on the lips. As she pulled away from him, blushing prettily, he felt the point of her fine breast brush against his arm. A tiny dampness occurred inside his trousers and he was grateful that the fashion of the day called for a long coat to be worn at all times. The wedding date was set for one week later.

Gently, carefully, he broke her membrane on their wedding night and Evangeline became his true wife. To his delight his silken touch and velvet tongue coaxed a deliciously wanton response from his bride. She was an eager student of the arts of love and like every eager student she was anxious to use her newly acquired skill.

Their lust for each other seemed to have no point of satiation. Joseph had never known such sensual pleasure, such heights of joy. He would smear her secretions on his wrist before he left for his office in the morning. He would of course be back for lunch, but three or four hours without a whiff of her sweet primal waters was more than he could bear. She was pregnant within a month.

The delicate body that he thought had fed only on sparkling wine and orchid hearts began to expand quickly. To his delight a map of blue veins appeared, tracking a road from her tender breasts to the center of his idolatry. He suckled her spreading nipples to prepare them for feeding and ended the therapy with gentle kisses on her darkened nethers. He rested his head on her belly and laughed when he heard what he knew to be two tiny heartbeats.

They prepared the big bedroom and lined up two cradles for the products of their great passion. She was brought to bed nine months to the day after the night she'd lost her guarded virginity. The first child was a large and lusty girl they named Eva after her mother. Smaller and quieter, the boy they would name Hoyt was born a quarter of an hour later.

Attended by the loyal Nurse Maggie, he massaged his wife's abdomen to contract the womb and complete the birth. He bit his lip and ordered Nurse Maggie to bring ice, lots of it, but still the organ was soft and bleeding. Evangeline grew white as the sheets spread with red and then she was gone.

After a decent interval, Nurse Maggie gave up Spiritualism, but not before Evangeline's spirit told her it was all right to return to the health-giving therapies. Joseph's heart was broken, he reminded himself, but his tackle was still in great shape.

Nurse Maggie arranged for her younger sister Beulah, the one with psoriasis and hay fever, to move in to care for the twins. Although the treatments might have helped her skin and her allergies, it never occurred to Dr Joe to offer them to Beulah.

CHAPTER TWO

'She has to finish her breakfast, Glory. You just wait and she'll come out once she's ready.' Mrs Reynolds was like a ghost inside of the screen door. Glory had to squint to make sure the woman wasn't somebody else who was trying to imitate Mrs Reynolds. Like on the radio plays. Spies could come in and take over, pretending to be other people. Of course she knew there probably wasn't a spy in the world who would want to imitate Mrs Reynolds, but it seemed like good practice just in case somebody came along who *was* a spy.

'I could wait inside and that way she won't dawdle.' Glory knew from long experience that Pammy could take hours and hours over a dumb bowl of cereal. Give that girl a piece of toast and they'd both be grandmothers before she was done.

'You can wait outside, Glory. I don't like Pammy to rush through things. Bad for the digestion and you two have all summer.'

'I'm ready.' The door burst open as Little Beau ran out onto the porch. 'Pammy's still eating, but I'm ready to go.' The small boy stood beside Glory and scratched at something scaly on his arm.

'You're not coming with us, LB.' Glory always called him LB because Little Beau sounded so dumb. Made him sound like something you'd find on a Christmas package and LB was more like something you'd find on the bottom of your shoe after you'd walked through a barnyard.

'Am so.'

'You do, you die.' She drew the last word out in a hiss. LB was always trotting after his sister like some little dog, only a dog would have been less work and more fun.

'Glory, you watch yourself or I'm calling your mama. I already told Pammy that I have an appointment and she's watching Little Beau this morning. If you don't like that you can make other arrangements.' Mrs Reynolds opened the door and glared down at the girl. The woman wore a dark blue dress with a string of Woolworth pearls around her neck.

'Yes, ma'am.' Glory looked down and noted with satisfaction that in spite of those pearls and that fancy dress the Reynolds porch needed to be painted, just like everybody else's. Uncle Hoyt said he didn't think a can of paint had been sold in town for over three years and she thought he was probably right. Even people like the Reynoldses with their hoity-toity ways didn't bother with things like paint anymore. More important things, the big people were always saying.

'I told Pammy and I'm telling you, so don't go pretending that you didn't hear me.' She put her hand under Glory's chin and lifted her face. 'Are you listening?'

'Yes, ma'am.' Mrs Reynolds's hand smelled like Lux soap and tobacco smoke. The woman was a secret smoker and most everybody knew it. Her mama always said it was the quiet ones, the prissy ones, those were the ones you had to watch out for.

'Stay out of the woods. There's been talk of hobos in the woods and you know what that means.'

'Yes ma'am.' The hobos had started coming through a few months ago. The men talked about the hobos a lot. They said they would stick to a route for a while and then they'd start going some other place. Somebody said that Charley who used to work at the Feed and Fuel actually became a hobo, but G. thought that probably was a lie. She figured you had to be hobo when you were born. Like being a gypsy or wall-eyed. It must be something that was in your blood and you couldn't help it. You could probably take a hobo baby and give it to the King of England to raise up, but you'd still have a hobo. One day that kid would tie a bandanna around a stick, steal a cherry pie and be on the road looking for the next freight car out of town.

'Your word, Glory. I want your word.' Mrs Reynolds put her hand to her own throat to straighten those pearls and Glory watched the little medal swing on her wristwatch. The Reynoldses were Catholics and Mrs Reynolds seemed to have a medal stuck every place she could think of.

The first time she'd been in their house when she was about five she'd gotten real scared because right there, big as life, was a picture of Jesus with his heart sticking out of his chest. Mrs Reynolds had another one of Jesus hanging on the cross and he was just dripping with blood. Aunt Flo said they were idol-worshippers, but her mama said they were just morbid. Pammy said they were Catholics because way back before they'd been Americans they'd been French. Glory thought that was even dumber than having pictures of bloody men hanging on your walls.

'You have my word, Mrs Reynolds.' LB was standing behind his mother making faces at Glory and pretending to wave his pecker at her. LB thought he was about the funniest thing this side of Laurel and Hardy. She was relieved to see Pammy walking toward her along the dark interior of the house. Even five minutes seemed like an hour when Mrs Reynolds was standing over you.

'We'll see you later, Mama.' Pammy stood on tiptoes and kissed her mother's cheek. As usual, she was wearing a clean dress and what most girls would consider to be Easter shoes. Pammy had a rich cousin in some city who was just two years older. Every few months this cousin would get tired of her stuff and send it down to Pammy.

'You girls take good care of Little Beau and have him home for lunch. And stay out of the woods,' she called to their backs as the girls scrambled down the steps with the younger boy close behind. 'You gave me your word, Glory Gorman.'

'Take good care of Little Beau.' Glory put her hand on her hips and pretended to be Mrs Reynolds.

Pammy laughed and pretended that she was prancing around on high heels. 'Stay away from the woods or the hobos might eat my precious boy.' Pammy's eyes glowed with her daring. Imitating her mother was pretty heady stuff for Pammy Reynolds. Pammy got the best grades in their whole class and was Teacher's favorite. Whenever Teacher needed a helper for anything interesting she'd ask Pammy. Teacher didn't seem to think that the other kids might enjoy pounding erasers or taking notes to the principal's office.

Once Teacher had to leave the room for a few minutes and had actually left Pammy in charge. Glory got so mad she ran around the room screaming with all the other kids even if Pammy was her best friend. Willis Harkin spit a great big gob into Teacher's desk that time, but Pammy didn't even try to stop him. All she did was stand at the front of the class like a statue. She wasn't nearly as responsible as Teacher thought.

'Where we going?' LB ran his fist under his nose and wiped the result on his already stiff corduroys. The only rich cousin they had was a girl, so LB looked as bad as all the other kids in town.

'The woods, Snot-Boy. You think we were taking you to a circus?' Glory was proud of her trashy talk and felt she had something of a duty to share it with other children whenever possible. She knew that a lot of kids weren't exposed to as many interesting conversations as she was. Wasn't their fault.

'I'm not Snot-Boy.'

'No, you're Winkie-Stink because you wet the bed.' Pammy wiggled her hips and rolled her eyes.

'No I am not! I haven't wet the bed all month!' LB started to run at his sister as she and Glory joined hands. Without a word they begin to sprint through the back yard to the alley and on toward the wood.

The air was already warm and the day promised to be hot and thick with humidity. Glory ran with pleasure, knowing she wouldn't be expected back home until dinner-time at six. Nine hours of pure summer spread in front of her feet.

She dropped Pammy's hand when it became slippery with sweat and raced ahead. All the soft leather shoes in the world couldn't match white canvas sneakers for running and jumping. Hers had a few holes, but they were still faster than Pammy's fancy Easter shoes. She could feel Pammy not far behind her and she could hear old Winkie-Stink whining through his nose about how they should slow down and how he was going to tell his mama and how they were going to be whipped.

'I'll send you home and my Aunt Flo will watch you if you don't shut up. I'll tell her to sit on you and fart on you and squash you like a big old bug.' Glory waved her hands above her head, delighted with her comments and the sound of LB's yelling behind her.

She kept running until she found herself completely surrounded by the green of the wood. Mama had told her that before the town, even before the farms, there hadn't been anything but woods as far as the eye could see. She liked to be far enough into the woods that she could imagine exactly what it must have been like before the farms and the town.

Glory turned around to see where the other two were. She could see the flash of Pammy's pink dress through the green, but was pleased to see that LB was nowhere in sight. She didn't exactly want to lose him, but it would be fun if he thought he was lost for a few minutes. She stepped backwards to look for LB from a different angle, but fell back against a soft pile of rags.

The pile of rags groaned and grabbed her ankle. It made a growling noise as it stared at her with huge red eyes and bared its ugly fangs.

'Mama! Mama!' She knew she was sounding like a baby, but the thing, the monster, was hanging on to her ankle and making horrible sounds and he smelled like that dark bottle Uncle Hoyt kept in the shed, all mixed up with a privy smell. 'Mama, help! Somebody, it's trying to kill me!'

'Mother of God!' Pammy stood ten feet away. She was jumping up and down, the skirt of her dress bunched in her hands. 'Holy Mary, Mother of God, pray for us sinners, now and at the hour of our death. Amen. Amen, Amen.' Pammy started crossing herself about a million times while she jumped up and down.

Suddenly, Glory felt the monster's hand release her ankle and she scrambled toward Pammy who was still crossing and jumping. She looked behind and saw the pile of rags scurry out of the woods toward the railroad tracks.

'What's going on? Who was yelling?' LB trotted up with a stick in his hand which he wielded like a sword.

'There was a huge hobo monster who tried to kill me. He was going to kill me.' Glory couldn't catch her breath. She could feel something wet like fire between her legs and knew she'd peed herself.

'How'dja get away?' LB swung his stick in a furious arc around himself.

'It was the Holy Mother.' Pammy stared at the spot where the hobo had disappeared. 'I prayed to the Blessed Mother and she made him disappear into thin air. She saved you, Glory. She cast out the demon and saved you.'

'He ran away.' Now her shoes were wet with tinkle and she wanted to cry, for a long time.

'No he didn't. He didn't run, he disappeared. The Virgin saved you, Glory. You had a miracle. The Holy Mother gave you a miracle.'

Beulah Jute moved into the small bedroom off the kitchen and took over the house. Although she was supposed to take care of the infant twins, Beulah was a self-starter and knew she could do more. There was something of the eraser about Beulah. She seemed to erase the memory of Evangeline a little more each day.

More than anything Joe wanted to remember Evangeline. He wanted to walk into a room and smell her scent, feel her presence, glimpse her out of the corner of his eye. Instead, everywhere he looked was Beulah with her plodding walk, and every time he sniffed the air he smelled the coal-tar soap she used to scrub her reddened skin.

Before Evangeline disappeared completely he called in Jarvis Matthews, a local carpenter, and commissioned something to be built. Into one of the corners of the big bedroom Jarvis built a platform and something that looked suspiciously like an altar. Jarvis, being a Baptist, complained at the time, but Dr Joe assured him that he was only building a display case for some hunting specimens he'd collected.

After Jarvis completed his work, Joe covered the part that looked suspiciously like an altar with Evangeline's favorite white damask tablecloth. On top of this he carefully arranged a lock of her hair which he had snipped while she lay in her casket. He lined up several pictures of her which had been taken during her short life. The largest picture was the one that had been taken on their wedding day. His sister-in-law, Judge Faber's wife, had been kind enough to give him the dressmaker's dummy on which Evangeline's wedding dress had been fitted. He carefully dressed the dummy in the handsome silk dress and stood it next to the pictures and the lock of her hair. He then locked himself inside the room, sat on the bed, and proceeded to drink a quart of sour mash whiskey.

Beulah heard him crying and singing through the locked door. She banged on it and begged him to open up so that she could comfort his breaking heart. She begged to be allowed to be a true mother to his children and a true wife to him. She confessed that she had always loved him.

The next day, after his hangover had allowed him to stand upright for ten consecutive minutes, he gave Beulah one hundred dollars and told her that her services would no longer be required. He didn't think it was right to lead the girl on.

Judge Faber's wife sent over Hilda Crenshaw who had looked after her own children when they were younger. Hilda loved children, but didn't think much of men, especially handsome ones. She made it clear to Dr Gorman that if he so much as looked at her funny she'd be out of the house, twins or not. He in turn assured her that her virtue was safe.

Hilda believed children were best left to their own devices. She felt that her responsibilities didn't extend too far beyond feeding and watering and the occasional wiping of noses or bottoms. Dr Gorman thought that his responsibilities didn't extend too far beyond paying Hilda's salary. Eva and Hoyt had an almost idyllic childhood. They learned early on that as long as they didn't touch the Evangeline Shrine their father would leave them alone. Hilda was kept happy by their display of hearty appetites and steady growth patterns. Apart from growing, eating, and Shrine-avoiding, their time was their own.

Of course, later on everyone would say that they knew things were going to go wrong. There was so much tongue-clucking later that it sounded like a hen house.

Hoyt was the sort of student that teachers just naturally ignored. He was a large, fleshy sort of a boy with a sweet smile and a quiet disposition. He was almost ten years old before anybody noticed that the only schoolwork he was able to do was to hand the stuff to his sister so that she could do it for him. Letters and numbers didn't mean anything to him. Just too many squiggles to bother about, was the way he looked at it. The only thing to do was to stick him back in school so far he wouldn't have been able to fit inside the little desks where the lower-grade students were expected to sit. Nobody thought that was a very good idea so he became an apprentice carpenter.

Some people have an affinity for certain materials and Hoyt was one of them. His hands and heart were made for wood. He loved the stuff, seeming to turn the wood into exactly what it was meant to be. Once he started working with wood the

Gorman looks and charm started showing up. He got good-looking and almost charming. At least charming enough to woo and win Florence Brodsky when he was just sixteen.

Florence was the prettiest girl in town, excepting Eva. She was blond and plump and almost every man who saw her immediately thought he'd be much happier if he could just stick a baby or two inside her sweet round body.

About three years after Hoyt started trying to stick babies inside of Florence, Joe started looking forward to joining Evangeline. He didn't mention it to anyone, but he made plans. He stopped giving treatments to Maggie Jute for one thing. He stopped giving those complexion-enhancing treatments to any one of several ladies. Even when the pretty new librarian complained of not sleeping and being awfully tense he told her the best thing to do was to take a brisk walk once a day. Truth was his treatment days were over.

Eva's girlfriends had been wrong about the examinations. By the time her girlfriends were getting their internals examined Dr Joe had closed that chapter in his life. His hands were still sweet and gentle and his face was still pleasing, but the foreplay was all in the heads of those young girls, who were more interested in a man's touch than they were willing to admit.

Joseph Gorman was preparing himself to meet his bride. He wrote her a letter each day which he would then burn and hope the smoke would take his loving words up to Heaven. He closed his office and stopped answering the door. For almost two months the town didn't have a doctor at all, but he didn't seem to care. He refused all patients.

Some of those people never forgave him for his seeming neglect. One of those was a young girl who had more sense of fun than common sense. Dr Joe had helped girls like this before. He'd never seen anything wrong with scraping out a few cells and helping a girl keep her monthlies flowing on a regular basis.

Eva had begged him, but by now he spent all day in his room writing letters to Evangeline and drinking ever increasing doses of laudanum. He died the same day she felt a tiny fishy flip inside for the first time. She didn't attend the funeral. She lay as quietly as she could on her parents' big bed and felt the fishy thing swimming toward her heart, hating the thing and its bids for attention.

Her plan was to give the fishy thing away. Hoyt hadn't managed to get any babies inside of Florence so she seemed to be the obvious recipient. Eva planned to give the baby and her half of the house to Hoyt and Florence and she'd go away, just like she'd always planned.

She started packing her bags the morning her waters broke. One less thing to do. No need to put everything off until the last minute. The baby eased out of her fine body with almost no trouble. A beautiful red-haired girl, she wiggled herself into Flo's hands as though they were the cradle she knew she'd find at the other end of the tunnel. Eva turned her face to the wall, refusing to look her daughter in the eye.

Eva awoke to the sound of a baby crying. Her feet refused to cooperate with her head's intentions and carried her into the next room where the baby wailed and waved at the air with tiny pink fists. Eva leaned over the cradle and felt her large breasts fill with milk. She pulled her nightgown open and lifted her daughter in her arms.

The baby smacked onto the big brown nipple as though she'd been doing that very thing all her life. Eva ran her hand across the downy red hair and knew she'd have to unpack her suitcase. She could almost feel the manacles that tiny baby was forging around her heart. Holding her fast to the ugly little town and the big old house with the wraparound porch.

Florence hurried up the stairs with the bottle of Carnation milk she'd been warming in the kitchen. She opened the door and knew with one glance that she had lost her baby and her house.

She went downstairs and ate a whole chocolate cake that Mrs Matthews had brought by earlier in the day to celebrate the baby's birth. It seemed to help so she started in on some stew and finished off the apple pie she'd made for Hoyt's supper two nights before. By the time Hoyt came home that night, she'd eaten so much it almost looked like he'd finally managed to stick a baby or two inside of her.

CHAPTER THREE

'See, here she is.' Pammy pushed the brightly colored picture under Glory's nose. 'And see, I've got a statue of her over there on the chest of drawers.' Pammy rummaged for a moment inside the ruffles of her pink dress. 'And see here, I've even got her on a medal around my neck. I never take her off, not even when I wash.' Pammy shoved the medal back inside her dress. 'I figure that me thinking about her all the time is one of the reasons she's chosen to show herself to me the same way she's been showing herself to those kids overseas.'

'*I* was the one who could have been killed, Pamela Beaumont Reynolds. If this Jesus-Mama was so excited about you, how come *I'm* the one she supposedly saved? Not that I think she saved me because all I saw was the worst-looking hobo I've ever seen. *I* didn't see any holy mothers or holy anythings.' At least she thought she was pretty sure about what she'd seen. She had been pretty upset, she reminded herself. Upset enough to tinkle down into her shoe. Glory couldn't even remember the last time something like that had happened.

Beau sat on the floor in his sister's bedroom and made funny faces, trying to get the girls' attention. Since he'd had nothing to contribute to the whole Virgin experience, he'd been trying desperately to turn their attention to something that could include him. In sheer desperation, he screwed up his face and forced out a small squeak of methane gas that rumbled against the floor before wafting up.

'He left because of my prayers to her. That's how these things work.' She turned to her brother and kicked him in the foot. 'Stop that, Little Beau.' Pammy rolled her eyes before continuing. 'She heard me and knew we needed her help. She made that man disappear.'

'How come I've never heard of her doing anything like this before? How come the only time you ever hear about her is during the Christmas pageant?' Glory studied the picture in the book that Pammy had opened. The sweet-faced woman looked a little like Evangeline, the woman who'd died in the big bedroom.

'We hear about her all the time at our church. You get told a lot more when you belong to the onetruechurch.' Pammy ran the words together in a heap.

'You don't belong to the onetruechurch because you're an idol-worshipping Catholic.' Being Presbyterians, the Gormans were considered to be fairly liberal and moderate by most of the townspeople's standards, but Glory remembered Reverend Harris's comments on idol worshipping and why it was such a bad idea. She hadn't brought it up before because she knew it was hard enough to be a Catholic in their town without having the idol-worshipping stuff shoved in your face by your very best girlfriend.

A lot of the other kids weren't nearly as thoughtful. Pammy had never been invited to Vera and Ivy Scott's house because their daddy was the Baptist preacher. Glory hadn't been invited either, but that was most likely because she was a bastard. To the Baptists a Presbyterian was all right, just. Bastards, however, would be visited by the sins of their fathers at some point.

'And you are probably going to spend eternity in Hell because you've turned your back on the Holy Mother.' Pammy closed the book with the picture of Mary as she heaved a long sigh.

'You mean I'm going to Hell, but old Winkie-Stink here is going to go to Heaven so he can wet the bed up there?' She was pleased to see that the corners of Pammy's mouth were twitching with a suppressed giggle. She didn't think they'd been chosen like those kids in Europe, but she could test that out later. Baiting LB was more fun than talking about church stuff any day.

'I don't wet the bed, not anymore.' LB's eyes looked like they were going to start leaking in a few seconds.

'Then you must be wetting your pants because I can smell you all the way across the room.' Glory took a sisterly-type kick at LB's foot just so that Pammy could see she was planning not to be too mad about those things she'd said about Hell.

'I'm telling Mama. She's going to spank both of you.' LB began to scuttle out of the room toward the back yard where his mother was drinking iced tea and reading the new *True Confessions* magazine. Mr Reynolds worked for Prairie Life Insurance and was gone all week, every week, collecting premiums for burial policies.

'You tell your mama about us being in the woods and I'll kill you, LB. As sure as I'm standing here I'll reach my hand down your throat and pull your guts out and wrap them around your neck.' Glory watched with satisfaction as the boy's eyes grew as round as saucers.

'Keep your mouth shut, Little Beau.' Pammy rubbed the toe of her shoe to remove a bit of dust.

'Can I tell her about the miracle?' LB looked from one girl to the other.

'Not yet. Holy Mother will tell me when it's time.' Pammy stood up a little straighter as she stared at the statue on her chest of drawers.

She sipped at her iced tea and listened to the drone of the bickering children. She glanced at her Timex and saw that in three hours he'd be done collecting Prairie Life burial insurance premiums for the day. She tried to keep track of his day through the length of her own after reading an article in *Ladies' Home Journal*.

It had been about helping your husband succeed in his chosen career. Thinking about his work was one way of supporting him and strengthening the sacred bonds of marriage, which in turn would boost his career. She thought about Prairie Life quite a bit.

Mr Reynolds's second cousin actually owned Prairie Life, and Lucille Reynolds felt very sincerely that family should take better care of family. She thought it would be the right thing if Mr Reynolds's second cousin would invite them to Chicago or Wichita or one of the other big cities and make him a Regional Manager. You'd think they'd look to family first, but just last year they had an opening at the main office and they went right out and hired someone else when they could have given the job to her Raymond.

A Mr Alan Rose, his name was. Probably short for Rosebaum or something. Those people seemed to worm their way into all the important spots. Wasn't enough that they'd killed our Lord, but now they were taking the best jobs away from decent Christians. Decent Christians who were in the same family and deserved a little consideration when fancy jobs were being handed out.

She wasn't ungrateful; that wasn't it at all. She always sent a beautiful bread and butter note and made Pammy do the same whenever a box of clothes was sent. It just seemed that a good-looking, hard-working man like her Raymond should move along faster in a family business. It didn't seem right, what with all his efforts, that he should be collecting nickels and dimes every week from the same sorry no-accounts year after year. Coloreds and trashy whites, mostly. Day in and day out, hardly ever dealing with people of quality.

Lucille Reynolds knew that she could be quite an asset to Raymond and his family given half a chance. It was such a waste to have her out in this ugly little place where nobody noticed or cared about quality and good manners. Anybody could see that she had that special charm and carriage that was unique to convent-educated ladies from New Orleans.

★

It did sound wonderful. It sounded so good she said it as often as possible. She loved to say it out loud, letting the words trip off her Southern tongue into the local ears that were used to listening to flat, farmyard vowels. Convent-educated.

Convent-educated almost had a taste to it. Close your eyes and it tasted of chicory coffee and sugary beignets. There was a smell of beeswax and magnolias when those words were spoken.

It was true, that was the best part. Anybody could check the facts and they would find that one Lucille Marie Beaumont had grown up in a convent. Sort of. St Dominic's was right next to the convent and completely staffed by the sisters from the convent. Every day the children were trooped next door to the convent for their prayers.

St Dominic's was not very big as orphanages in New Orleans went. Something about living in the Big Easy seemed to encourage situations where children were separated from their parents. The liquor, and the music, and the sad-eyed girls down around Bourbon Street; none of that seemed to contribute much toward family stability.

The nuns had acquired her from the lying-in ward at the Hotel Dieu. The orphanages took turns when one of the sad-eyed girls would slip out the side door a few hours after giving birth. Sister Mary Joseph named her Lucille after her own mother. Most of the nuns were an unimaginative lot and usually named the babies after members of their own families. Sister Mary Joseph loved the name Lucille and had given the name to three other baby girls from the Hotel Dieu.

The middle and last names were not left to chance. All the boys were given the middle name of Joseph, all the girls Marie. Twenty-six French surnames, one for each letter of the alphabet, were used on a rotating basis. The last child, two months before, had been named Theodore Joseph Alouette.

She didn't really know how the boys at St Dominic's spent their free time, but the girls spent theirs thinking and dreaming about who they really were. There wasn't a single poor child, not a single whore's daughter in the girl's dormitory at St Dominic's.

Some of the girls had been lost off the big boats that sailed down the river. Some of the girls had been left in St Louis Square or at the Café du Monde by lazy maids or thoughtless baby nurses. Young Lucille had reason to think she'd been kidnapped from one of the big, iron-balconied houses in the Quarter. One of the ones that you could sometimes get a glimpse of as the sisters traipsed you through. One of the ones where you glanced up and saw the carved ceilings and soft golden lighting. She was fairly certain that her real parents, members of the cream of New Orleans society, were in the process of paying a million-dollar ransom when the sloppy kidnappers accidently left her at the Hotel Dieu, where the nuns snatched her up and consigned her to life in an orphanage.

Not that any of that mattered, she'd remind herself. She was one of the most respectable women in town, if not the most. She'd overcome whatever misfortune she'd been dealt. She'd raised two fine children in The Faith and she'd been a good wife, even if Raymond didn't always make it easy. Not easy at all. He'd come home around eight o'clock on Friday night and she'd be lucky to get three words out of him. He'd sit in that big chair of his and drink beer after beer. He'd belch a few times and pick at the dinner which was usually ruined because it had been sitting in the oven so long.

She'd prayed about her marriage. She'd prayed long and hard and even talked to Father Greene when he came through town on his twice-monthly calls. Of course, he was an old drunk himself, so he hadn't been any help at all. If Raymond would just get that job as Regional Manager everything could be good again. She lit one of her secret cigarettes and finished the *True Confessions* story about the woman who found true passion with a good man after living a life of debauchery.

Glory put a pair of clean socks in her pocket before slipping into the big bedroom. Nobody slept in the big bedroom anymore. Once a week, her mama or her Aunt Flo would run a dust mop through the room, but the windows were always closed. The air smelled musty with hints of mice and mildew.

She went to the Evangeline shrine and ran her fingers along the wedding dress. Her fingers left a trail through the dust in the pleats like tiny snail tracks of yellowed silk. She glanced around to make sure the door was firmly closed and then knelt down before the shrine.

'I'd like some shoes. I'd like some shoes like the ones that Pamela Reynolds of 43 Endicott Road wears.' She only knew of one Pamela Reynolds, but thought adding the address was a sensible precaution. There might be another Pamela Reynolds somewhere who had awful-looking, clunky shoes and she didn't want a pair of those.

'If I get a pair of those shoes it will be a bigger miracle than the hobo leaving. If I get those shoes I'll tell everyone and praise your holy name.' She looked up and studied the pictures on the damask tablecloth. Evangeline wasn't the Mother of God, but she kind of looked like her. Even her wedding veil reminded Glory of the way Mary had looked on that Christmas card Aunt Flo had been sent by her sister. Mary had been sitting in the stable with the baby and all around her the snow had been covered with glitter that came off if you shook the card. The glitter stuck to everything and made everything look better than it did before.

It was easier to think about Mary when she looked at the pictures of her grandmother. Her grandmother had bled to death and so had Jesus, so that was something to think about. Uncle Hoyt said Grandpa Joe had died of a broken heart even if it took him another twenty years to finally die. That was another thing, because Pammy's mother had those open-heart pictures that had something to do with Mary.

Evangeline and Mary had so much in common they were practically like sisters or best girlfriends. Glory knew that if Mary and Evangeline were living in town right now they'd take turns going over to each other's kitchen for coffee right after their husbands left for work. They'd help each other run up clothes on their Singers and babysit each other's kids. In the afternoon they'd sit on each other's porches and drink lemonade and talk about how hot it was or how it looked like it was going to rain or maybe they'd gossip about how dumb Mrs Carver looked with that new perm in her hair.

Maybe they'd giggle about Mr Osburne, who gave piano lessons and directed the Community Players. They'd almost pee themselves talking about the scarf he'd tie around his neck when it wasn't even cold and how he wore clear nail polish on his big pink fingernails. They'd shake their heads and tsk-tsk their teeth about Vera Green having that nine-pound baby just six months after her hurry-up wedding last winter. They'd definitely be best friends.

Glory filled up the bathroom sink and rinsed out her panties and her canvas shoes so that she didn't end up smelling like old LB. She ran a washrag between her legs until the cloth turned cold and made her shiver.

Using the toilet as a step-stool, she perched herself on the edge of the white porcelain sink and ran more hot water into the basin. She eased her feet into the too warm water and let them soak for a few minutes until they started looking red and pruney.

Using her mama's fingernail brush she carefully scrubbed until the only dirty-looking places were where she'd built up calluses from going barefoot. She dried each foot carefully, making sure that even between her toes was dry and sweet. She sprinkled a little of Aunt Flo's talcum powder over each foot and carefully made her way downstairs, using as little of each foot as she could.

Once she got to the porch she settled into the rocker and pulled the pair of clean white socks from her pocket. She pulled them over her newly washed feet and sat back to wait for the shoes. She fell asleep and stayed out on the porch until dinner time.

Glory was just pulling her nightie over her head when she heard the slam of the front screen door and Mrs Reynolds's drawling voice added to the evening's noise. She knew in an instant that Pammy or LB had talked about the woods and what had happened. Mrs Reynolds had probably already told Mama that she'd never be allowed to play at their house again.

'Glory? Come on down once you get your nightie on.' It was Aunt Flo's voice and that wasn't a good sign. Aunt Flo was the one who jumped in when tempers were flaring.

'Coming.' Glory considered the possibility of climbing out the window, but she knew she'd have to face the music at some point. She smoothed her hair and tried to look as cute as possible as she headed for the stairs. Uncle Hoyt said all cats would be killed except they were so cute when they were kittens. She hoped the same theory would apply to children who disobeyed direct orders.

'Evening, Glory.' Mrs Reynolds sat in the big armchair in front of the picture window. She was still wearing her pearls, but she'd changed out of the dark blue dress into a flower-sprigged housedress. Glory stopped in the hallway before entering the room.

'Well, come here, Glory. Miss Lucille stopped by to see you.' Mama smiled and nodded her encouragement. 'Come here and say "hello".'

'Hi.' Glory walked in and stood about ten feet from Mrs Reynolds, but didn't look at her.

'I was just telling your mama that I came across something and I thought about you.' Mrs Reynolds reached into a brown paper sack at her feet which Glory hadn't noticed before. 'These came last year and silly me, I stuck them in the back of the cupboard until Pammy could fit into them. Wouldn't you just know it, she is shooting up so fast and I waited so long, now they're just too small for her.' Out of the bag came a pair of bright red-leather Mary Jane shoes. 'Try these on, Glory. Pammy says your feet aren't quite as big as hers. Nearly broke her heart when they didn't fit her.'

Glory grabbed the shoes and shoved them onto her feet without even sitting down. She wiggled her toes and found that she even had a little room to grow. She looked from her mama to Mrs Reynolds and smiled.

Mama laughed and that beautiful braid of hair bounced against her neck. 'I think they're just right, Lucille. Glory, what do you say to Miss Lucille?'

'I think they're the prettiest things I've ever seen in my whole life, Miss Lucille. Thank you.' She looked at the anniversary clock over the mantle and knew it would be at least two hours before the grown-ups fell asleep and she could sneak out the window to tell Pammy about the second miracle.

CHAPTER FOUR

Mama had insisted that she go to bed at her usual time. Glory had thought about telling her about the two miracles, but something held her mouth shut except to say good night to everyone.

Secrets were best held away from grown-ups, at least at first. Grown-ups didn't understand secrets. Tell a grown-up a secret and the next thing they do is run down the street to tell a few more grown-ups. They always have what they think is a good reason, of course. They always know better and they always understand things that kids wouldn't even begin to understand until they're real old too.

Glory sat up in bed, her new shoes, the miracle shoes, clutched to her chest. She listened as Uncle Hoyt climbed up the stairs and flopped onto his bed that he shared with Aunt Flo. The springs underneath his body squeaked and groaned as he found the right spot for sleeping. It had been that way every night since last spring when he did something to his knee.

He'd been over to Crocketts' farm to put a new door on their barn. Uncle Hoyt had made a real fuss that first morning about going to the farm because he hated that kind of work. He liked to do the fancy stuff. He liked making furniture and cabinets and he liked to carve fancy mantelpieces. Course, nobody had money for fancy anything anymore so he went and made the barn door for Mr Crockett.

It had taken him two days of working well into the evening to put the new door on the old barn. He'd come home the last night with a funny hitch to his walk and the knee had been stiff ever since. He complained about it a lot and made so much noise bouncing around in bed that nobody could get to sleep until Uncle Hoyt had gotten himself in position for the night.

The stiff knee certainly hadn't done much for his disposition, which hadn't been too good to start with. Uncle Hoyt figured that if the big house was sold, he and Aunt Flo could take their half of the money and move someplace else where a fine crafts-man could be appreciated and paid a living wage. Glory wasn't sure how this would help his knee, but somehow it would help everything, to hear Uncle Hoyt tell it. Her mama refused to sell because, well, she never really gave a reason.

Glory figured her mama was just too much a part of the big house to ever leave it. Her mama had wanted to leave once, but not anymore. The house smelled like Mama, or maybe Mama smelled like the house. She was thinking about the way her mama smelled when she heard the door close on her mama's room. It would be another hour before her mama fell asleep.

Next to her bed her mama kept a big stack of books she'd read every night to put herself to sleep. Her mama was always reading about paintings and art because she'd wanted to be an artist a long time ago. She'd been planning to run away to live and paint in Paris or Rome when she got the shock of her life. She'd never tell Glory what the shock had been, but it must have been a pretty horrible shock because she was still living right where she was born and she never painted anymore.

In a corner of the basement about thirty or forty paintings were stacked against the wall, their colored side facing the wall. There was also a big box of paints and brushes. She used to beg her mama to let her have the paints and brushes for playing with, but she finally gave up trying. Glory had looked at the pictures sometimes when her mama wasn't around. Whatever the shock of her life had been, Glory figured it was a good thing if it kept her from painting any more pictures like the ones in the basement.

They didn't look like people, or buildings, or flowers. They didn't look at all like the nice ones hanging on the wall in the parlor. The pictures were mostly wild smears of color and shape like a very angry child might make. There were half a dozen pictures that kind of looked like babies, but their heads were way too big and their backbones were curled up the way a snail's shell was. Some of the strange almost-babies had cords going through their middles so they looked almost like balloons on the end of a string. The worst of those pictures had the almost-balloon-baby all cut up and covered with purple-looking blood. She'd been planning to show Pammy the paintings until she'd found that one. She didn't want Pammy or anyone else to know what a bad artist her mother had been.

About a year ago her mama had gone to work in the library. Mama had been in there one day, just looking through the art books, when Miss Marshall the librarian dropped dead, just like that. One minute she'd been stamping a date in a book with that big wooden stamp and the next thing she was just gone except for her earthly remains. Mama had gone to get help and then applied for the job as quick as she could before anybody else had a chance to find out there was a vacancy. Now she opened the library four afternoons a week and looked at art books when things weren't too busy and they almost never were. The county had stopped buying new books two years before and most of the readers in town had read everything on the shelves at least twice.

Finally she heard Aunt Flo splashing around in the bathroom. Aunt Flo spent more time in the bathroom than the rest of the family put together. Glory didn't know why it took so long, but thought it must have something to do with either being fat or not having babies. She'd always run a lot of water and empty the basin two or three times. When she was done doing whatever it

was she did, she'd open the door and a little fog of sweet, soapy
smells would drift into the hallway. That fog would swing
through the hallway for an hour or two, filling noses with flow-
ery smells and almost insuring that everybody would dream a
little bit about summer gardens and damp flesh.

While she waited for Aunt Flo to finish up she rocked herself
back and forth and hummed a song about a dead goose as quietly as she could. When the song determined once and for all
that the goose was dead she hummed 'The Star-Spangled
Banner', the parts of 'Shenandoah' she could remember, and
finally a medley of Christmas carols. Her patience was finally
rewarded when she heard the click of Mama's reading lamp and
the liquidy sound of Aunt Flo's night-breathing. Just to be sure
that everyone was asleep she counted one-Mississippi, two-
Mississippi all the way up to two hundred.

The wonderful shoes in her left hand, she eased out of bed
and down the stairs, taking care to avoid the third step from the
bottom which Uncle Hoyt had yet to fix because he was sick to
death of all the nagging he was always hearing. She stepped onto
the porch and took a deep breath of the damp night air. She
decided that when she was a grown-up she'd stay up this late
every night. Every night she'd come outside and smell the night,
even if she lived at the top of the Empire State Building. She'd
buy herself some really pretty nighties like the women in the
movies had and she'd come out to the porch or the balcony (in
case she did end up living high in the clouds) every night and
take a twirl in her pretty nightie and have a smell of the air and
think about the miracle.

Almost nobody bothered to lock up their houses. Usually if
somebody locked the door it was because they didn't want the
dog or the cat to get out. The problem with locking the door
was if somebody lost the key they'd have to go down to the
Mercantile and buy another one, sometimes just to let themselves
in. The almost nobody who did lock her house up was Lucille
Reynolds.

What with her husband being away most nights, and what with her being naturally high-strung, she couldn't sleep until she'd checked the front and back doors and made sure they were locked up tight. She said she was worried about hobos and that was true. Once in a while a pie would go missing from a windowsill or something along those lines, but Lucille's concerns were of a darker sort.

She'd lie there in her dark bedroom and think about those men, those so-called 'knights of the road'. They travelled from town to town, never giving a care to tomorrow. Stopping here and there. She had to wonder if they ever missed the warmth of a real home. Missed the love of a good woman. Stood to reason that some of them would be driven half out of their minds if they knew that she was lying there in the dark, all alone and kind of lonely.

So she kept her doors locked. She pushed those thoughts out of her head and said two Our Fathers and an extra Hail Mary. She said her regular prayers and made a point of mentioning how she'd appreciate it if Little Beau could keep his sheets dry so she wouldn't have to worry about washing the linen again until Monday morning. She curled onto her side and fell asleep.

Glory pushed up the window and hiked herself over the sill. Still holding the shoes, she scuttled onto Pammy's bed and gently placed her hand over the girl's mouth.

'Wake up, Pammy, but don't make a sound. It's me, there's been another miracle!' She made the tiniest of whispers although she really wanted to shout at the top of her lungs until the whole town heard.

'Gloruphh merrr chii.' Pammy's words made a damp spot on her hand so she moved it away. 'What are you doing here? What time is it?'

'I had to tell you before morning so I came over as soon as Mama and the others fell asleep.'

'Tell me what?' Pammy yawned and her breath smelled foul, especially for somebody who usually looked so pretty.

'When I went back to my house I prayed for a miracle. I prayed for some shoes, shoes like you've got.' She held up the miracle shoes. 'See?'

'I can't see anything because it's dark.' Pammy leaned over and turned on the wall switch, flooding the room with light. She rubbed her eyes and yawned again.

'Can you see these?' Glory made the shoes dance in front of her friend's face. 'These are a miracle.'

Pammy shut the light switch off and fell back on her pillow. 'Those are the shoes my mother gave you because they don't fit me. That's not a miracle.'

'But I asked for them. I asked the Virgin for them. I told her I'd believe in her if she gave me some shoes and she gave me some shoes.' She poked at where she thought Pammy's side might be. 'Do you hear what I'm telling you?'

'Do you hear what *I'm* telling *you*? Those aren't a miracle. Those are my cousin's shoes that don't fit me.'

'But I asked her for them. I went up to the Evangeline Shrine and prayed to the wedding picture that looks like a Christmas card and she gave me the shoes.'

'That doesn't make it a miracle. My mama was just being nice to you because you're always eyeing my stuff.'

'How come when you say it's a miracle, it's a miracle? How come you get to decide?'

'I decide because I'm a Catholic, stupid. You're a Presbyterian and Presbyterians don't have miracles. If you had miracles you'd have Miraculous Medals and you'd have gold statues and parades and things.'

'Then if I can't have a miracle, what would you call that in the woods? It happened to me, Pammy Reynolds. It didn't happen to you!' Glory had forgotten completely that she'd been somewhat uncertain as to the validity of the first miracle.

'I was with you, Glory. I was the one who prayed to the Blessed Mother and she delivered you from the forces of darkness as a special favor to me.'

'I hope your tongue turns into a turd.' She pronounced the

last syllable with what she hoped was a tone of great importance. Still clutching the shoes, she threw her leg over to the windowsill and pulled herself up.

'We could test it. That would be the scientific thing to do.' Pammy's voice sounded almost friendly in the dark.

'How?' The shoes still seemed pretty wonderful, but somewhat less miraculous as she held them.

'We can ask for a sign. We can go outside and ask for a sign.'

'Well, come on.' Glory grinned and launched herself down the outside of the house.

'What kind of a sign should we ask for?' Much as she hated to defer to Pammy, it was clear that her friend had a clearer grasp of religion than she did.

'Anything. You just ask for a sign and then wait for it to happen.'

'How long do we have to wait?'

'Not more than five minutes, I don't think. Signs aren't like miracles. Signs are just that. They're like marks on a map to let you know you're going the right way.'

'Should we pray or something?'

'No, she knows we're out here. Just keep looking around.'

'I don't see anything.' Glory could hear some frogs, see some stars, but that was it.

'Look.' Pammy pointed her hand at the sky and made a sharp hiss between her teeth. 'Holy Mother Mary, you were right! Oh Glory! You were right!'

A third of the way up in the western sky, a shower of meteors played through the air. Careening and shooting, they lit the sky in tiny white spasms.

Glory stood in the middle of the Reynolds front yard and slowly began to twirl in her nightie. She held her head back and watched as all the stars began to shoot and career through the night skies. She twirled faster and faster until she fell down in a giggling, dizzy heap. Still staring at the sky, she felt Pammy plop down beside her and hug her arm.

'We've been chosen, Glory. Just like those kids overseas, we've been chosen.'

'Do you think this kind of thing happens a lot?'

'Not a lot, but it happens. Mostly in foreign places, I think. About fifteen or twenty years ago the Virgin even made the sun go backwards and dance in the sky.'

'She made the stars rain for us.'

'Lots of people saw the sun dance. That was the difference. That's why I know about it. It's real famous.'

'I'd like to be famous. I'd like to be on the radio and talk about the sun dance and stuff like that.'

'I don't think that's the way it's supposed to work. I think we're supposed to make the Virgin famous. I think we're supposed to get some secret messages or something like that.'

'The other kids got secret messages?'

'Ten or twenty of them. I think they told the Pope, but that was it.'

'What were the messages?'

'They're secrets, Glory. Nobody knows but the kids and the Pope.'

'Seems to me that if you had something really important to say you'd want to tell as many people as you could. I wonder if the Virgin really thought that one out.'

'She doesn't need to think it out, God does that for her. All she has to do is show up.'

'So she's kind of like Billy at the Western Union office. She delivers the telegrams that somebody else writes.'

'No, Glory. She is the most important lady that ever lived. She's one hundred percent holy. She's completely good and completely pure, so when she says anything you know it's true.'

A picture of her mama with her temper and her sharp tongue jumped into Glory's mind. The richly colored hair that could only be confined for a few hours by a piece of string. The way she walked like she was just daring everybody to say anything she didn't like. She'd never noticed if what her mama said was true or not because it was usually so interesting. She knew the names of all the plants and most of the birds. She'd read about every book in the world to boot. Holy was a wonderful thing and she hoped her mama had some of that too. She'd have to start looking for signs of holiness in her mama.

'What's the difference between being holy and just being real nice like Teacher or Aunt Flo?' She hated asking these things. Hated to show her ignorance to Pammy. She could almost feel Pammy swelling up with pride and importance as the questions were asked. It wasn't fair that only Catholics knew this stuff. They weren't exactly bad, but everybody knew there would never be a Catholic president because Catholics, even Catholic presidents, would have to do whatever the Pope told them to do. People like that, people who did what the Pope told them to do and people who worshipped idols shouldn't be given secrets. It wasn't right.

'Holy comes from God, I guess.' Pammy paused for a moment and Glory could almost hear the wheels turning in her head. Could almost hear the gears grinding over Pammy's ideas. 'Good is what you're taught and holy is what God tells you.'

'How do you know the Virgin was so holy? Maybe she was just really good.' After all, she reasoned, this was just stuff Pammy'd been taught. Stuff the Catholics told kids. Maybe it was like telling little kids about fairies and then when a kid actually sees a fairy the grown-ups laugh and say they were just making the whole thing up. The whole time they were just making it up while some poor little kid is out beating the bushes and getting skinned knees and about a hundred bug bites.

'God chose her to have His son. There were a lot of nice ladies around, but He chose the one who was holy. She was holy before she was even born. Everything about her was holy.'

'How can you be holy before you're born?' She thought of the almost-balloon-babies in the paintings that were turned to the wall. Maybe that was what babies looked like before they were born. Maybe those were something like human tadpoles.

'Even before she was born her parents knew she was going to be holy. Her parents Joachim and Anna had a big old hug and then she was born. Just like that. And when she was three her daddy took her to the temple to show her off and let everybody know just how special she was. Mary knew she was holy so she started dancing like nobody had ever seen before. She started dancing and dancing on the temple's steps. Pretty soon everybody gathered around and everybody fell in love with her because she was so holy and she was a good dancer too.' Pammy stood and started dancing around like the front lawn was a big ballroom.

Glory stood and watched, trying to hear Pammy's Catholic music, but she heard nothing and felt left out. She slipped on the red shoes and swayed slightly, hoping the rhythm would catch her and send her to wherever Pammy seemed to be going.

'Come here, Glory. Dance with me and we'll dance like Mary did. Maybe everybody will fall in love with us.'

Glory joined Pammy and, to her surprise, she began to hear the music. A sweet song of pipes and birds and maybe a touch of angel-humming. They swayed and swirled and kicked their legs high into the night sky. They held their nighties, damp with sweat, away from their bodies and finally pulled them over their heads with a giggle, discarding them where they fell.

Glory did it first, but Pammy was right behind her. She climbed up the porch stairs and began a rapid sort of tap dance in honor of Mary and the warm night air. Pammy's bigger feet joined hers until the whole porch seemed to throb with their wonderful Mary dance.

Glory felt the air against her body, cooling and heating all at the same time. Her hair clung to her neck and she lifted it toward the sky just as the screen door opened and knocked her against the side of the house.

'What the Hell is going on here? Jesus H. Christ, what do you goddamned kids think you're doing?' Lucille Reynolds stood in the doorway. 'Mother of God, where are your clothes?' Little Beau stood behind his mother, his eyes as big as saucers.

CHAPTER FIVE

'I hope you girls have an explanation, but I can't imagine what it would be.' Miss Lucille had sat them both down on the big green divan after wrapping them in damp bath towels that smelled like they hadn't been completely dry for two or three days.

'Don't be mad, Miss Lucille, we were just . . .' Glory looked at the toes of her wonderful shoes so that she wouldn't have to look at Pammy's mother. The woman had her hair tied up in a scarf and she was wearing some kind of silky robe that was the same color as moldy bread. Thick white face cream was smeared on her face and it made her look like something that had stayed in the bread box so long it had learned to talk and stomp around. The woman had been growling and fussing ever since she'd opened the front door.

'You were just doing what, Glory Gorman? I should have known better. I've been warned enough times, but I always gave you Gormans the benefit of the doubt and now I have to admit I've been proven very wrong.'

'Mama, you don't know what you're saying. Something wonderful has happened to us. Something so wonderful has happ—' Pammy, unsure about direct insubordination, began to get red in the face and her voice sounded like she could easily start gargling without the benefit of warm salt water.

'Naked. Naked as a couple of little whores. Dear God in heaven.' She reached into the pocket of the moldy bread robe and pulled out a pack of cigarettes. She fumbled with the matches before lighting the cigarette and taking a deep drag of smoke into her lungs. Glory and Pammy watched as her shoulders sank down and her hand stopped shaking. Glory hoped she'd blow the smoke out of her nose like the drawing of a Chinese dragon she'd seen in a book.

'That's not the only bad thing they done. They took me into the woods after you told them not to. They almost got me killed.' LB stood in the doorway to the kitchen with a big grin on his face. He was wearing a pair of ratty-looking underpants and some gray socks.

'Oh, Jesus Christ! What is it going to take for you girls to listen? Wait till your father comes home, Pamela. He will kill you. I'm certain it's the only thing we can do.' The tranquilizing effect of the cigarette seemed to have worn off very quickly. Mrs Reynolds wasn't known for her sense of humor and Glory half suspected that Pammy might very well be dead on Friday night.

'Tell her, Pammy.' Glory didn't know how she'd managed to keep quiet as long as she had. She wanted to yell and scream at Miss Lucille. Even if she had given her those wonderful shoes she shouldn't be able to say things without giving other people the benefit of the doubt. She was the one smoking and she was the one who came from down South and she was the one who talked funny and she was the one who didn't have a single dead relation in the cemetery. She swallowed hard, forcing down the big lump of anger that had wedged in her throat. Not only did her family have the biggest house in town, she reminded herself, but they had the biggest, fanciest plot in the cemetery.

Grandpa Gorman had a real nice headstone with crying angels put up for his mother, but he'd really gone whole hog when

Evangeline died. He'd had one of those fancy walk-in tombs built for the short-lived, but long-mourned Evangeline. It even had a little stained-glass window that made colored lights play across the dusty floor. Evangeline was put inside the wall of the tomb and when he died Grandpa Gorman had left instructions that he was to be slotted right underneath her in the same wall. Aunt Flo said it was a blessing that they would be together for eternity since their life together on earth had been tragically short.

Aunt Flo and Uncle Hoyt would take her there twice a year on what would have been her grandparents' birthdays if they hadn't died. Aunt Flo never knew Evangeline, but she always cried a little and talked about what a loss it was that she never got to know her babies. Uncle Hoyt would just stand there and watch as Aunt Flo took out the brown twigs that used to be flowers and replaced them with little nosegays she made up from whatever was growing in the yard or the fields. It always looked real pretty by the time they left. As far as she knew, her mama never went out to the cemetery at all.

'I can't tell her until I get a sign.' Pammy almost shouted out the words through the side of her mouth, but thought she was keeping things private since the words were centered around her dog teeth. Pammy looked kind of pale and shaky, like she'd been hanging upside-down too long on the monkey bars during recess.

'There's more? This isn't enough?' Miss Lucille was looking fairly pale and shaky herself.

'Your mama is threatening to kill you, Pammy. I think that's close enough to a sign, even for you.' She didn't want to alarm Pammy, but she felt that Pammy wasn't taking a hard look at the potential consequences of her sign-waiting behavior. Glory was concerned that as busy as the Virgin must be, she just might get distracted and forget to give Pammy the sign she seemed to need.

'I'll never tell. I won't tell until I've received permission. I will be like the saints and martyrs.' Pammy closed her eyes and folded her hands in prayer.

Mrs Reynolds shoved the cigarette into her mouth and grabbed each girl by the ear. She pulled each ear up until Glory was fairly certain that hers was about a foot above her hair. 'Tell me now or you won't live long enough to be a saint, but you will definitely be a martyr.' The woman's voice sounded dark and slurry. It didn't sound the way Glory's mama's did when she was threatening to skin her alive or take a coat hanger to her bottom. She was always saying that kind of thing, but Glory could never remember being hit by her mama or any other grown-up. Unless you counted Bubba Weston, who was as big as a grown-up, but only fourteen and dumb as a turnip. Bubba took swipes at almost everybody when Teacher wasn't paying attention.

'I'll tell, Miss Lucille. I'll tell you what happened.' Glory felt her ear drop back to somewhere around the side of her face. It burned and she wiggled her jaw to help it get back in its usual spot. Pammy made a whimpering sound, but Glory ignored her.

'Spit it out.' Mrs Reynolds put her face about an inch from Glory's, surrounding her in a cloud of smoke.

'This could take a few minutes. You might want to sit down.' Glory wanted to cough, but this would be acknowledging that the woman was smoking. Since no nice ladies smoked, it would be the same as saying that Lucille Reynolds wasn't a nice lady and she was sure that wasn't going to help things much. She didn't know if Miss Lucille could get madder than she already was, but she knew she didn't want to find out.

'Now!' The smoke curled in and out of the woman's teeth and even though it wasn't coming out of her nose, she still looked like a dragon.

'When we were in the woods a hobo grabbed me.' Glory glared at LB and hoped that her mean-eyed look was scaring him half to death. There were rules about kids telling on other kids and he knew it; she'd warned him before. 'Pammy prayed to the Virgin and he disappeared. He vanished into thin air. Pammy told me about the Holy Mother and I didn't believe in the Holy Mother, what with me being a Presbyterian and all, so I asked for Mary's help myself. I asked her for some shoes like Pammy has and then you gave me these.' She wiggled her feet in what she hoped was a friendly manner. She tried to move them in a musical fashion that would remind Miss Lucille of happy music and snappy tunes that were fun to hum.

'I came over here to tell Pammy about the shoes. She didn't believe it was a miracle so we went outside to look for a sign. At first we didn't see anything, but then we saw a great big part of the sky dance like fireworks on the Fourth of July.' She looked to Pammy and nodded in an encouraging manner. She felt that she'd softened Mrs Reynolds up, at least a little bit.

'So I told Glory some more about the Virgin because I'm teaching her about the onetruechurch. I was telling her about Mary and the time she was dancing at the temple and then I started hearing the most wonderful music. You should have heard it, Mama. It was the most beautiful music I've ever heard and I just had to dance to it. My feet were moving before I knew it and I was dancing like an angel.'

'I heard it too, Miss Lucille. I didn't hear it at first, but when I put the shoes on I heard it. We kept dancing and the air felt so good and pretty soon it seemed like our nighties got in the way of the music.' That must have been what happened because she'd never known anything like this to happen before. Sometimes her mama enjoyed walking around in her birthday suit, but only when Uncle Hoyt was at work. Besides, she did it mostly because she knew it irritated Aunt Flo.

Apart from that, being naked was something that happened accidentally, like the time Aunt Flo's nightie gave way or the time when Mr Heath was taking down storm windows last spring. It was almost like it had stopped being winter overnight. When they went to bed it was winter and when they woke up it was almost summer. The thermometer was reading eighty degrees, just that fast.

Mr Heath across the street decided, along with everyone else, to take his storm windows off that very day. He was almost done and he'd stripped down to just his trousers as had most of the men, what with it being a warm day and storm windows being hard work. He was reaching up to take down the last window and his pants dropped down around his knees. He couldn't do much because by then he had a forty-pound storm window in his hands. Most people on the street got a pretty good view of his butt before he was able to pull his pants back up. It got so quiet, a pin dropping would have made people blink. Nobody ever mentioned it, but Mr Heath kept pretty much to himself for the next few days.

'So you stripped off your clothes and danced buck-naked on the front lawn?' She wasn't smiling, but she no longer looked like a woman who was considering the eating of human flesh.

'It seemed like a very good idea. It sounds silly now, but it didn't then.' Glory raised her eyebrows and tried to position herself so that the light caught her red hair. This technique had proven itself to be especially effective with Aunt Flo, who would chuckle and call her a pixie.

'This isn't your first good idea, is it? I suppose you're the one who thought going into the woods would be a good idea?'

Glory lowered her eyebrows and looked down at her hands without saying a word. Mrs Reynolds had clearly formed her own opinions and it seemed rude to argue at this point.

'Eat up, Glory. I'll deal with you when I get back.' Her mama stomped out of the kitchen and slammed the screen door behind her. All the big people had been quiet and tight-lipped, because having Lucille Beaumont Reynolds on your porch with a naked child standing beside her at two in the morning makes people quiet and tight-lipped. Glory took a bite of her toast, but it tasted like a page in the dictionary.

After putting her own children to bed with the command to not even breathe, much less speak, Miss Lucille had frog-marched Glory back to the big house. As soon as they got on the porch she whipped the damp bath towel off of Glory and started pounding on the front door. Lights started going on in bedrooms up and down the street and Glory could almost feel half the town looking at her without so much as a pair of panties to cover her. For a second or two she thought about praying to the Virgin to kill her off then and there and give Miss Lucille a heart attack if she happened to have any more death left over to hand around.

Mama had opened the door and Glory had hurried in without saying a word. She ran upstairs and threw herself into bed and pulled the sheet over her head and listened to the drone of the women's voices downstairs. She couldn't hear what they were saying because Aunt Flo and Uncle Hoyt were running around asking who was dead. Within five minutes all the voices stopped.

She kept waiting for Mama to come into her room, but her door stayed closed. She heard the squeak of the bedsprings on Uncle Hoyt's side of the bed, the liquidy sound of Aunt Flo's night-breathing, and finally the click of Mama's lamp. Once all the house sounds were quiet she listened very carefully and heard just a few notes of the Mary music.

By the time she woke up, Uncle Hoyt had gone for the day and Aunt Flo just smiled a little and pointed her head toward her sister-in-law. Clearly, Aunt Flo felt she wasn't to talk to Glory even though Glory could see that Aunt Flo would understand what had happened and she'd feel a lot better if she could just climb up into that big lap for a few minutes.

Aunt Flo's lap was a wonderful place to be when things weren't too good. Her lap didn't end abruptly, but flowed down like a thick tablecloth. Any movement made while sitting on Aunt Flo's lap was answered with a friendly little wave of flesh that could rock a child to sleep if she were overtired or coming down with a cold. Her big breasts provided an ideal cushion; sweet-smelling and pliant, they could block out all sound but the beating of Aunt Flo's big heart.

She shoved her thumb in her mouth, something she hadn't done in broad daylight for at least two years. She thought about going upstairs to get Tilly, the stuffed rabbit, but it seemed like too much work and not enough comfort. She wasn't even sure where Tilly was anymore.

Aunt Flo was out back tying up the tomato plants so she didn't want to go there. It would be too tempting to talk to Aunt Flo and too awful if Aunt Flo looked real sad and told her that she was disappointed in her. She hardly ever got angry, but she could be so disappointed it would almost break her big heart, and that was a terrible thing to see and feel responsible for.

Glory moved in what she felt was a somber manner up to the big bedroom. Positioned at the front of the house, its window gave a broad view of the street and she'd be able to see if anybody was walking along the street. She'd be able to see, for instance, if somebody was walking to the house from the general direction of Pammy's house. Maybe if she saw Mama she'd be able to tell by looking at her whether or not she was still mad. Maybe.

She leaned out the window, but couldn't see anything but Mrs Clay tending her petunia bed. Mrs Clay was very proud of her petunias and would hand out little envelopes of her petunia seeds to the neighbors at Christmas. Everybody would ooh and aah over their little envelopes of seed, but Mrs Clay was about the only person around who grew petunias.

Because of a wall that had fallen down in New York City all the money was mostly gone. People didn't seem to care about petunias and things like that. Most people were too busy with their vegetable patches to grow things like petunias. Mr Heath had even grown runner beans around his front porch this summer. Told Uncle Hoyt it made a lot more sense than something you couldn't put in a jar and eat come winter.

Glory pulled her head in and took another look at the Evangeline shrine. She studied the wedding dress, which looked just the same, at least at first glance.

She moved a little closer and noticed the way the arms on the dress were positioned. For the first time she realized that the arms looked as though they'd just been dropped back down after being held up to pray. She was sure of it. She stepped back to look at the mannequin from a different angle as she scratched at an itching inside her left nostril with her little finger.

A moment later she felt a tickling warmth which she wiped

away with her hand. It happened again so she wiped at her lip with her other hand and made a loud sniff. She looked at one sticky hand and then the other. Blood streaked each palm, reminding her of the gory pictures hung on the Reynoldses' walls.

She fell to her knees without taking her eyes off the shrine. She continued to dab at her nose, which was dripping blood at a fairly steady pace. It fell with little plops on her dress, but it seemed like something that was supposed to happen. It didn't hurt and she didn't feel sick.

The blood started dripping faster and she thought about calling to Aunt Flo, but she knew that if Aunt Flo had wanted to talk to her she would have come looking for her. She lay down like she'd seen Teacher have one of the big girls at school do when blood had been dripping out of her nose. She tried to be as still as possible so that the blood would get the idea of staying where it was supposed to be.

She closed her eyes and thought about the night before and how the sky had danced for them. She made the night sky inside her mind and began to notice things that she hadn't noticed before. The stars danced and swirled in ever widening circles and behind the circles, back where it was dark, but not quite black, stood the Virgin Evangeline in her now black wedding dress with the sleeves that had just dropped down after praying. The Virgin Evangeline moved her head and a shower of shiny flakes, just like the ones on the Christmas card, fell on Glory's nose and made the bleeding stop.

CHAPTER SIX

He lay on his back and stared at the ceiling. He knew as soon as he moved from the pillow the whole thing would start up. His head would start pounding and he'd break out in a sweat. His stomach would start lurching, his bowels would rebel and then he'd be forced to get up. He hated mornings.

He heard the back door and the sounds of activity in the kitchen. It was part of God's punishment for his shortcomings, he was almost certain. Four parishes, four rectories, and four part-time housekeepers. All the housekeepers were ignorant but devout women and all of them made too much noise in the morning.

The footsteps left the kitchen and headed toward his bed-room. He tried to take a deep breath, but it made the front of his forehead hurt and that made his eyes burn. She was even hum-ming this morning. Some mindless little ditty that poked into his brains like Satan's own pitchfork.

'Father Greene, are you awake?' She was so loud. It sounded as though she was shouting the words into his ear.

'Yes, Judith, I'm awake.' His body responded to the news with some enthusiasm. A nasty taste leapt to his tongue and the contents of his stomach threatened to join the nasty taste. His neck informed him that he'd slept on it all wrong, and massive amounts of gas were converging inside his colon, ready to greet the day with a thundering announcement. He constricted his sphincter muscles to delay the announcement until Judith was back in her kitchen where she belonged.

'That's good, Father, that's very good. It's almost eight and I saw at least two people go into the church already for Mass. Two's not bad, do you think? Of course I'll be joining you so that makes three and that's quite good. I think that's good, don't you, Father?'

'Quite good, Judith.' He rolled on his side and saw that it was indeed almost eight. He could imagine the two who were already waiting. They'd be two of the ten or so Catholics in town. This time of day they'd most likely be two old women, widows. Widows who still found themselves getting up every morning at six to get breakfasts for husbands that had no use for earthly food. Not that it mattered to the widows. Most of them still cooked for two and were always surprised at the amount of leftovers from every meal.

'I got some fresh eggs on my way this morning. Can I fry up some eggs and maybe a little bacon for you?'

'No, just some tea if you wouldn't mind.' He'd never had her make him anything but tea for breakfast, but she bought fresh eggs anyway. He suspected that later in the day her shiftless husband would come by and make short work of the eggs and anything else in the rectory's larder.

'One more thing, Father.' He could just about picture her on the other side of the door. Judith with her hairnet and her crop of black chin hairs. She'd have her ear pressed to the wood, anxious to hear his every word. Judith felt it was a blessing to be able to serve a priest. She told him so at least once a week. Backbone of the Church, that's what Bishop Wrigley called women like Judith. Sweet-tempered, loyal, hairy-chinned women who felt cooking for a priest was a way of serving Christ himself.

'Yes, Judith?' His bowels rumbled, threatening to make a less than joyful noise that might blow the door off its hinges.

'Mrs Reynolds stopped me on my way here. She said she was coming by later with that Miss Gorman. You know the one I mean.'

'Miss Gorman?' He tried to think of his flock and couldn't think of a Miss at all.

'Miss Gorman is that one whose daddy used to be the doctor. He used to be the doctor, but then he died and she had a baby, but I think she would have had the baby even if her daddy had lived. Anyway, she lives in that big house with the wraparound porch and my husband says she's a whore even if she works at the library. He says he can't stand to go near the library since she's been working there.'

'That's fine, Judith.' He listened as her feet slapped their way back to the kitchen. He let himself relax and rather enjoyed the release of fumes that followed.

He stood in the shade as he bid the worshippers goodbye. A total of four in the congregation, Judith would remind him tomorrow. Of course, she and her slack-jawed husband made up half of that number.

He felt a little better now, a little steadier. He almost always did after Mass. A few sips of wine, a few prayers and the day ahead didn't seem so long. After Mass it was only three hours to lunch and a glass or two of wine. After that it was easy to take a nap and breeze through to four when drinking was the mark of a civilised man.

Prohibition had made things difficult for some, but not for priests. Even the Federal government recognised that. Production was still robust for sacramental wine. More sacramental wine was being produced that ever before. And it wasn't half bad. Thick and sweet, it went down like mother's milk. It gave him problems in the morning, he didn't deny that, but didn't everything have a cost, didn't every love require a sacrifice?

He crossed the yard to the rectory and went into his dark study to rest until Mrs Reynolds and the Gorman woman came. He shook his head at the thought of Judith's husband staying away from the library because of the Gorman woman. He doubted if the man knew what a library was, much less had ever been in one.

Each of his four towns seemed to have someone like the Gorman woman. Some foolish woman who spent her life paying for her lust. Women who'd given themselves up to sin and spent the rest of their days on the fringes, never being accepted wholly by decent people again. Perhaps, he mused, God put such a woman in each community to remind others of the wages of sin, the penalty for succumbing to the desires of the flesh.

He leaned his head back and closed his eyes in hopes of dropping off to sleep for a few minutes before the women arrived. His head was beginning to hurt again and his mouth tasted terrible. Mornings were a difficult time.

'Father Greene, how are you today?' Lucille Reynolds was wearing her dark blue dress and the string of Woolworth pearls.

'I'm fine, Lucille. It's nice to see you, as always.' He nodded to the Reynolds woman, but avoided looking directly at her companion. He recognised her right away, of course. The type men remembered even if they didn't want to, and judging by the way she carried herself, she seemed to know it.

'Father Greene, I'd like you to meet Miss Eva Gorman. Her little girl Glory is friends with my Pammy.'

'Miss Gorman.' He nodded and indicated the two chairs across from his desk. 'Please have a seat, ladies.' He wished they'd arrived later in the day, after his stomach had a chance to settle down. 'What can I do for you ladies this morning?' He put his fingertips together, forming a miniature steeple.

'It's about our little girls, Father. They've got something into their heads and I don't know what to think.' Mrs Reynolds fingered her pearls and looked out the window.

'The girls think they've seen the Virgin Mary and they think she's been performing miracles. Last night Miss Lucille found them dancing naked out in her front yard.' The Gorman woman had a low, slow voice and her right eyebrow went up when she spoke. Her mouth twitched slightly as though she might start laughing or whistling any second.

'Children.' He shrugged and smiled in what he hoped would be a reassuring fashion. 'They hear about things like Fatima and Lourdes and they naturally let their imaginations go wild.'

'Are you saying that this Mary person never shows herself?' The Gorman woman leaned forward slightly, her breast touching the edge of his desk.

'Not at all, Miss Gorman. There have been a number of sightings which the Vatican has recognised. There have even been several in this country, but I can't . . .'

'Well, then I think you should talk to the girls.' She sat back and started playing with the thick braid of hair at her neck.

'Are you saying that you think the girls have really been visited by the Virgin, Miss Gorman?'

'Reverend Greene, I'm a Presbyterian, and not a very good one at that. All I know is that some odd things seem to be happening to these girls and it seems logical to look at their explanations before anything else.' She looked up and stared at him for a moment before continuing. 'Aren't you supposed to believe in miracles and sightings? If you don't believe, who's going to?' She smiled, showing big, even white teeth.

'Now, about these so-called miracles that you mentioned.' He looked from one woman to the other.

'I don't think there have been any miracles, Father Greene. I told Miss Eva we shouldn't come here, but she insisted. We shouldn't have bothered you with this.'

'It's his job, Lucille. Isn't that so, Reverend Greene?'

'I suppose you could put it that way.' She made his head ache. Her voice, her appearance, he felt she was pushing him in a corner even though she was four feet away.

'Reverend Greene, in the last forty-eight hours I have found out that my young daughter is dancing naked in the moonlight because she thinks she's hearing something she calls Mary music. She tells me she was chased by a hobo who disappeared in a cloud of smoke when her friend said some Hey Marys.'

'Hail Marys, Eva, Hail Marys.' Mrs Reynolds tugged at her companion's sleeve.

'Hail Marys then. Yesterday morning I found her in front of my mother's memorial and she was covered with blood.'

'She'd had a nosebleed.'

'Lucille, I already told you, she's never had a nosebleed before. Even if it was just a nosebleed, she got it while she was praying to your Virgin and she passed out. She's never passed out, she's never had a nosebleed, she's never snuck out of the house and danced naked in the middle of the night either. I for one want to know what the hell is going on with those girls.'

'If it would put your minds at rest, I would be happy to interview the girls.'

Mrs Reynolds stood and pulled on the Gorman woman's arm. 'That's all we ask, Father. I'm sure the girls will listen to you and we can put an end to this.'

It was rather nice really. Not the kind of thing that normally went on in any of his four parishes. Catholics had never been popular in America, especially not in the places he'd been assigned. Being a Catholic was barely one notch above a Jew or an Oriental.

Being a Catholic, he'd always felt, required a community. The bigger the better. Catholicism was at its best in large groups. Protestants did pretty well on their own, but not Catholics. He'd grown up in Chicago, where it was fairly easy to be a Catholic in the neighborhoods that didn't recognise that Ireland, Poland, and Italy were five thousand miles away. They'd have wonderful processions through the streets on feast days. Poor as they were, they'd wear satin sashes and cover the saints with money. The women would make wonderful food and they'd eat and drink and sing long into the night.

Impossible to do when your congregation consisted of Judith, her odious husband, several widows over sixty, and Mrs Reynolds and her two kids. That was the troublesome part. Lucille Reynolds was from one of the finest families in New

Orleans, she'd told him so herself. She was convent-educated and who knew what connections she might have? Not the kind of woman to cross. She was just the kind who might have an uncle who's a bishop or a cardinal. Some of those New Orleans families had real tight connections in France and Spain, too.

She lived simply, that was clear, but old money was like that. Besides, her family might not approve of Raymond Reynolds and might not be forthcoming with funds because of it. Or they could have been hit hard in the Crash like almost everybody else. Not that it would make any difference in Church circles. She certainly dressed Pammy beautifully, preparing her for New Orleans society, no doubt. He'd have to tread lightly with her, he knew that. Wouldn't do to call Pammy and the other girl a couple of hysterical brats, even if that's what they were.

Eva Gorman had been a surprise. Didn't seem to be the least bit ashamed of her situation. She didn't even try to explain it the way most women would, at least Catholic women. Talking like she actually believed the girls had seen something. Handsome woman, even if she was on the big side for his taste, if he had taste. Which he didn't. A lot of priests fell into that old honey pot, but he wasn't one of them. He knew he could walk through a room full of naked Eva Gormans and not even blink if there was a bottle on the other side of the room.

It had been the seminary's fault. Filled with Irish boys. It would have been all right if he'd gone to one with Italians. Some wine with food wouldn't have done this to him. No, it had been the Irish boys with their sad songs and love of whiskey. They'd all go down to the docks before they took holy orders and dance with girls who looked hard and used. Then they'd start drinking in a very serious fashion. They'd drink because they couldn't go home with the hard girls, couldn't even think about any part of them but their souls.

He'd have to be careful with her, too. Another old family, even if a different sort. Fallen woman or not, she still lived in the biggest house in town and she ran the library. A person like that could have a lot of influence in the community. If she even half believed the girls, she might be a possible convert.

That would almost be a miracle in itself. When he was younger, he dreamed of bringing the beauty and mystery of the faith into the sorry little parishes he'd been assigned. How confidently he'd strode into those parishes with his message, with his medals and regalia, only to find that people had no curiosity about religion beyond the confines of their clapboard, white-washed little buildings. To make matters worse, the Baptists, the Presbyterians, and the Methodists were all convinced that Holy Mother Church in Rome was out to rule the world and destroy the American way of life.

He still included the dream of conversion in his daily prayers. One conversion would be enough. If his life had changed one person's that much, he'd be able to call himself a success.

'You're early. The girls won't be here for another fifteen minutes.'

'Miss Gorman?' He couldn't see where the voice was coming from. The long stacks of books were poorly lit.

'Right here.' She emerged from the last row of shelves with an ostrich feather duster in her hand. 'I try to dust in here once a month, whether it needs it or not.' She wiped her hand across her face, leaving a streak of dust and dirt across her nose. Dust seemed to be everywhere and he fought the urge to wave his hand in front of his face.

'I came a little early because I wanted to talk to you before I talked to the girls.'

'Why? I'm not the one seeing visions or claiming miracles.'

'I suppose that's why I want to talk to you.' He glanced around quickly until he noticed a small group of chairs in the corner. 'Could we sit down?'

'Sure. Are you thirsty? Would you like something to drink?'

'Something to drink?' His spine grew a little straighter at the words.

'I've got some iced tea in a thermos, but I could put some coffee on if you'd prefer that.'

'I'm fine, but thank you.' Disappointed, he thought, but fine. A drink would have made everything a little more pleasant.

She sat in one of the chairs, crossing one leg over the other. 'Talk away.'

He sat across from her and folded his thin hands over his belly before clearing his throat. 'You said some things this morning that interested me.'

'It's an interesting situation.'

'True, but I'm referring to your response to the situation. You said yourself that you're a "Presbyterian, and not a very good one".'

'That's right.'

'Yet you, more so than Mrs Reynolds, seem to give some credence to the children's statements. Why is that?'

She put her head to the side and began to toy with her braided hair. 'I've been trying to figure that very thing out since Lucille told me what the girls were saying.'

'And?'

'I see myself when I look at Glory. I guess every mother does when she looks at her daughter.' She shrugged and then bit lightly on her lower lip. 'My mother died giving birth to me and my brother. Obviously she was dead, but I remember seeing her. I remember seeing her looking down on me when I was in my crib. I couldn't have been more than about two, but I remember it. I remember seeing her on my first day at school. She was standing in the back of all the other mothers, but she was there. She was there whenever I was sick or sad.'

'That must have been a great comfort to you.' He'd heard variations on this story through the years. About half the widows would tell him similar stories and think they were telling something unique and quite true.

'I know what you're thinking. You're thinking that it was a child's way to cope with a void in her life, but I don't think that was it. I saw her. I saw my mother. She was looking out for me. She was a part of my life. She was as much a part of my upbringing as my father or the housekeeper. She was real.' There were tears in her eyes and she wiped at those, leaving another track of dirt on her face. 'I didn't imagine it, I didn't make it up.'

'Do you still see her?'

'No. They made her go away.'

'Who made her go away?'

'Everyone. Whenever I talked about her, or talked to her, I was told that I was making her up. She was one of the most important things in my life, but nobody would believe me. I had to choose between what everybody else believed and what I believed. I was just a little kid, so everybody else won.'

'So you think something like this is happening to your daughter?'

'I don't know. I know that somehow in Glory's mind the Virgin is mixed up with my mother Evangeline.'

'So she knows about your mother?'

'She knows that my mother died in childbirth. The shrine my father put up is still there in the big bedroom. My brother tried to clear it out a few years ago, but I wouldn't let him do it. I haven't told Glory that I used to see her, if that's what you're asking.'

'You said she died giving birth to you and your brother. Your twin brother?'

'That's what they generally call it when two babies are born at the same time.'

'Yes, well, did he ever see her?'

'I don't know. I always felt she was just interested in me, but I guess kids always think that way.'

'If I understand what you're saying, you believe your daughter because of what you saw as a child and you think she's seeing the same thing.'

'I think children might see things the rest of us don't. Maybe lots of people see things the rest of us don't. I know my world was a better place when my mother was a part of it. I made a bad bargain when I let myself be talked out of my mother. I don't want the girls to make the same bad deal.'

'I don't think you want the children to make up stories and live in a fantasy world either, do you, Miss Gorman?'

'What you talk about is religion and faith. What I talk about is stories and fantasy. Is that what you're saying?'

'Miss Gorman, I have almost two thousand years of history and tradition behind my beliefs and I don't feel the need to debate them with you.' He sighed and shook his head. Eva Gorman wasn't going to be his convert.

'You can take your two thousand years and do whatever you want with them, sir. I just think that whatever gets two little girls so excited and happy that they dance naked in the front yard in the middle of the night can't be all bad. Something that scares off a hobo who was trying to hurt my child sounds pretty good. Something that gives a child a pair of shoes her mother can't afford is something I'd like to see a little more of. And something that can make the stars dance is something this whole lousy town could use.' She stood, towering over him in what he thought was a menacing fashion. 'All this talking, I've worked up a thirst. I'm going to get me some of that iced tea. Sure you don't want some?'

CHAPTER SEVEN

'I think it's wonderful that you girls are so interested in the Blessed Mother, but as I listen to you it occurs to me that perhaps interest is all we really have here.' He spoke to the girls, but kept half an eye on Eva Gorman. A few minutes before she'd said 'Hey Mary' again and half winked at him when Lucille Reynolds corrected her. She knew the right way to say it, but she was one of those women who was only happy when she was making waves.

'You think we're lying, but we're not.' Glory knelt on the chair and leaned across the library table. She'd spent almost the whole time drawing while Pammy told the story. 'Are we, Pammy?' She didn't look at her friend as she busily added another star to her drawing.

'Are you drawing the sky you saw, Glory?' He glanced at her paper, feigning an interest.

'No sir, I'm just giving myself lots of stars like Teacher does when my work is real good. School's out and I miss getting all those stars.'

'I get as many stars as you do, Glory.' Pammy had sat with her ankles crossed and her hands folded during the entire interview with Father Greene.

'You get lots of stars because you're Teacher's favorite. I get lots of stars because I'm just that good at school.' She looked at Father Greene and yawned without covering her mouth. 'I'm ready to go outside now.'

'That's fine, girls. Miss Lucille and I are going to talk to Father Greene for a little while, but you two can go ahead and go over to our house. Your Aunt Flo is over there with LB and she'll keep an eye on you. Mind her, you hear me?' She called the last to the girls' backs because they'd run toward the door as soon as they heard the word 'fine'.

'What do you think, Father Greene?' Lucille Reynolds looked at him with her fine dark eyes. She looked weary, as though she hadn't been sleeping well for some time. Not a surprise really. A woman of her background and sensibilities had no business living the way she did.

'I think you ladies have two fine little girls who have fine imaginations. I think it's important to foster their interest without encouraging their flights of fancy.' He nodded to the Gorman woman. 'Ideas like this can enrich lives as long as they're not taken too seriously. We need to find a balance for the girls. I would be happy to instruct them in some Marian lore which I think they'd find most interesting.'

'Reverend Greene. Please forgive me for not calling you "Father", but I had a father and he and I didn't have a whole lot to do with each other. The day I call you "Father" you might want to leave town.' In spite of her words she smiled sweetly and her hazel eyes seemed to twinkle. 'Sorry to digress. Reverend Greene, this is kind of personal, but if you could change one thing in your life, what would it be?'

'I don't know, I'd have to think about that, Miss Gorman.'

'Why don't you just call me "Miss Eva"? That's what almost everybody around here calls me.'

'All right, Miss Eva.' He smiled back at her and glanced at the big clock above the door. It was half past three. At ten minutes to four he could pour himself a glass. He'd drink it fast, knowing he would savor the second one.

'Answer my question please.' She spoke in a tone he rarely heard. Brisk and authoritative were tones that weren't usually used toward men in clerical collars.

'Eva, please.' Mrs Reynolds paled and put her hand to her pearls.

'Lucille, whatever I say to this man in no way reflects on you. I know you think I'm going to burn in Hell for back-talking to a priest, but I assure you that if I'm going to Hell it's going to be for something a lot more interesting and amusing than this.' She turned back to him, her smile gone.

'You and I both know that you dislike yourself as much as the next guy. What is the one thing you would change?'

'We are all flawed, Miss Eva.'

'Damn right about that. Doesn't answer my question, but I can't argue with the statement.'

'I'm grateful that I was consulted today . . .'

'But you've got to go because you need a drink?'

'Eva!' Mrs Reynolds's hand flew from her pearls to her mouth.

'Lucille, you know as well as everyone else in town that Reverend Greene is a drunk. Not that I care. I sort of like drunks. Unless they're mean drunks, but he doesn't seem like a mean drunk. He just seems like the ordinary kind of drunk.'

He stood and walked toward the door; his chest and neck felt tight and hard. He could barely hear her over the pounding of blood in his ears.

'Maybe you can't help being a drunk, most can't, but that doesn't mean you have to be a coward.'

He turned and looked at her. 'Miss Gorman, I will not be spoken to like this by someone like you.'

'Someone like me? Like me? What kind of person am I, Reverend Greene?'

'You know what I'm talking about.'

'Ah, you mean Glory. I'm a bad woman and a whore because I had a child without being married?' She looked at him and stood up a little straighter. 'Mary wasn't married either.'

'That's blasphemy.'

'Well, here's some more blasphemy for you. Mary and I have a few other things in common when you think of it. We were both surprised, real surprised. And neither one of us ran away from what happened. I tried to, I admit it. I would have gotten rid of her before she was even born if I could have. I was planning to give her away to my brother and his wife, but I didn't. I faced up to my problem and it turned out to be the best thing I ever did.

'I didn't pretend to be a widow and I didn't go out and marry somebody just so I'd have a husband. I could have. I've had my share of proposals, but I don't want just anybody to be my little girl's daddy. We both deserve better than that. Not that I don't need men and I'm not ashamed to admit that either. Sometimes I just itch to feel a man's hand on my body.' She walked over to the door and closed it. She leaned back against the door and looked at him.

'I have been known to invite men into my bed. I choose who will keep my feet warm and when. I have never slept with a married man and I never promised anything I didn't intend to give.'

She winked at Lucille who looked as though she was hoping she could get sucked down into the floorboards so that she wouldn't have to hear another word of this. 'Enough about me. Is being a drunk the thing you'd like to change?'

He looked at Mrs Reynolds who was staring into her lap before he looked back to Eva. He nodded to the big woman. 'Yes, I'd like to stop drinking.'

'Why not kill two birds with one stone? Ask this Mary who seems to be hanging around for your miracle. You might want to ask the girls to help you. You wouldn't have to tell them exactly what it is you're asking about. That might make the test even better. If you find that your thirst has died off, you'll have to take another look at their "enthusiasm", as you called it.'

'Can I assume that nothing will be discussed outside this room?' The Bishop knew, or at least he thought he did. A common enough problem for men who were denied so much. Not a big problem if you looked at the things that others sometimes wrestled with. Women were a terrible temptation for many. Vulnerable, needy women who wanted and asked for comfort they hadn't been able to find outside the doors of a church. He knew that any of the poor, tortured souls who found themselves falling in love with the altar boys would have traded sins with him in a heartbeat.

Still, almost accepted as his type of problem was, it would never do to have it discussed in the parish. As long as it could stay behind closed doors, he was all right. The Gorman woman had probably just been fishing and got it right the first time. She might have made a good side-show gypsy.

'Reverend Greene, Miss Lucille and I know more secrets than you'll ever hear in that confession box of yours. Towns like this are built on kept secrets.'

'I'll talk to the girls if you'll tell me something.'

'What do you want to know?'

'What would you change about yourself?'

'I'd change the way I hate.'

'How do you hate?'

'I hate better than anybody I've ever known. I wish I wasn't so damned good at it.' She smiled again, and her eyes sparkled.

'Father Greene, I had no idea she would say such things. Had I known I never would have even introduced her to you.' Lucille Reynolds walked almost beside him to the Gorman house. She hung back slightly as though deferring to his position.

'I didn't expect her to be so . . . coarse, I suppose, is the best description.' 'Bitch,' he thought, 'bitch from Hell.'

'I hear she's always been like that. She and her brother grew up kind of wild, but everybody loved her daddy and she's always gotten away with whatever she wants to do or say. She's really not a bad person. I mean, I think she means well. I know she's basically got a good heart. She just makes her own rules.'

'Miss Lucille, God makes the rules. What would this world be like if everybody made their own rules? What would happen to marriage and the home if everybody did what they wanted?'

'I know you're right, Father.'

'I'm doing this stupid test of hers just because she's the kind of woman who makes trouble if she's not listened to. You know as well as I do that we Catholics have enough problems being accepted in this town without getting on the wrong side of someone like her.' He wanted to make sure that Lucille didn't think he was being bullied by that fat bitch. As if he could be afraid of Miss Eva Gorman. As if.

'I understand, Father.'

'I think you need to keep a close eye on Pammy's friendship with this Glory. If today is any example of what that child hears in her home I hate to think what she might be saying to other children.'

'She's a nice little girl, Father. Real sweet and mannerly, usually. She's a little bit spoiled because she's an only child with three adults, but she's a good girl and the Gormans are mostly real well thought of. Hardly anybody mentions about Glory being, well, an out-of-wedlock child.'

'Miss Lucille, the goodness in your own heart doesn't allow you to see the meanness in others'. I'm not saying she's not a decent child, but right now your two children are at this woman's house.'

'They're with Miss Flo and she's the dearest thing. She's a big fat girl, but she's got the sweetest, prettiest face.'

'Miss Eva is a pretty woman too, but you've heard the kind of things she can say.'

'About what she said, Father. I don't think you need to talk to the girls unless you want to. I know she was kind of forcing you, but I'll understand if you don't want to go ahead.'

'Miss Lucille, I appreciate your support. I have always considered you to be the backbone of this parish and you have just proved it. I do appreciate your concern as well, but I've given my word. I'll ask the girls to ask for intervention for my situation as agreed. When nothing happens, as I know nothing will, Miss Eva will drop it and the girls can go back to their dolls and games.'

'What if something happens?'

'What do you mean?' He stopped walking and looked at her.

'What if the Holy Mother intervenes and you don't want to drink anymore? What if the girls are being visited by Mary and what if these things that have happened are really and truly miracles?'

'Are you saying that you agree with Miss Eva?'

'Some of what she said made sense. Not all of it, not the sins she's committed, certainly not those, but the other things she said. Maybe God decided that some good things needed to happen here. Maybe He decided to send Mary to Pammy and Glory to give us all hope.'

'I don't think things are so awful here, Miss Lucille. Things are a lot worse in Oklahoma than they are here.' He liked to remind his flock of Oklahoma. A whole state blown away in a cloud of dust. They needed to count their blessings. Sure, money was tight and times were hard, but things could be worse.

'Maybe things aren't blowing away the way they are in Oklahoma, but not many people are working and everybody is wondering how they're going to get through the next year. We're all a little scared, you know that. People are scared and when they're scared they do things they wouldn't do otherwise. You're not the only one who's drinking too much and I know of at least three women who are getting hit because their husbands don't know who else to get mad at.'

'Times like this test our faith, Miss Lucille.'

'Maybe our faith has already been tested and found worthy. Maybe what's happening to the girls is a gift of the spirit, a sign of hope.'

'You might be right, Miss Lucille.' It wouldn't hurt to humor her, he thought. She'd have to face the facts soon enough. Soon enough all this would be forgotten and things would be back to normal.

'Girls, can you come down here? Miss Lucille is here.' Her extra chins vibrated as she called up the stairs. Miss Lucille had been right about her. She was pretty and sweet-faced, but he couldn't recall ever seeing anyone quite so fat. She was dressed in a pale green tent-like dress and she'd pinned a pink rose behind her right ear.

'I hope my two haven't been any trouble, Miss Flo?' Lucille touched the other woman on the hand.

'They've been as good as gold, all three of them. You just send them down to me anytime you want. They're a pleasure.' She smiled, revealing even white teeth that looked tiny against the expansive flesh of her cheeks.

'That's good to hear.'

'Didn't Eva come back with you?'

'No, she had to finish up at the library. She should be along shortly. I just stopped by to collect Pammy and Little Beau. Father Greene wanted to have a word with the girls so he came along with me.'

'Here they come now. What took you children so long? Didn't you hear me?'

'We were up in the big bedroom talking to Evangeline, Aunt Flo.' Glory swung and twisted around the newel post as she stared at the priest.

'I was talking to Mary.' Pammy tugged at her mother's arm to make the distinction clearer.

'Same thing. The words all go to the same place.' Glory kept staring at him.

'What were you talking to her about?' Flo smiled and nodded at the girls.

'We were asking for things. Pammy asked for her daddy to get that job from his second cousin and I asked for you to finally get a baby, Aunt Flo. I asked about a million times in a row, so you don't have to worry about it anymore.' Glory reached down and scratched at a large mosquito bite on her leg.

'I won't worry about a baby if you don't scratch at that, sugar. It'll get infected and be a real mess. I'll put some calamine on it for you.'

'Girls, Father Greene here wants to talk to you for a minute or two. Why don't you three go out on the porch and I'll just catch up with Miss Flo. Go along.' Lucille made a shooing motion to the three before turning to the fat woman.

'Pammy, Glory, if I ask you to do something for me, will you try your best to do it?' He'd sat down on the porch step so that his face was level with the girls'.

'Yes, Father.' Pammy looked at him intently with her large eyes.

'I want to know what you want me to do.' Glory was worrying a scab on her knee. She reminded him of a can full of fishing worms. Constantly wiggling.

'I want you to ask the Virgin for help, for me.'

'Ask her yourself. Pammy says your job is to talk to Mary and Jesus.'

'Pammy is right, Glory. This is just a little game we're going to play, just the three of us. The Holy Mother already knows what I want, but I'd like you to ask her especially nicely to help me.' Father Greene had always felt he had a way with children. He was certain that the girl would succumb to his charm and become as pliant as Pammy.

'Mama said we shouldn't talk about this anymore. She's mad because we took off our nighties in the front yard.' Pammy looked from Father Greene to Glory.

'She wasn't really mad, Pammy, but she was worried. That's why she wanted to talk to me. I've talked to both your mothers and we're going to play this game before we decide what we're going to do.'

'I don't care what you think because I'm a Presbyterian.'

'I care, Father.' Pammy lowered her eyes.

'I care, Father, I care, Father.' Glory moved her head bank and forth and sang out the words in an irritating sing-song. 'Pammy, can't you see that the lady is for us? If she wanted *him* to decide anything she would have gone to him first?'

'Glory, be careful what you say. He's a priest.' Pammy whispered the words under her breath.

'He might be a priest, but she came to us.'

'Glory, I don't think you understand how these things work.' He furrowed his eyebrows and lowered his voice to talk to the child, who was so clearly her mother's daughter.

'Why are you getting mad?'

'I'm not mad, Glory.'

'Yes you are. Your face is scrunchy.'

'My face is fine.'

'No it isn't. Your face looks like a drinker's, Uncle Hoyt said so. You smell funny, too.'

'Glory, stop it!' Pammy had started to cry.

'Stop it, Pammy.' She turned back to the man. 'We'll talk to her for you. We'll ask her to help you, but you'd better believe in her if it works.' She scratched at her knee again and the scab finally came off in her hand.

CHAPTER EIGHT

'Where are you going in such a rush, Glory?' Flo wiped the peach skin off of her fingers and paring knife as the girl charged through the room. Just three more peaches to be peeled and she'd have enough for Hoyt's favorite, peach crumble.

'I have to go up to the big bedroom and pray for that man, that priest man.' Glory reached into the bowl in front of Flo and quickly picked up a section of peach and shoved it into her mouth.

'I beg your pardon, Miss Glory, but I need every bit of this for tonight.'

'I'm starving and supper won't be for about a million hours from now. Besides, I don't know how long I'm going to have to stay upstairs and work on that prayer for the priest man.'

'Why are you praying for him and why do you need to do it up in the big bedroom?' She didn't care about the answers, not really. It was enough that Glory would stay around a minute or two and talk. For a minute or two she could peel peaches and pretend that the skinny little redhead was hers, hers and Hoyt's.

She'd spent almost six months thinking that the baby would be hers. Eva said all along that she didn't want it. Didn't even want to see it. If she'd only been faster with that bottle of milk. If only she'd grabbed the crying baby and taken her downstairs and *then* warmed up the milk, Glory might be hers today.

'He wants us to ask the lady to help him. He didn't say what he needs help with, but he said she knows what it is. I told him I'd do it, but he'd better stop thinking we're just telling stories if he gets what he wants.'

'Nothing wrong with telling stories, as long as you know you're telling stories.'

'I'm not telling stories, Aunt Flo.'

'I'm not saying you are, Glory. I'm just saying that stories aren't such a bad thing. I guess I like a good story as much as the next one.'

'If I was going to make up stories, it wouldn't be about this.'

'Why not?'

'Because it's no fun to have Mama and Mrs Reynolds all worried and upset with us. I didn't like having to go to the library and talk to the priest man today. Everybody is watching us and LB is making fun of us.'

'You know that your mama and Mrs Reynolds just want to make sure that you girls are all right. I have to tell you it gave me the heebie-jeebies when I heard that you girls were dancing around in the middle of the night showing your skinny little butts to anyone who cared to take a look.' She reached over and gave a playful slap to the aforementioned butt.

'If we decide to do any more naked dancing I'll let you know so that you can sell tickets and make enough money for that blue checked material you keep fingering down at the Mercantile.'

'I'd rather you just keep out of trouble and keep your mama happy.'

'Mama's happy now. She'll be even happier because I'm going to ask for a nice man for her. Then she can have a husband and I'll have a daddy.' She began to count off the likely events on her fingers. 'The priest man will get whatever he wants us to get him. You'll get your baby, Mama will get a husband, and I'll get a daddy. That's four things I need to ask for.'

'Maybe it's only three since the last two are really the same thing.'

'Okay, three. I better go upstairs and get to work because even if it's only three, it's still a lot of praying.'

'Any reason in particular that you have to do your praying up in the big bedroom?'

'She knows to look for me up there because Mary and Evangeline are friends, sort of. Not really friends, but they look alike and they both died and I just think they're kind of the same.'

'I don't imagine that Father Greene would want to hear you say that.' She knew a little bit about Catholics. Her grandparents had been Catholics when they came over from Poland. Stayed Catholic for a while until her father got into so much trouble with the union. He got all mixed up with the unions and the socialists when they lived in Milwaukee and then her grandparents were embarrassed to go to church. Once they stopped being embarrassed, they'd lost the Mass-going habit and never went back.

'I don't think Father Greene likes me saying anything at all. Pammy says it's because I'm a smarty-pants and a bastard.'

'Glory Gorman, are you telling me that Pammy has called you a bastard?'

'Well, I am a bastard. Everybody says I am.'

'Oh, my sweet girl.' She wanted to cry. She'd warned Eva. She'd begged her to say that she was a widow. Of course, the whole town knew it was a lie, but everybody would have played along. Everybody was entitled to a private lie or two.

'Mama says it just makes me different. Like my red hair. She says everybody is different. Course that's all going to change when I pray her up a nice man. Then I'll have a daddy and I won't be a bastard anymore.' Glory swiped another section of peach from the bowl and ran upstairs.

She snuck another look inside the oven to make sure the crumble wasn't getting too dark. Hoyt didn't like it too dark and she wanted things to be right for Hoyt. At least the things she could do anything about.

Just last night he'd started in again about how good things would be if they could just leave town. In his mind the good jobs and interesting work were all about a hundred miles away. He even thought a baby would finally catch hold and stay put if they had a house that was just their own, one that they didn't have to share with Glory and Eva.

She tried to tell him that she didn't mind Eva, but he wouldn't listen. He'd never gotten over her refusing to leave the house and the baby. Being Hoyt, he just assumed that Flo must feel exactly the same way.

Hoyt had trouble imagining that other people saw things in a way that he didn't. For as long as she could remember, and that was over ten years that they'd been married, his favorite expression, the thing he said ten times a day, was 'I just don't understand'. Poor Hoyt didn't even understand why he should understand. His world was wood and tools and something pleasant on his plate.

So she tried to keep things the way he liked them. She was careful about how brown the crumble might get. She always double-checked the dinner table before she called him in. Made sure that there were four slices of white bread on a plate to his left. Checked to be sure that his glass, the biggest one in the house, was filled with iced tea that had been sugared down with three spoonfuls of C&H sugar.

While the cobbler cooled, she went out on the porch to rest for a few minutes. Her feet hurt and her legs felt shaky, but that was nothing new. Sometimes, she'd catch a glimpse of herself in the mirror when she wasn't expecting to and she'd wonder who the fat girl was. At night, when she got ready for bed, she always draped a towel across the bathroom mirror so she didn't have to be surprised so close to bedtime.

She'd been so pretty, that was the thing. Beautiful, really, ask anybody and they'd tell you the same thing. She'd had Hoyt in such a fever that the two families and half the town breathed a sigh of relief when they got married. Hoyt could barely work, couldn't keep his mind off of her. Not that she wasn't the same way. One day she'd almost got herself killed because she'd walked in front of a truck on the road. Hadn't seen a thing because she'd been thinking about Hoyt and the way his hair curled at the back of his neck.

They'd meet after school and he'd kiss her so hard she thought she was going to faint. He'd kiss her so sweet, too. He'd start up at her eyes and end up kissing her nipples, right through her middy blouse. She'd feel like she'd been sitting in warm egg whites when he did that.

The first time the middy blouse got lifted she almost cried because it felt so good she knew it had to be bad. She knew men liked to look at pictures of them, but who would have ever guessed that they liked to suck on them like babies? Maybe it was because his mama had died bringing him into the world that he went at her with such gusto. He could've done that one thing for hours, it had seemed.

One night things went too far and before she knew what was happening those clever fingers of his that could make such pretty things out of any piece of wood were sliding around inside her egg-white panties and she knew she was going to explode if something didn't happen, even if she wasn't sure what it was. It happened. It happened a lot. It happened fifteen times in one day when her parents went to see her sister's new baby in the next county. She still wore white to her wedding because her family didn't want to think it could be any other way.

She and Hoyt had lobbied for, and got, a hurry-up wedding. They were so sure, the way they'd been going at it, that something had started. Flo had stood at the altar in her wedding white just knowing that Hoyt had stuffed her up with at least one baby. After they'd done the business in those days he'd always rub her belly and call it his hope chest.

Her monthly had started on the honeymoon. Right there in the honeymoon suite of the Stanley Hotel on Lake Acadia. And every month after that. Never so much as a day late. Every twenty-eight days her womb would cry for its loss. That's what the book her father-in-law had given her on her wedding day had said. The monthly was the red tears of her useless organ.

'That was good, Flo.' Hoyt laid the bowl, now empty of crumble, on the porch floor.

'Nice out here tonight. The air's cooled off and we should be able to sleep real good.'

'Long as everybody stays in their beds. I was glad that Glory managed to stay put last night. Don't know what's gotten into that girl.' He stretched his legs out in front and leaned his head against the back of the porch swing.

'I think it's just kid stuff. Glory and Pammy just don't have enough to do in the summer. If they were a little older I'd give them some chores that would keep them busy.'

'Course it's kid stuff. I don't understand why Eva doesn't just wash her mouth out. Same with Miss Lucille. Let these kids get away with it this time and next time they'll just have a bigger whopper. And that stuff about taking their clothes off and jumping around out front. That's not right. I just don't understand.'

'How do you know what to do when someone asks you to put a carving on a mantelpiece? How do you decide what to carve?'

'I wish somebody would ask me to carve something. Flo, I am so sick of fences and mending porches and junk like that. I wish I did have a mantelpiece or a cabinet coming up.'

'I know, Hoyt, but just imagine that you did. How would you decide to carve it?'

'I'd think about what would look good and I'd just do it. Why?'

'Honey, I'm trying to tell you what this is that Glory's talking about. You put your dreams into wood and she puts hers into words. She's just dreaming out loud, the way kids do. You carve, she talks. Do you understand that?'

'No, but if it makes you happy, I'll try.' He reached over and took her hand.

'Do you know what she told me?' She hadn't been planning to tell him. He'd think it was silly and she didn't want to hear that. It was such a nice idea and she wanted to hang on to it, at least for the next fourteen days when the red tears would start up again. She wasn't going to say a thing, but he'd smiled and taken her hand. Hadn't just taken it, but had entwined his fingers with hers. An old signal of his. He used to stand next to her in church and do that.

He'd entwine their fingers when the service had forty-five minutes left to go. She'd have to sit there for all that time and feel his big hand in hers and feel his thigh pressed up against her skirt. Sometimes, during the sermon, he'd press his thigh a little harder and she'd press back. He didn't do it much anymore. They usually stayed for coffee and cake after church these last few years.

Eva used to tease them about needing sleep more than most because they were usually in bed by nine, but not anymore. They stayed up until ten, ten-thirty most nights. Mostly she didn't mind. She'd gotten so big, so awfully big. Hoyt never said anything about it, but it had to make a difference to him. *He* didn't look that different. If anything he just got better-looking. She'd be a fool not to think that he might start looking around, find some woman who didn't weigh a hundred and fifty pounds more than he did.

'Well, are you going to tell me?'

'What?' She'd been thinking of Lucille Reynolds and how she'd asked him to come over twice. Both times she said it was about having some shelves put up, but she never actually hired him. Lucille seemed like a nice enough person, but her husband was gone most of the time.

'You were going to tell me what Glory said.'

'She told me this afternoon that she was praying that I'd have a baby. Let me see, she was getting us a baby, she was getting something for Father Greene, and she was getting a nice man for Eva.'

'That'll be the day. I don't think there's a man in the world who'd want to be with my sister for longer than it takes.'

'Hoyt Gorman!' She was hoping he'd like the idea of Glory praying up a baby for them. She couldn't recall the last time he'd put his hand to her belly and called it his hope chest, but she knew it had been a very long time indeed.

'It's true, Flo. Eva is a bitch and more trouble than she's worth.' He lifted up their entwined hands and kissed the back of hers. 'She's not like you.' He took a gentle nip at her thumb. 'What else was Glory asking for?'

'She was asking for something for the priest.'

'Well, I hope he gets it. I can't understand why a man wants to spend his whole life without a woman, but I hope he gets what he wants.' He took another nip at her thumb and looked up with a broad grin. 'Maybe that's what he's having Glory pray up for him. Maybe he's hoping she'll get a woman for him. Maybe Jesus' mama will fix him up with Eva.'

'Hoyt.' She tried to sound annoyed with his silly talk, but the egg-white feeling was coming back. That fifteen-times-in-one-day feeling was coming back.

'What was that other thing she was wanting to get?'

'She said she's asked for a baby for us.'

'A baby is a pretty big thing for one skinny little kid to pray up, even if she is talking to the Mother of God.'

'Not as big as praying up a man.'

He moved her hand down to the front of his trousers. 'Your man is feeling pretty big tonight.' He leaned toward her and she could smell the peach crumble on his breath. 'You know, we should really help the kid out a little, don't you think? If she's going to go to all the trouble of praying like that, I think we should do everything we can on our end.'

'Hoyt.' She gave his zipper a tug.

She tried not to move once he rolled off of her. She wanted to hold on to every drop this time. It wouldn't take because it never had. That was simple enough to understand. Some women just didn't have babies. It might not even be her fault, she knew that too. Of course she'd never talked to Hoyt about that. He wouldn't believe it and she didn't either, not really.

It was her problem, she was the one. Only had to look at the other Gormans to see that. Why, Hoyt's mama had got twins, probably on her wedding night. Poor Eva, she certainly didn't have any trouble getting a baby. The problem was definitely hers.

Unless this took. Unless Glory really could talk to the Mother of God and Mary was willing to listen and grant some favors. The Bible said all you have to do is ask. Not that she hadn't asked through the years, but maybe she didn't ask the right way. The Bible also said a little child would lead them and maybe that meant that kids like Glory could do things other people couldn't.

Maybe her child would be able to do it too. Her child. In a few months, less than a year, she could hold a child of her own. A child that nobody could change their mind about letting her have.

She reached over and touched Hoyt where he was still damp and sticky. It jumped slightly in her hand and his arm fell across her breast as he turned toward her.

'You still awake?' He adjusted her breast like a bolster and sank against her.

'Just thinking.' It jumped again and seemed to be growing in her hand.

'What were you thinking about, Flo?'

'I was just thinking about . . . different things.'

'Want to know what I'm thinking about?'

'Sure.'

'I'm thinking about that time your parents went out of town and we did it fifteen times in one day.'

'That was a long time ago.'

'Not that long ago.'

She giggled as he ran his finger lightly down her stomach. 'This thing in my hand is kind of useless unless you do something with it, Hoyt.'

'I think you're right, Sugartit. I think I'd better get it inside the hope chest and put it to work.'

CHAPTER NINE

He glanced at the clock and was surprised that it was only five to five. It seemed later.

Judith had been waiting for him when he got back to the rectory. She had a message or two and she wanted to know about the flowers for Sunday. She chattered and mumbled and fidgeted until he wanted to scream, but he didn't take a drink.

Not that he ever would in front of Judith, or any of the other parishioners for that matter. In spite of what the Gorman woman had said, and he had to assume she had simply made a lucky guess, no one knew. Even Judith and the other housekeepers didn't *know* about the drinking unless they actually saw him drinking.

He was as careful as he could be. He was the only one with access to the wine cabinet and he always kept the empty bottles in the trunk of his car. As soon as he left whichever town he was staying in, he'd throw the empties into the underbrush along the side of the road and be on his way. Nobody knew. As long as he wasn't seen, it didn't happen.

She finally left after asking him if he wanted eggs in the

morning. He'd almost screamed at her. After all that stupid chittering and chattering she wanted to know about her damned eggs which he never wanted and never ate.

He thought about not pouring a drink. He'd thought about not pouring a drink ever since he'd seen the girls. However, he told himself, if the Blessed Mother was going to stop him from drinking, she would stop the craving, wouldn't she? Would the miracle come in the form of nothing more than increased will power? It seemed unlikely. If she were going to intervene, she would, and she clearly wasn't.

He'd poured a glass and put his lips to the rim before he felt the blow to his back, knocking the glass out of his hand and across the room. Instinctively, he crouched to the ground and looked behind him. A large crow was flying around his study, frantic with confinement. He crawled over to retrieve the glass, but the animal kept flying into his face and he finally retreated to under his desk.

The north window was already open, no doubt the point of entry for the bird. Crawling out from under the desk and hitting his head in the process, he scuttled over and opened the western window to offer the bird some choice as to its egress. This seemed to excite the crow even more as it now flapped against him once again, forcing him backwards against his desk. This time he heard the tumble of glass and felt the wine splash across his leg from the broken bottle.

He reached behind him and grabbed the first thing he could to help fend off the bird. His hand closed on something that he brought around from behind. He lifted the object and glancing up saw that he was holding a carving of the Madonna, about nine inches high.

'Mother of God!' The bird stopped flapping and landed on the floor next to him. It looked up and seemed to cock its head before nodding at him. It took several steps back, appeared to nod again, then flew out the window.

Father Greene looked at the carving again and felt half sick, so he sat down and looked at the shattered remains of the bottle and glass. 'Mother of God, most blessed among women, make me worthy of this miracle.'

He cleaned up the mess, carefully putting the broken glass in a paper bag for later storage in the trunk of his car. He blotted up the wine and rinsed the tea towel for several minutes to make sure he'd removed all trace of the spillage. He closed the windows and drew the curtains shut.

Father Greene could have opened a second bottle, but to his surprise he felt slightly light-headed, no doubt from hitting his head on the desk. His stomach also felt off. He tried to eat the dinner that Judith had left in the dining room, but couldn't manage more than a bite. Judith's food was at best plain and filling, but this meal of pork stew and dumplings tasted so strongly of pig that he could almost smell the barnyard. He tried to put a second forkful to his lips, but found himself retching at the smell of it as an image of a four-hundred-pound sow wallowing in the filthy mud sprang to his mind.

It hadn't been a miracle, he realised that now. It had been startling and a coincidence, but nothing more. There was an old folk-tale about what happens when a bird gets inside a house, but he couldn't quite recall what it was. It was a bad omen, he thought. Something to do with someone dying, perhaps. Utter nonsense, of course. Typical of superstitions that never quite fade. It had been absolutely nothing. A confused bird was all it had been.

Maybe it hadn't even happened quite the way it seemed. Clearly he was ill. His temperature was no doubt elevated and that was known to cause confusion under certain circumstances. Or it may have been something he ate earlier in the day. The mind plays tricks. How easy it was to assume the supernatural when a simple explanation was obvious. He'd often scoffed, privately of course, about some of the saints. Especially the women with their well-known inclination to hysteria and exaggeration.

The bird was probably flying around outside and wasn't even in the study. Seeing it had startled him and he broke the bottle and dropped the glass in a panic. As for picking up the statue, it didn't seem the least bit strange for a statue of that sort to be on a priest's desk. Naturally it was the first thing he picked up.

He had definitely felt a blow to his back, but that could have been nothing more than a muscle spasm. That would make sense. It had been a stressful day and muscles do tense up in those circumstances. Easy enough to see why two little girls and their mothers could start finding miracles in the commonplace. Hysteria of that sort was somewhat contagious. One only had to look at the Salem witch trials and more recently those poor colored boys who had been tortured and killed on the word of an unreliable girl who'd cried 'rape'.

Slowly he made his way down the hall to his bedroom where he threw himself onto the bed after removing his coat and shoes. He pulled his trousers off and left his shirt crumpled on the floor. Judith would no doubt find it an honor and a blessing to clean up his clothes tomorrow. Poor, stupid Judith probably thought it made her the bridesmaid of Christ or some such nonsense that her sort seemed to get in their heads whenever they got inside a church.

It was still early, barely seven, but he felt weary. As though he'd been toiling. Toiling in the fields of the Lord. Just what his mother always told him he should be doing.

His father had tried to keep him out of the priesthood. It wasn't manly, he'd told his son. A man works with his hands. A man works with his hands and has sons of his own. Shouting down the road after his son, so that the whole neighborhood knew how Jocko Greene felt about his son becoming a priest.

It had all been his mother's idea, he knew that even back then. She'd groomed him to be a priest because it was the thing her husband hated. If Jocko had hated plumbers, she would have given him a box of pipes to play with. If he'd hated farmers she would have turned their tiny back yard into a garden for him.

She'd filled him with her sweet peasant's faith and the Church's dogma. She'd pressed prayer cards and medals on him with whispered promises of protection and good fortune. Every day she would describe his holy future until it was as real as the doors of the church and as bright as a votive candle. She shoved him under the priests' noses and made sure that he was always scrubbed cleaner than the other boys when altar boys were being chosen. She stood over him while he did his homework so that the nuns would recognise his studious nature and relate it to the priests.

He took holy orders and his father was dead within the week. His mother smiled sweetly at the funeral, a testimony to faith and hope in the resurrection, most people thought. Of course he knew different. She'd insisted that he hear her confession. He never saw her again after the funeral, couldn't bear it. Couldn't believe it, not really.

What had the Gorman woman said? Small towns were built on lies. Small towns, small lives. He'd told his mother the Bishop didn't allow priests to see their families for the first five years. She believed him and he prayed that she would die within those five years and she did. And just as well. She had believed so in the power and faith of the priesthood. His lack of power and faith would have killed her, if her heart hadn't.

He rolled on his side and tried to think about the children and what they'd said. His head hurt and his stomach felt unsteady underneath his ribs. Felt like it might want to jump into his throat if he so much as thought about putting something, even water, inside of it. He closed his eyes and tried to stop thinking at all.

'Father Greene?' He could hear Judith on the other side of the door. He reached for his watch and saw that he'd slept almost thirteen hours. 'You awake, Father?'

'Yes, Judith, I'll be up shortly.' He lay as still as he could, waiting for the first waves of morning nausea to begin, but they didn't. Cautiously, he sat up in bed and gently moved his head back and forth. He waited for the blinding pain behind his eyes, but it wasn't there.

'Was there a problem last night, Father?'

'I wasn't feeling very hungry, Judith, that's all.' Judith, and all other women, it seemed, like to see a man finish his food. It hurt their feelings if a man did less than lick his plate dry.

'I meant your study, Father.'

'My study?' He thought he'd picked up all the glass, mopped up all the wine.

'Some bird must have gotten in there. There's bird shit, I mean manure, on the floor and some feathers on the curtain. I thought you knew about it because the windows are all closed. I guess you didn't see it when you closed the window.'

'Bird shit and feathers?' It *had* been inside after all.

'That's right, but don't you worry about it. I cleaned it up.'

'Thank you, Judith.' Bird shit and feathers. The thing had probably nodded at him too.

'You're welcome, Father. Will you be wanting an egg this morning? I've got some nice fresh ones.'

He was about to order his usual tea when he remembered that he'd eaten almost nothing the night before. 'An egg would be fine, Judith, and perhaps some bacon and toast, if you wouldn't mind.'

'Coming right up, Father.'

He climbed out of bed and took a deep breath of the morning air. He looked at the small carving of Mary on his dresser and smiled at it.

He noticed her right away, and not just because she didn't know when the right time was to stand or kneel. She took up the space of two large women and a little extra on top of that. She'd come in about halfway through Mass, taking a seat in one of the pews at the back.

He hadn't expected to see her, but after last night he wasn't completely surprised. He felt the way a child starts feeling two months before his birthday. Hope was starting to stir, but he told himself it was way too soon to get excited. He approached her as soon as the service was over.

'Miss Florence, isn't it?'

'That's right. How are you this morning?' She smiled sweetly and he recalled hearing that she'd been a beauty once. Hard to believe, but not impossible when she smiled.

'I'm fine, and how are you?' Her gaze kept going to the door as though she were afraid to be found inside of his church.

'I'm fine.' She looked down at her hands. He noticed that her hands and feet were quite small. She reminded him of a horribly overweight cat he'd once seen with its ripples of fat supported on impossibly tiny feet.

'Did you enjoy the service?'

'I didn't understand most of it.'

'That's the Latin.'

'Is that the way Jesus talked?'

'No, but it's always been the language of the Church.'

'I thought Jesus started the Church.'

'Saint Peter founded the Church.'

'And he was Latin?'

'Not exactly, but the Church uses the same language through-out the world to make it possible for everyone to understand. Because we use Latin you can attend church anywhere at all and understand what is going on.'

'I live two blocks away and I hardly understood a thing.'

'Miss Florence, you seem like a nice person and I don't think you're here this morning to discuss Latin with me.' How he envied priests who served in Catholic neighborhoods. Neighborhoods where nit-picking, Low-Church Protestants didn't ask inane, even obnoxious questions.

'No, I don't want to talk about Latin. I want to talk to you about Glory.'

'What about her?'

'She told me yesterday that she was praying for something you wanted and I just wondered if you expected to get it.'

'Why do you ask?'

'She asked for something for me, for me and Hoyt. First I just laughed, but something happened last night, it happened twice in fact, and I just started thinking that maybe it would really happen. I thought I'd talk to you, you being a man of God and all, because I can't talk to Reverend Harris about this because it just sounds like something that isn't very Presbyterian.'

'What happened last night, Miss Florence?' Now interested, he sat down beside her.

'I don't think you, I don't think I should talk to you about this.'

'Miss Florence, I'm a priest. When you talk to me, it's as though you're speaking to God.'

'It's kind of personal.'

'Most things that people really worry about are personal, Miss Florence.'

'Well, I don't know if you know much about us since you're not around that much, but me and Hoyt, that's my husband, Glory's uncle? We don't have any children, not of our own. We like to think of Glory as ours, because Eva was going to give her to us, except I was warming up a bottle of milk and the baby's crying made her own milk come down and once she put that baby to her she wasn't about to give her up, not that I blame her. A little, I blame her a little. Hoyt blames her a lot, but I understand that too. If I had a baby I wouldn't give it up to anybody for anything.

'We've been married for ten years, Father. On the day we got married, if anybody said that Flo and Hoyt weren't going to be having a baby a year, they would have been laughed out of town. I don't know if you've seen my husband, but he's real handsome and I didn't always look like this. I used to be real pretty and . . .' She looked at the man and hesitated for a minute. 'There's no ladylike way to say this, Father, so I'll just say it. Hoyt and I were like a couple of cats in heat.' Her face turned dark pink and she bit her lip.

'Three, four times a day, but I never caught a baby. Things have changed the last few years, what with my getting so big and all, but we still love each other. We just don't show it quite as often. Not nearly. Until last night.

'Last night was like the old times. After Glory told me she was praying for us it was like all this blubber fell away and the two of us just forgot about it. Hoyt even talked about the hope chest and he called me his Sugartit. He hasn't called me that in years.'

'I see.' He allowed his gaze to rest on the altar, willing his thoughts away from sugartits. These farm girls, he thought. After years of being around animals they tended to forget that some things should never be discussed, even with a priest. At least not outside the confessional and certainly not in such detail. 'Sugartit' indeed!

'So that's why I'm here. I've got another thirteen days before my monthly starts and I don't want to spend all that time hoping for something I can't have.'

'That seems reasonable.' He didn't hear her say 'monthly'. That was impossible. Even unmarried girls in trouble would just say they were late, and they said it when they were in the confessional. Not out in the middle of the church at nine in the morning.

'So I started thinking. I thought if you get what you want, what Glory asked about, maybe I'll get what I want too.' She looked at him and nodded. 'Well?'

'Well, what?'

'Did you get what Glory asked for? Did you get the miracle you need?'

'I don't know.' It was only a bird, after all. A crow at that. Maybe if it had been a dove, but it hadn't been.

'When do you think you'll know?'

He looked at his wristwatch. 'It's nine o'clock right now. Come back here, same time tomorrow morning.' The words were out before he'd thought about them.

'You'll know then?'

'I think I'll have a better idea.' Twenty-four hours added to the time yesterday would be longer than he'd gone without a drink in years.

'I'll be back, nine sharp, Father.' She smiled and her whole face seemed to light up.

'I'll look forward to seeing you, Miss Florence.' She must have been something in her prime. One of those milk-fed girls with strong limbs and wonderful skin. He escorted her out into the warm sunshine and watched her walk away on her impossibly small feet.

She probably wouldn't be pregnant, he knew that. He had a better chance of staying sober. The thought of his possible sobriety cheered him and he considered the idea of Florence Gorman becoming a convert. Perhaps he could show her how the Church could become a substitute for what her poor bloated body refused to give her. She'd be a pleasant addition to his little flock.

CHAPTER TEN

'Yesterday, after the priest left I went up and did some praying.' Glory swung upside down from the monkey bars in the school-yard. She allowed her fingers to sweep through the dry dirt as she watched the world turned upside down.

'That's not so special. I pray every single night, even Little Beau prays every night.' Pammy had sat herself on the brown grass, her skirts arranged around her in a circle.

'Aren't you going to ask me what I prayed about?' From upside down, Pammy looked like a flower with blond curly roots.

'My mama says we shouldn't even talk about this anymore until Father Greene decides what's going on.'

'Why?'

'Because it's up to him to decide what's going on. She said this could be something bad instead of miracles.'

'Pammy Reynolds, that's a bunch of cow poo and you know it.' She put her hands on the monkey bars and flipped herself off onto the dirt.

'What my mama says isn't cow poo and that's disrespectful to say that. Especially after she gave you those shoes.'

'I'm not being disrespectful, but I don't see what the priest has to with what we know. It happened to us, so why should he decide what happened?'

'Because he knows more about this stuff than anybody else.'

'*We* know more about this than anybody, Pammy. I don't see any Blessed Mothers hanging around his smelly old head.'

'Maybe it was just our imaginations that got away from us. Have you thought about that?'

'Our imaginations are always getting away from us, have you thought about that? Our imaginations are always getting away from us, but the grown-ups never got worried before. We've never taken off our clothes and danced around the front yard in the middle of the night, either.' She sat next to Pammy and pulled on one of her blond ringlets.

'Ouch! Why did you do that?'

'Because you're sitting there all prissy and trying to act like you're so smart.'

'I'm not being prissy.'

'Are too. I bet you haven't even thought that Mary doesn't like hearing you say that everything is just stuff that comes from inside our heads. That just seems like bad manners to me. If you ask me, I bet she's angry at you right now because you're listening to your mama and the priest instead of listening to her.' She still hadn't even had a chance to tell Pammy that Aunt Flo was going to have a baby and her mama was going to marry and she was going to have a daddy. Course, if Pammy had just got one of her stupid boxes from the rich cousin, she'd have to hear about that. Pammy always thought her stuff was so interesting.

'She's not angry with me.'

'I'm angry with you because you won't let me talk about it and I know she is too. The poor thing gives us miracles and the next thing she knows you're pretending they didn't happen. It's like she gives us a great big present all wrapped up so pretty and you don't even say "thank you". I think we should be telling everybody what's happened.'

'What if the grown-ups get mad?'

'What if they do? Grown-ups are always mad half the time anyway. What if they get mad? What are they going to do? You think they're going to run us out of town? They can't do that because we're kids.' Pammy was always a cluck-cluck chicken, but it wasn't really her fault, not all her fault at least. Her mama said it was because of Miss Lucille and her nerves. Even Uncle Hoyt said that people from Louisiana were difficult to deal with because they were sort of French and they tended to over-spice what they ate.

'Mama told me not to say anything. We're supposed to honor our parents. It's one of the ten commandments.'

Glory crossed her eyes and stuck her tongue out at Pammy. 'Which you don't follow because you're Catholic and worship idols and all anyway.'

'We don't worship idols.'

'I don't really care if you do or not, Pammy Reynolds. What I care about is having some man and your mama decide what I think. What I think is we've been given two miracles and I'm praying for three more.'

'What are you praying for?'

'First, I'm praying for that thing the priest wants. Then I'm praying for Aunt Flo to finally have a baby. Then, the best one is for Mama. Well, Mama and me. A man, a really nice one is coming for Mama and they'll get married and then I won't be a bastard anymore.'

'Can you stop being a bastard just that easy?'

'You bet. Once Mama marries this man, I won't be any more of a bastard than you and LB.'

'Why don't we both pray for that? It would make things easier for me, too, if you weren't a bastard anymore.'

'Why's that?'

'Because it isn't easy having a best girlfriend in the whole world who's a bastard. Especially with everybody knowing about it. Mama says your family should have had the sense to keep quiet about it instead of just going about their business like you all were normal.'

'And I suppose you think it's easy being best friends with the only Catholic girl in town? Do you know what that's like for me? I'm always having to tell people that you're a Christian, even though most of them won't believe it because you worship the Pope.'

'What's going to happen when you stop being a bastard, but I'm still a Catholic? Are we still going to be best friends?'

'Sure. We're going to be best friends for ever and have a double wedding and have babies on the same day.' They'd agreed on this plan several months before. Their houses would be next to each other and their first babies would be girls. Glory was going to name hers Evelyn and Pammy would name her daughter Estelle.

'I don't know if I can get married now.'

'Why?'

'Because it seems like when kids get visited by the Blessed Mother they always go off and be nuns when they grow up. I think it might be some kind of rule.'

'How can you be a none? None is nothing. How can you be none?'

'A nun. N–U–N, nun. You live in special houses and you never get married and you wear long black dresses because you're married to Christ.'

'You just said you don't get married.'

'Not to a man, you can't be married to a man if you're a nun. But you still get to get married, except it's to Christ. You get a ring and everything.'

'Do you get a wedding dress?'

'I guess so. If you get married, you have to have a wedding dress.'

'How about babies? Does Christ give you babies?'

'I don't think so. I think nuns just get other people's babies, but I'm not sure.'

'It sounds pretty dumb to marry somebody who's dead and can't give you babies.'

'Your Uncle Hoyt didn't give any babies to Miss Flo.'

'And that's about to change, isn't it? I wouldn't be surprised if she ends up getting twins because I've been praying so hard.' To whoever. It seemed to her that the Blessed Mother, being a Catholic and all, wouldn't really be interested in a girl who was a Presbyterian. She especially wouldn't be interested in a girl who knew lots of swear words and made fun of Catholics.

'That sure would show everybody, her getting twins, wouldn't it?'

'Sure would.' Getting twins just like Evangeline had done. Evangeline who would have loved her if she hadn't died having Mama and Uncle Hoyt. Evangeline who looked down from Heaven and saw that some things needed to be done to make folks happy. Evangeline who was practically like a sister to Mary already.

'Why don't we go talk to your Aunt Flo and see if she thinks she's caught a baby yet?'

'Good idea.' Glory jumped to her feet and started running toward home. 'Race you, Pammy!'

The house was empty so they headed toward the library because if there was anything to know, they knew that Glory's mama would know it. There was a sign above the door that said 'Quiet please', but Glory's mama didn't care how much noise went on in the library because she was mostly the only one who ever used it. Glory had even heard her mama singing in the library and seen her dancing around like she was in some show.

Glory shoved the door and stepped into the familiar gloom, Pammy right behind her. 'Mama?' She said the word before she'd bothered to look around.

'Right over here, Glory.' She heard her mother's voice from behind a stack of uncatalogued, unwanted books that people had brought in as donations to the library. Her mama was always complaining about these because she said they were a mere reflection from dull bulbs. Her mama said it was frightening to think what people were reading behind closed doors if this was the kind of thing they were willing to admit had been in their homes in the way of reading matter.

'Aunt Flo wasn't home and we wanted to know if that baby I told you about has started yet. Does she know yet when the baby is coming?' Glory called through the stacks before she turned the corner and saw her mama standing next to two other women, Mrs Weston and Miss Weesie Cartwright.

Mrs Weston was Bubba's mother. Glory didn't like her much, mostly because she was Bubba's mama, but also because her mouth smelled bad and she liked to lean down and talk right into her face so that Glory could actually taste the bad smell herself. What with Bubba being slow, she was always looking for someone to talk to and she didn't care what she talked about. Glory's mama had said that the woman didn't seem to have any connection between her mouth and her brain.

After her mama had said this about Mrs Weston, Glory had taken a real good look inside her own mouth. She studied herself in the mirror for some time, but couldn't find any place where her mouth connected to her brain. She couldn't find her brain either, but she knew that was inside her skull because Teacher had a picture of a skeleton in a book on her desk and Teacher had said that the brain sat inside the skull.

Miss Weesie was probably the oldest person Glory had ever seen, but she had a mother living in her front bedroom who was even older. Glory had never seen her and couldn't imagine that anyone could really be that much older than Miss Weesie. Miss Weesie was so old that her daddy had died during the Civil War. Of course Miss Weesie didn't recall any of that because she'd just been a little thing when he died.

Miss Weesie Cartwright stood two or three inches shy of five feet and was as thin as a child. Her face was all wrinkled and puckered up and she looked like an apple that somebody had forgotten to get out of the back of the cellar. In fact, Miss Weesie's face looked like an apple that had been in the cellar since around the time that her daddy went off to join the church triumphant during the battle of Gettysburg, Pennsylvania.

Miss Weesie was the owner of the town's newspaper, which she published every Friday. Every Friday for the last fifty-three years, Miss Weesie had published her one-page paper and there wasn't a soul in town over seven, except maybe for Bubba Weston, who didn't read every word that was printed.

The Guide provided the town with a reliable supply of information and gossip. Towns the size of theirs were never lacking in gossip, but *The Guide* lent to information a veracity that was sometimes lacking in the type that was exchanged over back fences and cups of coffee. Miss Weesie was the person in town who kept track of the daily comings and goings on a larger scale than anyone else.

Miss Weesie was also the town's unofficial historian since she and her mama were the only ones who were old enough to remember back that far. Miss Weesie remembered Evangeline and she'd even taken singing lessons from the Widow Gorman, although she'd been a little too old to take a fancy to young Joe. Miss Weesie had seen it all and she hadn't forgotten any of it.

'Outside with you two. Go on now, I'm talking to Mrs Weston and Miss Weesie. Go on.' Her mama had lines on her forehead and looked like she might start growling, but Glory didn't notice that until it was too late to stop talking.

'I just wanted to know if Aunt Flo said if there's a baby yet.' By now she'd noticed her mama's face and the surprised look on the other women's faces. 'Hi, Miss Weesie, Mrs Weston.' She started to back out of the stacks. She didn't want to smell Mrs Weston and all the thick, ropy veins on Miss Weesie's hands made her a little nervous. It reminded her of that song about the worms crawling in and out after you got yourself buried. Judging by her hands, it appeared that the worms weren't waiting for Miss Weesie to actually die and be buried before they started doing that crawling around.

'Florence is in a family way? Praise Jesus, after all these years!' Mrs Weston was a Baptist, but that wasn't surprising because only Baptists would call their boy 'Bubba' when his real name was Arthur. It was supposed to be 'brother' in baby talk, but it was really stupid. Sounded like somebody's lips were dry and stuck together.

'Eva, is this true?' Miss Weesie turned to Glory's mama with her little dried-apple face and looked up from behind her wire-rimmed specs.

'What's happened is that the girls were . . .' When she started to speak, Glory's mama glanced over at the girls with a look that meant 'I'll handle this'. Glory stopped talking, but Pammy didn't speak Gorman, so she didn't understand what the look meant.

She stood there like a statue with her arms down at her sides. She held herself real still and her face looked pale and damp. 'It's part of the miracles. The Blessed Mother has shown herself to us, to me and Glory here, and she's already given us two miracles, three if you count the music and the dancing, but we're the only ones who think much of that. Glory has asked for three more things to happen and one of them is for Miss Flo to finally catch a baby.'

Suddenly the room was as quiet as that sign over the door said it should be. Mrs Weston stood there with her eyes bugging out like a frog and Miss Weesie seemed to have developed a tick in one of her rheumy blue eyes.

Miss Weesie kept ticking, but she was the first to speak. 'That sounds real interesting, girls. Are you saying that Mary has come to you?'

'Yes, Miss Weesie, just like those children overseas.' Pammy's lower lip was trembling, but she still stood still, except for her mouth.

'Eva, do you know about this?' Mrs Weston found her voice finally and the look on her face made Glory wonder if she was finally getting a whiff of her own bad breath.

'Of course I do.' Her mama crossed her arms over her bosoms and just looked back at Mrs Weston.

'If my Bubba ever came to me with such a tale I would wash his mouth out with laundry soap until he was foaming at the mouth. This is blasphemy and you are encouraging it!'

'Well, I guess that's the difference between us.'

'What is that supposed to mean?' Mrs Weston's halitosis bounced around the small space between the stacks of books.

'It means I'm not going to wash out my daughter's mouth just because she tells me something that doesn't agree with your view of how the world is stitched together.'

'This is not my view, Eva. There is nothing in the Bible about Mary doing miracles.'

'There's stuff about angels if you don't like Mary.' Glory gave a quick, if pained smile in Pammy's direction. Pammy had tears in her eyes, probably from Mrs Weston's breath. 'There's a lot of stuff about angels and I'm almost certain that whoever is helping me is an angel. Maybe the Blessed Mother is helping Pammy because she's a Catholic like those kids overseas, but I think Evangeline is the one who's been listening to me.'

'Evangeline?' Glory's mama and Miss Weesie said the word together like they'd been rehearsing it for days to make sure that it came out just right. Her mama knelt down and squatted so that she was looking right into Glory's eyes. 'Baby, why do you think Evangeline has been listening to you?'

'Because when I'm up in the big bedroom it feels like she's up there with me. When I ask for things it feels like I'm asking you for something sensible that doesn't cost any money so I know I have a pretty good chance of getting it.'

'Is that all? Is that all, Glory?' Her mama looked at her like she could see all the way down to her socks and back.

'Remember when my nose started bleeding and I fell asleep?'

'Of course I remember. It scared me half to death when I saw you up there with all that blood.' Now there were tears running down those fine-skinned cheeks. Each tear acted like a tiny magnifying glass against her mama's face.

'I closed my eyes and I could see Evangeline, except her wedding dress was black. She sprinkled something on me and it made the blood stop and it made me fall asleep. You told me we didn't have ghosts, you said there was no such thing, so I guess she must be an angel.'

'Listen to me, Glory. Think real hard and tell me if you ever saw her before that day up in the big bedroom.'

Glory scratched at a bug bite on her elbow while she decided how much to tell. She wished the others would go away because she didn't think she could trust the other two women, but her mama didn't even seem to know that they were there. 'Sometimes when you and Uncle Hoyt fight, or sometimes when I'm sad, there's something that happens.'

'What happens, Glory?'

'I'm not sure how to say it because it's not like other things. It's like the air, only it's like real soft cotton, too. When I'm real sad it comes into my room and it fills it up with something that makes it good again. It's something warm and safe and when it happens I know it's okay.' She swallowed hard because the tears were coming out of her own eyes and the ones that didn't come out her eyes were going down her throat. 'And that time when I had the scarlet fever she sat in the corner of my room. She sat right there, even when you and Aunt Flo went to bed she stayed there. I didn't want to tell you because I didn't want you to be mad and make her go away.' Glory ran her hand under her nose to stop the dripping.

'Oh Glory, Glory, Glory!' Her mama grabbed her and held her tight while she half laughed and half cried into her neck.

CHAPTER ELEVEN

She checked again, but there was still nothing there. Flo sat down in the kitchen and thought that nothing had never been quite so good. Nothing had always sounded bad, like something was lost, but not now.

That Father Greene had told her things seemed to be going the way he wanted them to. He'd looked good, the last time she'd seen him. Ten days ago he'd headed off to some other town for a few days, but not before promising to call once he came back into town. It was too bad he wasn't around all the time, being so nice and all.

Funny thing about his being nice. What she knew of him, which wasn't much because of his being a priest, but she could-n't recall anyone ever saying that Father Greene was nice. Surprising that it never came up, compliments about the man. Usually folks were anxious to think and say the best of preachers, which he technically was, even if he was a papist. Some might hold that against him, but she didn't. If her daddy hadn't gotten mixed up in the union and embarrassed her grandparents out of going to Mass, she might have been a papist too.

He listened and that was another thing you'd think folks

would mention because that wasn't what you might expect. Especially for a *man* to listen. She'd told him all about things she normally didn't even talk to Hoyt about, but he sat there and nodded and didn't even look too embarrassed about what she'd had to say.

Since nobody was around, she pulled up her skirt and took another peek. Still none. Twenty-four hours of sweet and nothing none. For the first time since she was thirteen, she'd missed her monthly. She heard a knock on the door and rose to answer it after smoothing her skirt down. As she walked toward the front of the house she couldn't help but notice that she was walking a new way. Her legs and hips felt kind of loose and she knew her body was walking with a rhythm that felt right today, but would have felt wrong and forced only two weeks before. She smiled as she opened the door, thinking of Hoyt's hope chest and the little angel that must finally be growing inside of her.

'Morning, ma'am.' He was about thirty and wearing the kind of brown suit that nobody in town owned. He was holding a fedora which he'd shed as soon as she opened the door, so she knew he had nice manners to go with those nice eyes and teeth he was showing her. 'I hope I haven't come at an inconvenient time, but I was told at the Mercantile that the Gorman family lived here.'

'That's right.'

'Ma'am, I'm Elmo Robinson. I'm a reporter with the *Wichita Eagle* and I wondered if I could talk to you about something that Miss Cartwright wrote about in *The Guide*.'

Flo felt a little unsteady and thought this seemed like a scene from a movie. Felt almost like she'd stepped up into that big screen. She'd never met a real reporter before, not unless you counted Miss Weesie and nobody did. Miss Weesie ran a newspaper because her uncle had run the newspaper before her and left it to her when he died. That was a long time ago as Miss Weesie had been running *The Guide* since she was about twenty, but word had it that her uncle had been worried that Miss Weesie would never find a husband and would need something to keep body and soul together. Body, soul, and that old mother of hers who seemed to be aiming for an age of biblical proportions.

'They get *The Guide* all the way over in Wichita?' She couldn't imagine anyone in Wichita caring about what went on so far away. Especially as it was mostly the kind of thing that wasn't interesting unless it was about you. That was why most people read *The Guide*, anyway. It was always worth a peek just to see if your name was in it.

Most folks could count on being mentioned about ten or twelve times a year, more if they made an effort to put themselves out for Miss Weesie or her mother. Lucille Reynolds was always over at the Cartwrights' house with cookies or flowers. Always going on about Pammy and Little Beau and what exceptional children they were. Either Miss Cartwright believed the Reynolds children were really that interesting or maybe she was just being polite, but Pammy and Little Beau were mentioned an above-average number of times.

'We get a lot of the small papers, ma'am. Once in a while we see something in one of them that we want to take a look at.' He smiled his nice smile and nodded at her. 'The editor on the rural desk came across the story about the two little girls having some kind of religious vision and he asked me to come and meet you good people and find out more about it. Are you the mother?'

'The mother?' For a second, less than a second, more like a tenth of a second, she thought he knew. She thought he knew about what was surely growing in her. Her wish come true. Her miracle. 'No, I'm the aunt. My sister-in-law, Miss Eva, is Glory's mama, but she's not down yet this morning. I could go and get her for you.'

'I wouldn't want to bother her. Maybe I could talk to you for a few minutes?'

'I've got some coffee, just fresh made in the last half hour.' She opened the door and waved him in.

★

She tried to be careful about what she said to Elmo, he insisted that she call him Elmo. She was careful because she didn't want to steal Eva's thunder about what had been going on, but it was all she could do to keep quiet about what she knew had happened to her. Instead she talked about Glory and Pammy and what nice little girls they were. Finally, when the words ran out, she called up to Eva to come down and meet someone. She had to call three times, the last time shouting like some fishwife.

'Flo, what are you yelling about? I was trying to finish Glory's dress.' Eva came into the room wearing her oldest housedress and clearly she'd decided to wear nothing under it because of the heat. Attached to the front of the faded fabric, through which her brown nipples could clearly be seen, were half a dozen needles with thread still running through their eyes. She hadn't bothered to braid her hair that morning, but had made a haphazard knot on top of her head and secured it with a wooden knitting needle.

Flo couldn't help but notice that Mr Elmo Robinson jumped to his feet so fast his knees must have been placed under a terrible strain. 'Eva, we have company. This is Mr Robinson, Mr Elmo Robinson. He's a newspaper reporter from Wichita. Miss Weesie sent him a copy of *The Guide* and he wanted to talk to us, to you, about Glory and Pammy.'

'Mrs Gorman, I . . .' He tried to greet her in a gentlemanly fashion, Flo could see that, but Eva turned and walked out of the room.

'I don't think she realised anyone else was here.' Flo smiled weakly. 'If you'll just make yourself at home for a minute or two, I'll go talk to her.'

Eva stood by the front door, smoothing her hair in the mirror of the hall tree. She'd already wrapped a shawl around her shoulders even though it felt like it was easily going to be over a hundred degrees by the afternoon. 'Why didn't you tell me someone was here?'

'I did, Eva, you just didn't hear me.'

'All the way from Wichita, and here I am looking like some

kind of slutty housewife.' She pulled this way and that at the dress. 'Dress is so old and faded you can see right through it. You could have warned me, Flo.'

'You look fine, Eva, just fine. You always do.' She couldn't recall ever having to reassure Eva about her appearance. It was one of the things she admired about Eva, the way she was so comfortable with the way she was. She'd never cared about what was fashionable or what was in season.

Not that any of the women could do much of anything about it the last few years, what with money being so tight. They'd still look at the pictures in the magazines and try to make what they had look a little more like what they were wearing in New York or Chicago. Women would scrimp and save and go without so that they could buy a new lipstick, some nail polish, anything that could make them feel a little special, a little prettier than the mirror told them they were.

While the other women were busy with magazine pictures and lipsticks and doing each other's hair, Eva Gorman always looked exactly the same. She rarely looked in mirrors, but she always seemed pleased with what she saw. The closest she ever got to make-up was some Vaseline on her lips in the wintertime.

Yet there she stood, acting just like some fifteen-year-old whose big brother's best friend was taking her to a dance for the first time. Frowning into the mirror and moving her chin from side to side like it was a foreign object and one she didn't much like at that.

'What's he doing here, anyway? What's a reporter want with us?'

'I told you, Eva. He said that somebody read about the girls in that stuff that Miss Weesie wrote up and he wants to find out more.' She put her hand on her sister-in-law's shoulder and patted it. 'You look fine, Eva, just fine.'

'What have you told him?'

'I just told him what good girls they are and a few things about the town. I thought any real telling that needed being done should be done by you or Miss Lucille.'

'Where's Glory? Is she down at Pammy's?'

'They went off right after you were done measuring her for the dress. I expect we'll see her again as soon as Lucille gets tired of her or she gets hungry, whichever comes first.'

'What exactly has he asked about?'

'He said something about religious visions. He hasn't said anything about miracles and neither have I, if that's what you're asking.'

'That damned paper of Miss Weesie's. Nothing but an excuse to gossip and carry tales.'

'What are you so worried about, Eva?'

'I don't want my little girl subjected to a bunch of reporters and writers who'll pick over everything she says and does. I don't want that to happen to her. Right now she's having a good time because she thinks her grandma is making visits like all the other grandmas, only better because her grandma is a guardian angel. Pammy is happy because she thinks that the Virgin Mary has chosen her like she did those kids overseas. Basically, those two are having a wonderful summer. A magical summer, and that guy in there could ruin it for them.'

'I agree with you, Eva. The girls are having a wonderful time, but you know as well as I do that something else is going on. How long did you think you could keep all this quiet?'

'Keep what quiet?'

'The miracles, Eva.'

'Don't you see, Flo? The miracles are only going to be miracles as long as nobody takes too close a look at them. I want those babies to believe in miracles. Damn, *I* want to believe in miracles! The thing is, if you take a good look at any of these miracles, they're just nice things that happened. We are so unused to nice things these days that when something good happens we call it a miracle.'

'I think you're wrong, Eva Gorman, and I think you know it. I don't even want to think what that hobo might have done before Pammy prayed and he disappeared. He disappeared, Eva. Right into thin air.'

'He ran away and the girls were too upset to see him go.'

'Those shoes that Glory prayed for. Miss Lucille has been getting pretty things for Pammy for years, but she's never shared so much as a ribbon before the shoes.'

'You heard her, Flo. The damn things got shoved into the back of a cupboard and Pammy got too big for them. Lucille couldn't very well throw away perfectly good shoes, could she?'

'Father Greene stopped drinking after the girls prayed to the lady. They prayed to the lady and he stopped drinking. You're the one who told me he was a drunk.'

'And I bet he's still a drunk. He might have stayed sober for a few days, but it won't last. Mark my words, Flo.'

'I've missed my monthly, Eva.' She'd planned to tell Hoyt in a few days, but Eva needed to know now. 'I haven't been even an hour late since my curse started when I was thirteen. Glory prayed to her lady and I've finally caught a baby.' She put her hand to Hoyt's hope chest and sighed.

'Flo, I want you to be right more than you'll ever know. I think a baby would be the best thing that could happen to you and my brother, but I don't want you to get your hopes up.'

'They are up. I'm going to have a baby and if that's not a miracle, I don't know what is.'

'Florence, I don't want you to be counting on that. The mind is very powerful and your mind just might be telling your monthly to stay away.'

'Eva, I'm not going to argue with you because we'll all know soon enough whether I'm finally going to have a child I can call my own or not.' After those first horrible hours when it seemed pretty clear that Eva was going to stay and raise up her own child, she'd never brought it up with Eva. She knew how Eva must have felt about the baby, even if Hoyt didn't.

'Do not try to work on my conscience, Florence Brodsky Gorman, because I had every right to keep my own child and half of this house.'

'I'm not trying to make you feel guilty, Eva. I have always wanted you to be happy because the best thing for Glory is a happy mama. I have done everything humanly possible to make your and your daughter's lives good. You know that and shame on you for making it sound like something bad.' Florence could feel her throat turning sore and funny and she willed herself not to start blubbering. Wouldn't do, not anymore. Not with that Elmo Robinson in the house and not with the miracle growing inside of her.

'I'm sorry, Flo. I didn't mean anything. I just have this bad feeling. I'm afraid this reporter and maybe some others will be sniffing around and making things bad for us. First we'll be getting reporters and the next thing you know we'll get the priest and preachers of every stripe. All of them will be poking at my baby girl and then somebody will bring in some damn doctor or three.

'This one will be poking and that one will be measuring. They'll badger her and Pammy until they won't know what to think. She's going to feel like a bug in a jar, we all are.'

'Then you better be careful about what you say to this Elmo Robinson. Make him your friend and maybe the others will stay away, if they need to stay away.'

'Of course they need to stay away.'

'Maybe they don't.'

'What are you talking about?'

'Eva, I'm talking about gifts. Gifts of the spirit. Things like healing and other good things. Maybe this isn't just about the girls. Maybe this is a gift for everyone, not just them.'

'I guess it wouldn't hurt to talk to him. You might be right about making him a friend and getting him on our side.' Eva glanced in the mirror one more time before heading down the hall toward the kitchen.

She opened the bottom drawer and pulled a few of the things out. She hadn't even looked in the drawer for at least three years. That was about the time she had well and truly given up. Or thought she had.

She'd started making them even before she'd married. Her

older sister had been expecting and she'd started in sewing her own layette, right alongside the older girl. She smoothed a tiny yellow sweater across her lap. That first winter they were married she'd knit it up in yellow so it would be good for a boy or a girl. Booties and a little cap to match too. She's kept them out for the longest time, but Hoyt said it looked messy and seemed like it was only trying to rub the pain in deeper.

She'd cried then. Told him he didn't understand and never would, all time knowing that he'd wanted children as much as she did. He left the house angry that day, but when he came back he'd bought the first of her ceramic shepherdesses. He'd even had Becky Johnson, the girl who'd been working part-time at the Mercantile, wrap it up like it was her birthday or something.

Not that a collection of figurines made things better, but they were something to look at. She would take them down once a week and wash them in soap flakes and warm water. She'd worry about them in case a cat got in the house and knocked one over and broke it into a hundred shards. That time that Eva had deliberately broken one had been as close to wanting to do murder as she hoped she'd ever come.

She held the little sweater up to her stomach before tucking it back into its drawer with the other things. She figured the baby would be born in April and sometimes that could be a cold time of the year. She'd need to knit at least two more sweaters, and one cap would never be enough. Course, her sister and Eva probably had some things she could borrow from when their babies were tiny.

CHAPTER TWELVE

Glory stopped when she saw the car out in front. There were only eight cars, not counting trucks, in town and this wasn't one of them. She approached it cautiously and touched it just to make sure it wasn't another of those things she could see but couldn't quite touch. There had always been some of those things, but now there were more than ever. She'd seen pictures of white cars before, but she'd never touched one. The top was down and the seats were made of red leather, almost the same colour as her shoes. Satisfied that it was real, she beat a short tattoo on the fender before going up the walk toward the house.

Even Pammy didn't seem to see half of the things she saw, but that wasn't unusual. Pammy only saw what she wanted to see because she was a stuck-up poo-head. Pammy was just so sure about everything and Glory hated that. Miss Lucille had decided that she and Father Greene knew everything and that was that. Miss Lucille even said that the Virgin had a message for the world and she was going to be telling it through Pammy.

Glory had asked Miss Lucille why she'd seen stuff too if the Virgin was talking only to Pammy, but she got all huffy the way she was inclined to do. Her voice would get all funny when she got huffy and she would sound like she had the sore throat and had to gargle. Miss Lucille had never been her favorite person anyway. Mama said she put on airs and Mama was usually right.

At least Father Greene wouldn't be back for a couple of days and that was a relief. Aunt Flo said he was a fine man, but Glory didn't like him. He'd make a big fuss about Miss Lucille and always go on about the Reynoldses like they were the most important people in the whole world. The last time she'd seen Father Greene she'd made a point of telling him that her family had the best spot in the cemetery. He'd given her a dumb look like he didn't know what she was going on about, but he knew. That's why he'd been so nice to Aunt Flo and had stopped by just to talk to her three times. He knew they had the best spot in the cemetery even if he wouldn't admit it.

'Mama?' Glory stood in the dark front hall and shouted. 'Mama?'

'I'm in here, Glory. Come in and meet someone.' Her mother's voice called to her from the front room.

'I'm never speaking to Pammy again, Mama. Miss Lucille said . . .' A man was sitting on the divan. He was leaning toward her mama as he held a pad of paper in one hand and a pencil in the other.

'Glory, this is Mr Robinson. He's come all the way from Wichita to talk to you and Pammy.'

'Hi.' She took a step back and looked to her mother. She didn't like strangers. They looked funny, unfamiliar. They acted funny too. Either they fell all over themselves to be friendly or they pretended you weren't even there. It was hard to talk to people unless they knew your whole life.

'Hi, Glory. You can call me Elmo, if you want.' He smiled and nodded at her.

'I can't call grown-ups by their first name. Not unless it's a lady and then I can say Miss, like Miss Lucille or Miss Becky, if I know them real good.'

'Real well, sugar.' Her mama corrected her with a little twitch of her mouth. It was that kind of twitch that says a person knows they're being a little bit rude and bad-mannered, but something's got to be said right away. She knew sometimes when people corrected each other it was just to be show-offy, like Pammy and Miss Lucille, but her mama wasn't being show-offy, not a bit. Gormans talked good and used the right words, almost all the time. She wasn't sure why, but it had something to do with the biggest house and the best place in the cemetery.

'You could always call me Mr Elmo, if it's all right with Miss Eva, that is.' He looked over toward her mama and gave her the same kind of look that Uncle Hoyt gave Sunday lunch. It was that 'I've been waiting a long time for this and I'm going to enjoy every minute' look.

'Is that your car that's parked out front?'

'That's mine, Glory.' He'd managed to pry his gaze away from her mama and was looking directly at her.

'If I had a car like that I'd be out driving around instead of being in here.' It had been so hot the last few evenings that they'd all sat on the porch after dinner instead of the front room. All that front-porch sitting had made the air in the front room smell musty and unused.

'Glory!' She knew her mama wouldn't like what she said. It was like she'd practically told him to take her for a ride, but she didn't want things to happen the way they had with Father Greene. He'd talked to them for a long time and asked boring questions. When he decided he was through all he'd done was make some kind of magic sign with his hands before he mumbled something and left. If she had to talk to someone it would be nicer if she could at least get a ride in his car.

'That's all right, Miss Eva. I think your daughter has brought up an excellent point. Maybe a ride around town and lunch over at the diner could be my way of thanking you two ladies for your time.'

'Can we, Mama?' Maybe they could drive right up to Pammy's house and blow the horn until Pammy 'Poo-Face' Reynolds came out and started crying because she was so jealous. And Miss Lucille would come outside to see why her little cry-baby was crying this time and she'd see Mama sitting next to a man who was about ten times better-looking than Mr Reynolds and then maybe she'd start blubbering and grabbing at those pearls she liked to wear around her skinny chicken neck.

Her mama glanced down at the floor. Like she was surprised or even embarrassed. 'Glory, I don't think we should take too much of Mr Robinson's time.'

'Miss Eva, trust me when I tell you that I can't think of a better use of my time than spending it with you two ladies.'

'I have to open the library at two, so I couldn't be gone too long.'

'It's only eleven now, so we've got plenty of time.'

'Yeah, Mama. We've got plenty of time and I can't remember the last time I ate something at the diner.' She could remember, of course. A meal at the diner wasn't something that a person wouldn't remember. She'd had a grilled peanut butter and banana sandwich. It had been for her birthday last year and Miss Alma at the diner had even put a candle in a cupcake and brought it around to the table after she'd finished her sandwich.

'You poor, deprived child.' She was smiling in that nice soft way she had when things were good. It wasn't that hard smile that was worn when she was covering up something bad. 'If you two will just give me two minutes, I'll change into something suitable.' She hurried out of the room without looking back.

When she heard her mama's feet on the stairs leading up, she turned to the man and asked the question she'd wanted to ask ever since she had walked in the door and seen him sitting there, leaning toward her mama. 'Are you married?'

'No, I'm not married.'

'Good. Mama's alone too.' He looked good sitting in the front room, but a man who was going to be her daddy would have to do more than look good.

'What happened to your father?'

'Nothing, I just never had one, but I'm going to be getting one pretty soon.'

'So your mother is planning to get married?'

'She's not planning anything, but I've already asked for it so it's going to happen.'

'You're sure about that?' He looked at her with that same look grown-ups always use when they think kids are being silly.

'Yes sir, I'm sure.'

Miss Alma's diner was almost empty. It was almost empty most days and had been for the past three years. Alma Osburne ran the diner, but her brother Virgil was the owner. Once a week he took care of the books, but he left the day-to-day operations to his sister. He did eat all his meals at the diner and it was understood that the corner booth was reserved for his use. An invitation to join Virgil in his corner booth was not refused or disregarded lightly because Virgil was known to cultivate only the most interesting people in town.

Alma and Virgil lived down the street from the Gormans and had done all their lives. Neither had ever married; Alma because of a shortage of men after the Great War and Virgil because of what he'd discovered about himself during the Great War. Devoted to each other, their interests included knitting and the poetry of Mr Walt Whitman. He was a special favorite of Virgil's and he could listen to Alma read from the collected works (boxed edition with deckle edging) for hours and hours.

Virgil had been sent home early from the war. His family said it was because of an ulcer and most folks in town decided that was as good a reason as any. Ulcer or not, it was generally agreed that Virgil wouldn't hurt a flea and maybe it was nobody's business as long as he didn't try anything.

They were a quiet couple, model citizens and as solid as they come. Everybody said so. Alma was a good if uncreative cook and Virgil was a credit to the community. He directed two different church choirs each Sunday morning. At half past nine he made sure that the eight Presbyterians in the choir stall were all singing the same thing. After the recessional, he'd hurry the eleven blocks across town to the Baptists and make sure that they were all on the same page of their hymnals.

In December of each year, Virgil would organise a community sing on the last Sunday before Christmas and in the summer he would direct the Community Players. Sometimes the occasional remark would be made about the scarves he always tied around his neck or the clear nail polish that some swore he wore, but most people thought his musical contributions far outweighed his bold fashion sense. Also in his favor was his almost legendary devotion to his sister and his excellent advice dealing with affairs of the heart, which he dispensed freely. Women would flock to his corner booth and spill out the contents of their broken hearts, hoping that he could help in their mending. They'd tell him things they wouldn't even tell their sisters or best friends because whatever was told to Virgil didn't travel to any back fences. Virgil could be trusted with secrets, and that was more than could be said for most sisters or girlfriends.

'Miss Eva, over here, my dear!' Virgil attempted to stand up in his corner booth to wave them over.

'Hello, Virgil.'

'Miss Eva and Glory, too. This is my lucky day.' His eyes widened slightly as Elmo Robinson followed the pair to his booth.

'Virgil, I'd like you to meet Mr Elmo Robinson. He's down from Wichita.'

Elmo Robinson extended his hand to the older man. 'A pleasure, sir.'

'The pleasure is mine. The pleasure is mine. Please, join me, I insist. From Wichita, gracious. That's quite a ways away. What brings you down here? Don't tell me they've heard about our Miss Eva way up in Wichita?'

'Virgil, we'd love to sit with you, but Mr Robinson has some . . .'

'Say no more, Eva. I've got eyes and I know what I see. Two handsome young people, excuse me, Glory, two handsome young people and a beautiful child have no need of old bachelor me. You three take that table in the other corner and I'll make sure that Alma gives you a meal you won't soon forget.' He made a shooing gesture with his hands. 'Go on, get yourselves comfortable.'

'This isn't what I expected.' He crushed his napkin and put it to the side of his plate.

'What isn't what you expected?' Eva had hardly touched her food.

'You, your daughter. I thought you'd be some dyed-in-the-blood-of-the-lamb type.'

'I think that's supposed to be washed in the blood of the lamb.'

'Who washes in the blood of lambs?' Glory picked her way through a piece of Alma's mile-high lemon meringue pie, which was only about three and a half gluey inches high.

'Nobody, baby. It's just an expression people use.' Eva moved another piece of Veal Bird around her plate before looking at Elmo. 'Are you disappointed?'

'No, I'm not disappointed, just surprised.'

'By what?'

'By everything.' He shrugged his shoulders and stared at the milk-shake machine behind the counter.

'He's surprised because he didn't know he was part of one of the miracles. I was surprised when it started, so I know how he feels.'

'Hush, Glory.'

'You can hush me all you want, but it won't change anything. I don't think these things stop once they get started. They just have to run themselves out.'

'Glory, I'm warning you.'

'Father Greene comes back tomorrow so you can ask him if he got what he wanted. Aunt Flo must have a baby started because she's going through her baby drawer again and now he's here. Put that together with the other two and we've got five miracles. It's rude to pretend they didn't happen, don't you think so, Mr Elmo?'

'I don't think I know enough about it to say much, not yet, Glory.'

'Nobody knows much, that's what makes it miracles instead of ordinary good stuff.' She took one last bite of pie before pushing the plate away. 'Can I go see Pammy now? I want to tell her about Mr Elmo.'

'I thought you were mad at Pammy.'

'I am. That's why I want her to know right away that Mr Elmo came to see me and not her. And I want her to know that he'd so much better-looking and so much nicer than her daddy.'

'Well?' After he stopped the car in front of the library she turned to him.

'Well, what?' He climbed out of the car to open her door.

'What are you going to tell your editor? What are you going to write?'

'Miss Eva, I don't want to be the laughing stock of the newspaper.'

'Then you won't write about it.'

'No, I will write about it.'

'You said you didn't want to be a laughing stock.'

'Exactly. I don't want to be a laughing stock because somebody else got in here and wrote the story up because I couldn't see it for what it was.'

'What is it? It's two little girls. Can't you find a nice murder or scandal to write about? Isn't there some politician in Wichita who's stealing money from widows and orphans?'

'I'm sure there are lots of other stories, but not like this. Why would I want to write about that when I can write about miracles and ghosts and beautiful women?'

'I'm not beautiful.'

'I know, I was talking about your sister-in-law.' He grinned at her, offering his hand to help her out of the car.

'Very funny.' She pushed his hand aside. As she stood he took her wrists in his hands.

'Listen to me, Eva. This isn't going to stay where you want it to. My editor saw the story and so did other people. Work with me and I'll do everything I can to keep things from getting too crazy. I don't want you or your little girl to get hurt, believe me.'

'Why should I believe you?'

'Well, according to your daughter, I'm going to marry you.' He grinned again and she pushed him away.

'Don't you dare say something like that in front of Glory.'

'I was just joking.'

'It wasn't funny and kids don't have a very well-developed sense of humor. Talk like that in front of Glory and she'll reserve the church and borrow a wedding dress for me.' She unlocked the door to the library.

'That wouldn't be good at all.'

'No, it wouldn't, and I'm glad you realise that.'

'I do indeed. I would hate for you to get married in a bor-rowed wedding dress. You deserve one of your own.' He winked and climbed back into his car as she slammed the door of the library behind her.

She opened the door and stuck her head out. He hadn't started the car, but sat watching her. 'If you'd like to come in here for a few minutes, Mr Robinson, I think there's a few things we need to get settled.'

'The thing is this, mister: I'm not some small-town slut that you can just flirt with and forget about. I'm not going to roll on my back and piddle just because you drive a fancy car and wear fancy clothes.'

'I didn't think you . . .'

'No, you didn't think, did you? You roll in here and see a sit-uation and you think you can control it. You come in and you take over and tell everybody it's for their own good. My daugh-ter tells you she's been praying for a daddy and you pretend that you could be that man just to get a story for a newspaper. Or maybe it just makes you feel important. Men like to feel impor-tant, don't they?'

'I don't know about . . .'

'You don't know much, do you, Mr Elmo Robinson? You don't know much at all. Well, I'm going to tell you a few more things you don't know. I will not be trifled with. I am a person and I'm not a joke and neither is my sister-in-law. This town is not a joke and our lives are not jokes.'

'I just . . .'

'You will keep your mouth shut until I tell you that you can speak. This is my life, and my daughter, and my town. After you leave this will still be my life, and my town, and I will still have my daughter. You can make your jokes and have your fun and write your story, but you sure as Hell better remember that real people are going to have to live with what you leave behind. Do you hear me?'

'Yes ma'am, I do.'

'Good. Don't mess with me, Elmo Robinson. My baby may be talking to angels, but I will be the Devil herself if you make trouble for me or mine. Do you hear what I'm saying, Elmo Robinson of Wichita, Kansas?'

'Yes ma'am, I truly do.'

'Good, now get the Hell out of my library because I have work to do.'

'Yes ma'am.'

Chapter Thirteen

Miss Eva was the first person in town to read the story that Elmo Robinson had written. Although the county no longer provided new books for the library, the long-standing subscription to the *Wichita Eagle* had never been canceled. To her surprise, his story had a sweetness about it which made her think of his nice smile and the way he'd helped her out of the car at the diner. He'd written some nice things about the innocent faith of children that made her regret her own comments about his work in general and him in particular.

He'd written about her town in a way that reminded her of what she would have written if she could. He'd made it clear that times had been bad since the mill had closed, but that people were still trying hard to keep their lives together in the best way they knew how. He even mentioned the worn clothes that were spanking clean and freshly pressed. He'd disguised the name of the town, which she knew he didn't have to do, but somehow it made a big difference. Naming her town would have seemed like he'd pulled a few chunks of wood off of her house. Chunks that would have left holes that anybody could stare through whenever they wanted to take a look.

Eva pushed aside the book on Monet she'd been studying and wrote him a letter on the library's Underwood. She wrote that she enjoyed the story and would be saving it so that it could be put with Glory's baby book and report cards. She thanked him for not mentioning Glory or Pammy by name. Eva added that a few people besides Glory and Pammy thought they had seen the lady since he'd last been in town. The town seemed pretty evenly divided between those who had seen the lady or wanted to and those who thought the whole thing was mass hysteria or a joke. She offered to make herself available should he be interested in more information about what had gone on since his visit.

How to end the letter took a lot of thought. She tried to really focus on that, but sometimes she'd think about his hands. His hands had nice long fingers with big knuckles. He'd been wearing a long-sleeved shirt, so she couldn't be sure, but she thought he probably had nice wrists too. Kind of bony, but strong and not too hairy.

She could end the letter 'sincerely yours', but that sounded like the kind of letter you'd write to someone you'd never met. Not the sort of thing you'd write to someone who'd bought you lunch and driven you around in a convertible. She could end it with 'best wishes', but once again, that wasn't quite right. That sounded too much like a birthday card or a note of congratulations.

She finally settled for 'yours'. 'Yours' had a nice ring to it and it sounded warm without sounding too forward. It could be used if it was being sent to a man or a woman. It sounded better than 'sincerely'.

'Yours.' She said it out loud and listened to it to make sure it was indeed the right word. 'Yours. Yours and mine. What's mine is mine and what's yours is yours.' She smiled at the sound of her voice and the thought of Elmo Robinson.

Eva dropped the letter in the mailbox, holding on to the envelope for as long as she could. Once she sent it she knew she'd be waiting for a reply that most likely would never come. He'd have a lot more stories to work on now. Those politicians would be acting up as usual and then there would be the stories about Mr Roosevelt and what he was doing. Right now, Elmo was probably sitting across from some other woman and hearing about an armed robbery or an epidemic of rabies in calico cats.

Not to mention his private life. Silly Glory had come right out and asked him if he was married and he said he wasn't, but men often lied, especially about that. Even if he wasn't married he was just the sort of man that women would want to see married. Mothers and daughters would be flocking around him because it wouldn't be natural for a man like that to be on his own. He might not be married, she reasoned, but he no doubt was just as good as, even if he didn't know it yet.

She was probably about twenty-two and had gone to some fancy college Back East. She'd be slim and have dark hair which she would comb in soft waves down her back. She'd never had a child, of course, and was probably still a virgin, or pretty much a virgin. Her nipples would be small and pink instead of big and brown because she'd never had a baby sucking on her for twelve out of twenty-four hours. Her belly would be flat and smooth without a single bump or silvery line to give testimony to its previous occupant.

The main thing was she would be so full of life and hope. She'd have all her dreams intact. She'd be the sort of girl who'd say she was going to Paris and she'd do it. She would do it. Love would be so different for Elmo Robinson's girl, whoever she was. Love would be going to nightclubs and dancing in beautiful clothes. Love would be laughter, and caressing, and long, long kisses that tasted fresh and sweet.

It was what he would expect. If Elmo Robinson was going to fall in love he'd want it to be about all those things. All the good side of love. He wouldn't understand that love could be such a dark thing which chained you down to a life you hated. A dark thing that you couldn't live without even on the days where you thought it might kill you if you thought about it too hard. A thing that sucked away at you and your dreams.

Finally, she gave the mailbox a foolish little pat and turned away from it. From it and from him because Flo wasn't feeling well and she'd told her she'd make supper. Poor Flo was so nauseous, so excited and so certain. Kept asking if she was showing even though Eva told her it was way too soon. Even if she wasn't way too big to show anything smaller than a baby elephant. Not that there was anything to show.

His sleeves were rolled up and his wrists were just how she thought they'd be. Bony, strong, and resting on the arms of the old rocker on the porch. Flanked by Glory and a green-tinged Flo, he smiled at her in a way that made her feel like he'd touched her skin.

'Afternoon, Miss Eva.'

'Mr Robinson. I didn't expect to see you again so soon.' She hadn't expected to see him at all. Until she saw him on her porch, and he looked like he'd spent a lot of time on that very spot.

'Glory, you come along and help me make dinner. I'll let you use the peeler.' Flo heaved herself off the porch bench.

'Flo, I told you I'd make dinner tonight.' His shirt was big and white and made his shoulders look real broad. He was still wearing a tie, but he'd pulled the knot down several inches. She felt herself blushing, just a little. Maybe just enough for her to feel it without him seeing it.

'No, you have a guest. Glory and I will make dinner.'

'We've got it all planned out, Mama.' Glory grinned and followed in Flo's wake through the front door.

She shrugged and looked at him. 'I saw your story.'

'Was it okay?'

'It was good. In fact I wrote you a letter about it this afternoon. I just mailed it five minutes ago.' She climbed up the steps to the porch.

'I'm glad you're happy with it.' He stood when she reached the porch.

She nodded to the rocker. 'Have a seat.' She sat on the bench left empty by Flo.

'If you insist.' He sat next to her on the bench, his leg an inch from hers.

'Why are you back so soon?'

'I told my editor I need more time down here. I told him I needed to talk to this Father Greene and a few others. He wasn't too keen at first, but he came around.'

'I thought you got pretty much everything in your story.'

'When a story is good it doesn't hurt to make it better. This is the kind of story that gives people a good feeling, and there haven't been that many of those around, not lately.'

'How long are you planning to stay?'

'I don't know. I'm going to have to see how things go. I think I'll be here at least two weeks.'

'Two weeks?'

'Well, I thought I'd do something real in-depth about the whole area, not just this town. My editor thought it would be a good idea to see how the county has been affected by the Crash, the bad weather, everything.'

'Where are you going to stay?' Mrs Weston used to keep a spare room that she would rent out, but then Bubba got so big and unruly. Not that there'd ever been much call for rooms. Almost the only strangers who came around were hobos and they never wanted a room, even if they could afford it.

'Your friend Virgil Osburne is putting me up. Seems he has a back bedroom they never use.'

'That's good. I hope you like Walt Whitman.'

'Why?'

'Miss Alma and Virgil read Walt Whitman to each other while they knit things up for some mission in China. Not much in the way of nightlife, not what you're used to at least.'

'What do you think I'm used to, Miss Eva?'

'More than Walt Whitman, I imagine.'

'Compared to how I usually spend my evenings, Walt Whitman and knitting for the Chinese mission sound almost exciting.'

'I bet.'

'I mean it. I live by myself in a little apartment by the paper and I spend most of my evenings, and a lot of my nights, writing.'

'For the newspaper?'

'No, that's my day job. I'm working on a novel, which will never sell, but I'm working on it anyway.'

'Why don't you think it will ever sell?'

'Because almost everybody I know who writes for the papers has written a novel that will never sell. It's a tradition in the trade.'

'Maybe you'll be the exception.'

'And maybe I won't.'

'Why do it then? If you're so sure it won't sell, why do it?'

'Maybe I'm like your little girl. Maybe I believe in miracles.'

'No, I mean really. Why do it?'

'Because I believe in having dreams. I believe that if you don't have dreams of something different, everything stays the same.'

'Dreams are a luxury you can afford because you have nothing holding you down.' She could picture his little apartment that would stay clean because only one person lived in it. There was probably a Chinese laundry down the street where he could drop his clothes off once a week. He'd come back the next day and pick up a paper parcel that smelled of soap and starch and not even think about laundry for another week. He'd eat all his meals in some cafe or diner and never spend a minute worrying if he could make the food stretch if somebody just happened to drop by around suppertime. Somebody who you knew was feeling the times even worse than you and yours. Some friend or neighbor who'd never admit that you were their only chance of a square meal that day.

'People who are held down need dreams most of all.'

'Bullshit.' Red leather upholstery and he was talking about people who felt held down.

'I mean it.'

'I mean it too. Bullshit, horse pucky, and cat piss. Dreams don't feed the kids, make the beds, or butter the bread. Dreams are for people who have too much time on their hands and not enough brains in their heads.'

'So, Miss Eva Gorman has no dreams, none whatsoever?'

'I had dreams, but I outgrew them.' The Left Bank for one, St Mark's Square for another.

He leaned back in the bench and closed his eyes against the setting sun. 'Tell me what your dream was, Eva.'

'I can't even remember what it was now.' The Bridge of Sighs had been part of the dream as well. Hyde Park and London Bridge had both played their parts as backdrops to her dream.

'You are not only foul-mouthed, Miss Eva, but you are a liar. You're not even a very good liar.' He made a throaty sort of chuckle that made the bench vibrate and buzz.

'I'm not lying.'

'Only simpletons don't have dreams of something better, something different. It's one of the things that sets us apart from the animals.'

'You've got your dream all set up in front of you. It sits there and you can keep walking toward it. I can't do that anymore. My dream is behind me. I can turn around and look at it, but I need to go forward. I need to put one foot in front of the other. I can't afford dreams.' She knew she was sounding melodramatic, but he was sounding like some damn inspirational speaker on a lecture tour.

'Maybe it just feels like it's behind you, Eva.' He put his hand over hers and put their hands between them.

'What are you doing with my hand?'

'I'm holding it.'

'Did I give you any indication that I wanted you to hold my hand?' She didn't pull her hand away, didn't even consider it, not for a second.

'No, but you did indicate that you needed your hand held.'

'I think you should get your sorry self over to the Osburnes'.' Her hand stayed inside of his.

'If I go over to the Osburnes' I can't court you and that would be a terrible loss to both of us.'

'Court me?'

'That's right. I've already asked for Glory's approval and you'll be relieved to know that she's given me the green light.'

'I warned you about that. I told you not to encourage this idea she has about you.' This time she pulled her hand away.

'Eva, listen to me.' He took her face in his hands. 'I'm not a bad guy. I've got a steady job, my own teeth, and I've never kicked a dog. I don't drink gin and I don't smoke cigars. I am not now, nor have I ever been, involved in the selling of human flesh.' He smiled again and in the dimming light she couldn't tell if his teeth were his own or not.

'I've only got your word to go on.' She smiled back at him and pulled his hands from her face.

'You could call my landlady.'

'She'd probably lie just so that you don't get run out of this town and go back to Wichita. You being gone is probably like a vacation for her.'

'Oh, so you've met my landlady?'

'Elmo, you're going to be here for two whole weeks. Now if you want to have a good time and have some local girl on your arm I will be happy to give you a list of names of young ladies that would be thrilled to drive around with a nice-looking man who drives an even better-looking car.'

'I found the local girl I want on my arm.'

'No you haven't. I've got a daughter in there who thinks you're the answer to one of her prayers and I'm not going to let you encourage that kind of thinking. Glory's bound to get her heart broken, but I don't want that to happen until she's at least sixteen.'

'Why am I going to break her heart?'

'Because you're leaving in two weeks, but Glory and I are here forever. You'll drive back to Wichita and do all those big-city things and we'll never see you again.'

'You don't know that, Eva.'

'I know it. I know what my life is and I know how I have to live it.'

'You're too young to be living like this, Eva.'

'Like what?'

'Alone. Don't you ever miss having a man in your life?'

'I have men in my life. I have my brother and I have my friends like Virgil.'

'That's not what I meant.'

'I know that. I also have the occasional man who comes to my room late at night after my daughter is asleep. We get whatever we can from each other and then he leaves before my daughter wakes up.' She watched as he pulled himself away from her, only an inch or two, but away.

'So you're . . . attached?'

'No, I'm not attached. I make sure I don't allow myself to be attached. I rarely see the same man twice in a row.'

'I didn't mean to pry.'

'Well, you did pry.'

'I'm sorry.'

'About prying or the men?'

'About the prying, I guess. I'm just jealous about the men. Some guys have all the luck.' He smiled again, but not in her direction.

'If you want you can still stay for supper.'

'I'd like that, I really would.'

'I'll go see when it's going to be ready.' She rose from the bench, but he took her hand.

'You never told me what your dream used to be.'

'I used to paint. I was just about to get on a train headed for a ship in New York harbor. I was going to live and work in Europe and never come back here again.'

'What happened?'

'You give that thirty seconds' thought and I reckon that you'll be able to figure it out all by yourself.' She pulled her hand away and went into the house, leaving him to blush in the fading light.

CHAPTER FOURTEEN

Aunt Flo had tied fifteen cents, two nickels, and five pennies inside the handkerchief that she'd shoved into Glory's pocket before she sent her down to the Mercantile. She'd tried to give Glory a list, but the girl insisted that she'd be able to remember everything.

A week ago Aunt Flo wouldn't have let her go at all. Aunt Flo had always loved going down to the Mercantile herself, where she could catch up with the other women while she made her careful purchases. It wasn't unheard of to spend an hour or more buying eggs or picking over a basket of okra while women visited, laughed, looked shocked, or clucked their tongues and wondered what this world was coming to because it surely wasn't like that even five years ago.

Six days ago, Aunt Flo had started walking around with a wet wash-cloth pressed to her lips. She said that smells made her sick and she couldn't hold anything down. Glory's mama had fried up some bacon and Aunt Flo had run upstairs twice as fast as she'd ever seen her move before. Usually by suppertime she could eat a few saltines, but before that even water came right back up.

This morning when she didn't know Glory was in the room, Aunt Flo had been telling Mama that her bosoms hurt so much she could hardly stand it. Glory had been worried about that because Aunt Flo had the biggest bosoms she'd ever seen and that was an awfully big part of a body to be hurting. Then her mama started in about how much her bosoms had hurt and how big they had gotten. That went on for a long time before it got boring and Glory snuck out, leaving the women to their bosom talk.

Last night she'd heard her mama and Aunt Flo talking on the porch after she was supposed to be asleep. Her mama told Aunt Flo that she'd better get herself to a doctor, but Aunt Flo wasn't having any of that. Aunt Flo said all those years the doctor hadn't given her any kind of help or hope and she wasn't about to turn herself over to him now. She said she wasn't about to let him have anything to do with her or her baby. Her mama had told her it might not be safe to let nature run its course, but Aunt Flo said Jesus and Mary wouldn't let anything happen to her miracle. Aunt Flo said that for the first time in years she felt really happy.

Even Uncle Hoyt had seemed happier the last few days. There'd hardly been so much as a raised voice in the house or around the yard. Aunt Flo was generally the one who kept the peace, but with her feeling poorly the twins seemed to have figured out how to get along. Three nights ago at supper he'd asked her mama if she wanted any more of the mash potatoes. She couldn't recall his talking at the supper table, much less asking his sister if she wanted more of anything.

The women on the porch had laughed and giggled like two schoolgirls. That was happening a lot lately and she couldn't remember it ever happening before. They sounded the way she and Pammy did on those rare occasions when they were allowed to spend the night with each other. Their mothers didn't like them spending the night together because they always ended up making the same kind of racket that Mama and Aunt Flo made out on the porch. As she fell asleep she could even hear them

singing some kind of song or lullaby that sounded almost like the
music she'd heard the night that the stars danced.

She'd turned the corner onto Main and was headed for the
Mercantile when she saw something strange in front of Miss
Alma's diner. There were two cars out in front that she'd never
seen before and there seemed to be some kind of commotion.
She could hear the buzz almost a block away as people hurried
and pushed to get into Miss Alma's.

She glanced at the Mercantile because Aunt Flo had been real
clear about going directly to the Mercantile and buying exactly
what she'd been told to buy. She looked over at the diner again
and saw that Mr Elmo and Reverend Harris were both looking
into the windows so she had to assume that something important
was going on there. Certainly more important than six eggs, a
loaf of bread, and a bar of soap.

She hurried over to the diner's windows and stuck her face up
to the glass along with the others. She couldn't see anything in
spite of all the oohing and aahing that all the big people seemed
to be doing. She took a tentative tug on Mr Elmo's pant leg and
he looked down right away.

'Hi there, Glory. Not surprised to see you here.' She liked the
way he looked down at her and she liked the way his voice went
a little higher when he talked to her. He didn't act like a kid
exactly when he was around her, but he acted like somebody
who remembered what it was like to be a kid.

'What's going on?'

'Can't you see, right through there, on the back wall?' He
pointed through to a section of the wall that seemed to be
smudged or singed.

'They have a fire or something?'

'Mr Virgil says there was a little flare-up of grease last night.
They thought they'd cleared all the smoke out before there was
any damage, but I guess they didn't get it all. Seems that when
Miss Alma opened this morning there was that up on the wall.'

'What is it?'

'Can't you see?'

'Just looks like a smudge or something.'

'Here, let's try this.' He picked her up like she hardly weighed a thing and held her so that she was sitting on his forearm. He pointed to the smudged spot again. 'Now, tell me what you see.'

'I just see a . . . oh, Mr Elmo. It's her! Put me down, put me down!' She squirmed out of his grasp as he lowered her to the ground and she rushed inside the diner to stare at the wall along with almost two dozen others. Set inside the smudge, as though she was stepping out of a cloudy mist, was Evangeline, still wearing the veil she'd worn in the wedding picture. The smudge also looked like Pammy's Mary, at least a little bit. 'It's her.' She looked at the other people in the room as she realised that they were all watching her. 'Do all of you see her?'

She knew that speaking up in such a way was a little bit fresh and sassy, but she didn't really care. Normally she would have felt shy with all those grown-ups looking at her, but they all looked so interested in what she had to say. Ever since Miss Weesie had written that story people had been interested in what she had to say, even if they didn't believe in the lady or the miracles.

She jumped a little when she felt a hand on her shoulder. Mr Elmo squatted down beside her so that his face was right next to hers. 'Does it look familiar, Glory?' He kept his hand on her shoulder and it made her feel even more important because he was so nice-looking and he lived in Wichita and drove that nice car.

'Sure she does. Why did you go outside to look at her?'

'I wanted to see if I could see her through the glass. I thought maybe she was some kind of optical illusion.'

'She's real. She's always been around, it's just that she didn't show herself much.' Some of the eyes that had been watching her got big and round when she said that.

'Who is she, Glory?'

'Evangeline Gorman. She died back when Mama and Uncle Hoyt were born. Her dead part is down at the cemetery.' She didn't recognise everyone in the diner and quickly added some more information for their benefit. 'You can't miss where she is because it's the biggest plot in the whole cemetery. My grandpa had it built special for her.'

'Her dead part? What do you mean her dead part?'

'The part of her that died. I guess only part of her died because now she's an angel.'

'The child has a point, Mr Robinson.' Miss Weesie Cartwright stood there in her long skirt staring up at the smudge on the wall. 'I knew Evangeline Gorman and that does look like her, at least from certain angles.'

'It looks just like her, if you ask me. Especially right around the jawline.' Maggie Jute, now approaching her sixtieth year, took a step closer to get a better look.

'I just see a smudged wall and I'd advise all of you that this isn't doing anybody any good.' Brother Cletus Scott, the Baptist preacher, held his hands in front of his chest as though he was clutching a large ball. 'This sounds like Spiritualism and necromancy. We are told to beware of false prophets and witches.'

'If you shut up, Cletus, I'll give you a cup of coffee on the house.' Mr Virgil put a friendly hand on Brother Scott's arm.

'No, Mr Virgil, I don't want your coffee. I want you to go in the back and get me a bucket of soapy water so that I can clean this abomination from our midst.' Brother Scott pushed away Mr Virgil's hand and swiped at where it had been. He kept flicking his hand there as if to pretend that Mr Virgil had left something nasty on his shoulder.

'No!' Glory pushed her way through the others and grabbed at Brother Scott's arm. 'You can't wash it away. That's Evangeline and you can't wash her away because she's here to do miracles, for all of us!' Everyone, every last one of them was staring at her. All the buzzing and humming had stopped and they were all staring at her to see what she would do or say next.

'She's good and she makes good things happen. She saved my life and she gave me some shoes, and now Aunt Flo is having a baby and something good has even happened to Father Greene, the priest man. All you have to do is ask and she'd give you what you want.'

All the quiet stopped then. It sounded as noisy as the time Mr Heath's father, who was so old that he wasn't right in his head, got hold of Mr Heath's hunting rifle and started acting like he might shoot up the Mercantile. There had been about ten women in there that time and they'd all started screaming at the top of their lungs. They screamed so loud that pretty soon people from as far as two streets away rushed in the Mercantile to see what the fuss was all about. Nearly scared Mr Heath's father half to death.

There didn't seem to be a single person who didn't have a very strong opinion about Glory's comments. Since it was so noisy, each voice got louder and louder as it tried to be heard above the din. Brother Cletus started jabbing Mr Virgil in the chest and then Miss Alma jumped on Brother Cletus' back, which made Mrs Weston pull on the roll of hair that Miss Alma had pinned to the back of her head. After that things got plain rowdy.

Glory felt herself being lifted by the back of her overalls and the next thing she knew she was across the street in Mr Elmo's arms.

'Are you going to tell Mama that I started that?' She pointed to the diner where she could see Miss Weesie scuttling out the front door followed by a man she'd never seen before.

'You didn't start that, Glory. That smoky picture on the wall is what got everything going.'

'It didn't start until I said what I did.' She wasn't entirely sure that she wanted to give up responsibility for events in the diner. It had been pretty exciting and she was sorry that Mr Elmo had removed her without even asking if she wanted to go. Not that she was going to tell him that. He needed to think the best of her if he was going to be her daddy.

'Nothing gets people more inclined to yell at each other than religion, Glory. People don't like to have their beliefs questioned and being told that your grandmother is handing out miracles and showing up on the wall of the diner isn't something that most people can believe.'

'Pammy says it's the Mother of God doing everything. She says that the Mother of God has done this before overseas and I don't think anybody tore up the diners over there.'

'Different beliefs, Glory. Some people, like the Catholics in Europe, halfway expect something like this to happen. People around here just don't expect it. I think you've scared them more than anything.'

'Why would I scare them?'

'I guess they don't like the idea of people being around twenty-five years, or two thousand years, after they've been buried.'

'I thought I'd make them happy if I told them about the miracles, but that's when it got crazy.' She looked at him and grinned. 'Did you see the look on Miss Alma's face when she grabbed Brother Scott?'

'Yeah, who'd have thought she had it in her?'

'I still don't get it. When I found out about the miracles, I was so excited and happy, but they just got mad.'

'A few of them got angry, but just as many were mad at the ones who were mad. There are people in there right now who are just itching to talk to you and Pammy and find out more. You think you're the only one who'd like to have a miracle?'

'You want one too?'

'Yeah, I think I do.'

'Which miracle do you want?'

'I'm not saying, not just yet.' He stood and took her hand. 'I think we better get you home before you start any more riots, Miss Glory.'

'I've got to get to the Mercantile first. I promised Aunt Flo I'd do it because she's so sick she can barely stand up.'

'What's wrong with Miss Flo, Glory?'

'Mama says it happens to some ladies when they get a baby growing. They can't stand the way things smell and they have trouble eating without sicking up. Sometimes they even faint dead away, but I'm hoping that won't happen to Aunt Flo, at least while I'm around. What with her being so fat she could just about squash me flat if she fell on me.' She looked up at him and grinned. She knew it was kind of mean, but she could usually get a smile out of people by mentioning things like that about how fat Aunt Flo was. Everybody liked Aunt Flo because she was real sweet, but a good fat story was something that most folks just couldn't help enjoying.

'I heard what you said about your Aunt Flo in the diner. You're sure about that?'

'Yeah, I'm sure. Mama says that when a lady's got a baby starting all kinds of weird things start happening. I was telling Pammy about it, but Miss Lucille heard me talking and she sent me home because she said I was talking about things that children shouldn't even know about. She told Pammy that the doctor brings the mamas their babies in his black bag, but I know that's a lie because I remember when Vera Green got so fat and then she had her baby. Her baby was way too early because she hadn't been married very long, but right after she had her baby she wasn't fat anymore.'

'Glory, I mean are you sure that your Aunt Flo is going to have a baby?'

'Of course I'm sure. I prayed for it and so did Pammy. A few days after we started praying for it, there it was.'

'I don't know much about having babies, but I think it takes a while to find out for sure.'

'It usually does, but I heard Mama say that since Aunt Flo is sick the way she is, and her bosoms are hurting, and since her monthly something or other didn't come, she must be growing a baby.'

'You're certainly well informed for a little girl. You'd make a good newspaper reporter.'

'That would be good. Then I'd have the same job as my daddy.'

'Your daddy?'

'Well, that's what you're going to be after you marry Mama, isn't it?'

'I don't think your mama has much interest in me, Glory. In fact, she's made me promise that I won't encourage those kind of ideas in your head.'

'I don't need any encouragement, Mr Elmo. You and Mama seem to forget that you wouldn't even be here if I hadn't asked for you in the first place.'

CHAPTER FIFTEEN

He stood at the door and counted them as they left the church. Of course he'd counted them about three dozen times during the Mass, but their numbers gave him so much pleasure he found that he had to count them again. Fifteen people, and seven of those were new. It wasn't exactly a booming congregation, he reminded himself, at least not yet.

There was a suggestion of fall in the morning air and he walked toward the rectory at a brisk pace. He hadn't had a drink in weeks, hadn't even wanted one. Even the tiny taste of wine on his lips during the Eucharist didn't tempt him or remind his body of what it used to crave. If he awoke in the middle of the night now, it wasn't with the aching bladder and head of the drinker. If he awoke it was with the excitement of his epiphany.

He'd started talking about his epiphany openly. He'd even told the Bishop last week. The Bishop hadn't laughed in his face as he'd been afraid he might do. Instead, he promised to keep Father Greene, his ministry, and the town in his prayers. He'd also promised to write to the Cardinal and look into the possibility of sending out an investigative committee. No word on that yet, but the Bishop usually kept his promises.

Even though greed was one of the seven deadly sins, he had hoped for an even more dramatic interest in Mary and her position in the Church once she had appeared for all to see in the diner, the Reynolds kitchen (sadly, Pammy was the only witness to that event), and Mrs Clay's petunia bed. The sighting in the petunia bed had been made by almost ten people, but only five of them thought they saw Mary. Two others thought what they saw was nothing more than the shadow of a passing cloud, and the remaining three thought they were seeing the late Evangeline Gorman.

He had to lay the blame for most of this Evangeline nonsense squarely in the lap of that Elmo Robinson, the young reporter from Wichita. It was quite clear that he was much more interested in the side-show appeal of the sightings than in exploring the theological implications. If only he'd spoken to the Reynolds family before encountering the Gormans. Lucille would have set him straight and things would have had a very different outcome, no doubt about that.

The Lord works in mysterious ways, he reminded himself as he stood outside the rectory. Elmo Robinson may have even thought he was presenting the true story. Men could become so blinded. Inevitable really. Nice-looking young man comes to town and is immediately thrown in with the likes of Eva Gorman and after that he has trouble thinking straight at all.

He'd had a number of conversations with Eva Gorman over the space of the summer and nothing had changed his original opinion. She was nothing but a small-town slut who didn't even have the decency to be ashamed of herself. He had no doubt that she had encouraged her daughter to see the Mary manifestations as some sort of visitation from her long dead mother. Insane really, and so unfair to the child.

Not that he knew of anything going on between Eva and Elmo. Elmo always stayed with that sodomite Virgil Osburne and his sister Alma. He didn't have to actually see something to have his suspicions, though. Elmo Robinson took a special interest in that woman and her family and no one could doubt that.

Miss Flo would have been in his flock by now if she wasn't under the thumb of her sister-in-law. Not that he didn't wish Miss Flo well, because he did. Wonderful that the gift of motherhood was being given to that poor woman after ten years of marriage. She was a good soul and who knew, she might come around yet.

It didn't help matters that the child seemed to have a certain talent for asking for things that the Holy Mother was already in the process of granting. Sheer coincidence that Raymond Reynolds's promotion came through after Glory Gorman started praying to 'Evangeline' about it. Poor little Pammy had been praying for two months with no result until Glory got into the act. In every way, Pammy was the more attractive child, but Glory seemed to be the proverbial wheel that squeaked. No doubt she'd picked up that mouthy behavior from her mother.

Things could change, they always did. A year from now the town could be a place for devout pilgrims instead of something to do until the County Fair started. Yesterday there must have been half a dozen rubes walking around and asking stupid questions. One of them had even stopped him and asked him where he should go if he wanted to see a miracle. The fool seemed to have been under the impression that miracles and visions were being dispensed from some storefront on Main Street.

Still, there had been fifteen people for Mass and he wasn't the least bit interested in having a drink. Nothing to snort at, he told himself. Nothing to snort at.

Just as he was about to step into the rectory a pair of crows flew into the yard, settling in a tree a few feet away from him. They'd be leaving soon, he thought. Flying to some place warmer for the long winter. Since his epiphany he'd seen them as a reminder of the great blessing that had been granted. He raised his hand and made the sign of the cross. 'Bless you on your long journey.' He glanced around to make sure that his actions had gone unobserved.

★

Hoyt made a mark on the wood and then shoved the pencil back behind his ear. He figured he would need another day before he could turn it over to Eva for the painting.

They used to do that kind of thing a lot when they were kids. He'd hammer something together and she'd paint it up in some wild colors that would almost make your eyes hurt. Even if he didn't like the job she'd done he'd keep his mouth shut because there was no sense in getting Eva's back up. He'd never been able to quite understand her, even if she was his twin.

His daddy, their daddy, he corrected himself, had tried to explain that because they weren't identical twins they were really just a regular brother and sister that had been born at the same time. It felt that way now and had for some time, but it had been different when they were kids.

Just the two of them had practically made up the whole world back then. Eva was the last thing he saw before he fell asleep and the first thing he saw in the morning. She could be mean and bossy, even back then, but she'd always been his. When Glory had first talked about the lady it reminded him of something, but it was something he hadn't understood then and now he had only the memory of forgetting.

Eva had been his world, but he hadn't been Eva's. She could bury herself in books and take herself to places he couldn't follow. She always seemed to be coming up with solutions before he'd figured out that there was a problem. He'd been slow and unsure to her quick and certain. Not really twins, as their daddy often reminded him.

Flo had changed all that for him. Flo was beautiful, and every boy in town had plans about what he'd like to do to sweet Flo Brodsky. The boys would wink and strut in front of each other and make bets about who was going to do her and how many times. Shy in front of her, they were bold and brash with each other. They were bold and brash, but he was the one she chose.

Those early days had been like a Christmas dinner that you never finished and kept finding that no matter how much you ate, you were hungry for just a little more. At first it was just a little hand-holding and then a little kissing, but that didn't last long. The hand-holding and kissing only served to make them hungry for things they hadn't even heard about. He kept finding his hands and his mouth on places he hadn't even known existed a few days before. He'd look down and see her doing things that had to be wrong and unnatural, except they felt so damn good he thought he might die then and there, but go to his grave a happy boy.

Even without babies they'd been happy. He'd had his share of ribbing about that and plenty of joshing from men offering to do his job if he couldn't, but that was just the way of men who were jealous that he had Flo. The work had been good and he was married to the woman he loved. Even when the work wasn't worth doing anymore, even with Flo getting so big, he'd never stopped loving her, not for a minute. Even that one time he strayed it was just because she'd reminded him of the way Flo used to be. Just wanted to close his eyes and feel a body that felt the way hers used to feel.

Funny thing about that night this summer. Flo had told him what Glory said and somehow the years in between didn't matter anymore. He'd felt the way he used to feel when they had to sneak around and thought they were doing things nobody had ever done before. And finally something had caught. It took him a while to believe it, but she'd finally caught. After all these years he was finally building the cradle he'd promised her so long ago.

It was the first time they'd done it. She got a little scared later and started worrying about what would happen if she'd caught that first time. He'd never forgotten what happened then. He pulled her into his arms and held her, just held her. He'd never felt so big or so grown up as he did that night. None of the stuff about being dumb in school and never being a doctor like his daddy had mattered that night. He was holding the prettiest girl in the world and he'd never let her go. She asked again what they would do if she'd caught. He held her face, that sweet, heart-shaped face, in his hands and told her that first he'd marry her and then he'd build her the most beautiful cradle in the world.

He put the wood aside and slapped his hands clean against his work pants. It kept happening like this all the time, ever since she caught. He'd start thinking about her and the next thing he knew, she was all he could think about. Felt like he wouldn't be able to breathe unless he touched her, put his arms around her. Maybe if she wasn't busy and nobody was around it could be like it was this morning before he'd gone out to the workshop. Couldn't get enough of that woman. Just like in their early days.

She turned the canvases so that they caught the light. Painting the cradle hadn't been her idea, but Hoyt wanted the cradle to be different from the ones in the attic. He said he'd promised Flo a beautiful cradle years before and he meant to keep his promise.

She tried to palm the job off on Mrs Clay down the street. Mrs Clay did china painting and she was pretty good, if you liked that kind of thing. Eva thought a cradle covered with cabbage roses would be pretty, but Hoyt had something else in mind. He wanted clouds, trees, and animals. A man not known for his flights of fancy, he'd surprised her by his plans.

She'd told him she hadn't so much as picked up a brush since before Glory was born, but he said that didn't matter. Said it would be like the old days when they did things together and had lived in each other's back pockets.

Eva almost told him to put off the cradle until Flo was further gone, but the words wouldn't come out. They were so happy, and so hot for each other, just like when Hoyt had first brought his bride home.

All that romping and rolling had done wonders for old Flo, as anyone with eyes could see. She'd been so sick the first few weeks she'd hardly eaten a thing and a little bit of her had just evaporated. She was still the fattest woman in town by a good hundred pounds, but some of Florence Brodsky was coming back. Her skin and hair shone like a young girl's and people seemed to smile whenever they saw her.

Well, good for them, she thought. True love wins in the end. She held up the last picture she'd ever painted. She'd thought if she could paint it, make it gory enough, it would happen. The thing would fall apart and drop right out of her. She could be herself again and leave the old man to his laudanum and his death and Hoyt and Flo could carry on like a couple of dogs in heat.

She'd started hating them in earnest right about then. All three of them. Probably the beloved Dr Joseph Gorman most of all. Of course he'd always hated her, but been too much of a coward to admit it. Hoyt had been a small baby and the second one, but she was the one who'd killed off Evangeline. So eager to come into the world, she'd ripped her own mother open to the point where her incompetent husband couldn't save her.

He'd always pretended that the ignoring of his children was a philosophical stand. He'd talk about the noble savage and how children learned more in a world free of constraints. Free of love, too. By the time she was fourteen she'd found that men and boys would hold you and love you if you gave them what they wanted. As long as you held their penis, you held their attention. Treated her like a queen until they were done.

She'd had it all worked out for herself. She arranged for contraception by going through her father's drawers. She carried them first in her book bag, and later her purse. She didn't ask Joe Gorman for his advice or his approval. A good thing too, because the one time she'd asked for something, he'd closed the door in her face. To this day she wasn't even sure if he'd heard her. He had one foot in the grave by then, and the other was on a wet cow flop. He'd been too busy writing love letters to Evangeline to pay any notice to the child, now grown, who had killed her.

Flo had watched her those long months like a dog watching a three-legged, toothless cat. She'd felt her and Hoyt's gaze follow her wherever she went. Because of the pregnancy she had lost herself and become a laying hen for their empty nest. Flo had almost force-fed her with the foods she wanted the baby to be fed, doing her bit to build a baby. Hoyt hovered around Flo like she was the one who was carrying the child they wanted.

She'd listen to them late at night when the kicking inside of her would keep her awake. Always at it, always grunting and smacking and squealing until she changed all that by keeping her child.

Eva rummaged in the box of brushes until she found a straight-edged knife she had used to use for cutting canvas to the right size. She lined up all the paintings of unborn children and carefully cut them from the stretcher bars. She laid them on top of one another and, pressing as hard as she could, cut through the pile until all that was left was a heap of narrow strips.

She put a large pad of paper on her easel and sharpened a charcoal pencil. That was all from before, she told herself. This was now and it was time for something new. She began to sketch what Hoyt had asked for. She wanted to make sure that they agreed on the painting of the cradle. No more fighting or anger. No more children born under a cloud, not in this house.

Lucille Reynolds would have preferred that Raymond's promotion had taken them out of town. Father Greene told her he was quite certain that God wanted her family to be right where it was, which was fine in principle, but she still couldn't help but think it would be nicer to live in Wichita or maybe Kansas City.

Of course things weren't as bad as they had been. Things were actually pretty good. Raymond was still gone all week, which was nice, and now they had some extra money she could enjoy her free time more. One of the Jute boys was coming by tomorrow to start painting the house. It was nice thinking that hers would be the only freshly painted house in town until the Jute boy said he had to finish up the Heaths' house before he could start in on hers.

That was disappointing, having to wait and all, but then he told he had a big job coming up because he was doing the

Gormans' place when he was done with her. She felt her house was a pretty big job itself and almost told him just that.

It was nice having some new people in the church, except none of them knew what to do and it was distracting with them sitting and standing and kneeling, almost always at the wrong time. Father Greene had asked her to help him instruct some of the 'newcomers', as he called them, but she declined. She didn't say it to him, but that was his job and it wasn't as though he hadn't had plenty of time on his hands through the years.

Lucille had been tempted to remind him that none of those new people would even know where the church was if it wasn't for the interest that had been generated by Pammy's visitations from the Holy Mother. Not that you'd know it to hear people talk. Glory this, and Glory that. Damned Gormans with their big house and fancy cemetery plot.

That was the problem with not being a native to the town. It would be different if this had all happened in New Orleans. It might even have allowed her to find her parents. A sympathetic story in the newspaper about her early years in the convent just might jog the right memories and she could claim her heritage once and for all.

She'd said that very thing to Raymond last Friday night when he got home. He'd laughed at her and said her parents were in some Potter's Field somewhere, but of course he'd been tired and cranky like he always was when he came home.

CHAPTER SIXTEEN

'Mama says this whole thing has just turned into a circus and we shouldn't have anything to do with it.' Pammy looked at two more strangers going into the diner. She had her nose curled up like she did when she was standing too close to LB.

'I guess your mama can say any old thing she wants to say, but that doesn't mean I have to listen to her.' Miss Lucille had been keeping Pammy on a pretty short leash for weeks and this was the first time in three days that Pammy hadn't had to go home directly after school. Miss Lucille said the reason was that Pammy needed to study more, but everybody knew she was Teacher's favorite, which usually meant she had to study less.

'Well, maybe you don't have to listen to her, but I do. She said it's disgusting what they're selling over at the Mercantile now. Mr Strikings even had Father Greene come over and bless that stuff and then he put up a sign that said it was all holy and blessed and everything.'

'I'd think she'd be real happy Mr Strikings is selling all those medals and statues and stuff. Now everybody can have a house that looks just like yours. Your mama has started a new fashion of having pictures of blood and guts on the wall. I should think she'd be real pleased about that.' She knew this might make Pammy mad, but she didn't care anymore, at least not today. Pammy had been acting like a gutless wonder lately and she was seriously looking around for a new best friend.

Unfortunately, the pickings were slim. There were the Scott girls, Vera and Ivy, who were sort of fun. Especially Ivy, who prided herself on being a PK. A PK was a preacher's kid who was known to be a little wild. Ivy was two years older than Glory, so that was a problem because two years older was enough older that she could be awfully bossy. She did use a lot of cuss words, which was a nice change, especially when you've been spending the last two years with Miss Pammy 'I am an angel and even my poo doesn't stink' Reynolds.

In spite of the age difference Ivy might be willing to be friends with Glory because she knew it would make her daddy Brother Scott so mad. Almost every day, at least for an hour, Brother Scott would walk up and down Main Street carrying a picket sign.

He'd change the message every few days just so people wouldn't get bored. People actually looked forward to seeing what Brother Scott's signs said from day to day. To help folks keep track he'd even listed them and handed them out for ready reference. His latest list read:

Beware of false prophets!
Repent, for the end is nigh!
Protect yourself from the whore of Rome and her offspring!
If God wanted to visit us why would he send a woman?
For God so loved the world, he gave his only begotten son, not the boy's mother!
Renounce the Devil and all his works!
Beware the sin of pride!
Even children can speak with the tongues of serpents!
FDR is a secret Mason!

Brother Scott was so angry that he wouldn't even allow Virgil Osburne into his church to direct the choir anymore. He told his congregation that Virgil Osburne was a sodomite and a moral degenerate. They listened, nodded their heads and a few of them even shouted the random 'amen' to his comments, but Monday morning most of them made a point of glancing into the diner's window, just to make sure that the image was still there, and it was.

Brother Scott had organised a prayer vigil to remove the image. For twelve hours, he and seven of his stalwarts had prayed on their knees outside the diner. They only came up off their knees when they wanted to speak in tongues or give their legs a good stretch. Twelve hours, but her smoky self stayed up there, big as life.

'Do you still see her?' Pammy wasn't looking at her. She was studying the sidewalk, making it seem like the pavement had gotten real interesting since the last time she'd looked at it.

'Who?'

'Mary, of course.'

'I see her, but I'm not sure she's Mary.' Mostly at night, but she still saw her. 'How about you?'

'Well, if you still see her then it only makes sense that I would see her, doesn't it?' Pammy was still looking at the sidewalk.

'You know, Pammy, if you weren't seeing her much anymore it would be okay. When I see her now it's just a little bit of her, more of a feeling her than seeing her.'

'Yeah, I think it's been like that for me too.' Pammy stopped looking at the sidewalk and finally looked at Glory. 'Do you ever wonder if people like Brother Scott are right?'

'Right about what?'

'About this being something bad or something that didn't happen at all.'

'If it didn't happen, there wouldn't be the miracles and we're still getting miracles, more all the time.'

'We are?'

'Sure we are. Just last week, Becky Johnson got a letter from a lawyer in New York City, or maybe it was San Francisco, but anyway, he's sending her lots of money because some uncle she didn't even know about died and left her his money.'

'And there was Charley coming back home. I guess nobody expected to see him again. I suppose that was a miracle even if Father Greene isn't too sure about that one.' Charley Little had turned hobo two years ago after a brief career of dragging sacks of grain at the Feed and Fuel. Two days after Charley returned his father suffered a near-fatal stroke while arguing with Charley. In spite of the fact that his father's stroke had come about because of the argument with Charley, most people felt it was a miracle that he had come back in time to help with the harvest.

'That's right. That's two miracles in one week.' Glory did a little sidewalk-studying of her own for a minute. 'And maybe it's not quite a miracle, but things are starting to get painted again. Mrs Weston put up some new curtains in her front room and Mrs Matthews said she's going to organise a Christmas tree at the top of Main Street this year.'

'You know, I haven't actually seen the stuff that Mr Strikings is selling over at the Mercantile. Mama isn't expecting me home for another half an hour. Maybe it wouldn't hurt if we went over and just took a look?'

'You haven't even seen it? There's one statue of Jesus that even has blood dripping on his feet.' Glory grabbed Pammy's hand and led her across the street to the Mercantile.

Strikings Mercantile (High-Class Wares for the Family) had been in the same location for over one hundred years. With the exception of two new roofs and three different Strikingses manning the till, not much had changed.

The present owner was Darryl Strikings, the grandson of the original purveyor of high-class wares for the family. Darryl was more than aware that the Mercantile needed a few changes. Folks might joke that Darryl was selling some of the same things his grandfather had ordered and Darryl would chuckle right along with the wags, but in fact it was true. Just last week he'd sold Miss Weesie a buttonhook for her boots which still left fourteen hooks from his grandfather's days. He also had a stock of washboards, butter churns, pails, spittoons, and chamber pots that had been part of the original inventory.

Darryl, an innovative thinker, immediately saw the possibilities for his business when the Lady sightings started. He promptly arranged for a line of tasteful medals and statues to be delivered as quickly as possible before whatever was going on decided to go someplace else.

As soon as the new stock came in he had Father Greene come right over and bless them. He wasn't sure why that was important, but Judith who kept house when Father Greene was in town said it would make them better. Being a free thinker and a humanist, he hadn't put much store by the blessing, but after what happened to Becky a lot of others did.

Becky Johnson used to work for him three days a week, week in and week out. Business had been slow after the first of the year so he had to let her go on the understanding that she would fill in on an as-needed basis. It almost broke his heart to do that. Becky Johnson was the one thing in his life that he really enjoyed.

Not that Becky knew anything about it. Nobody did. As far as everybody was concerned he was just Darryl Strikings, husband, father, and owner of the Mercantile. His wife Selma had not left her bedroom since their second daughter had been born. Nothing wrong with her, she just didn't feel like leaving the bedroom. Her mother lived with them and she took over the running of the house and the children while her daughter stayed in her room.

His own mother had warned him about marrying Selma. She had known Selma's mother and aunt for years and the elder Mrs Strikings had never approved of the way that Selma had been raised. His mother said she'd been peaked as a child and indulged to the point of spoiling. She'd warned him, but he hadn't listened.

He'd tried with Selma, he really had. He'd go in every morning and try to lure her downstairs, but she'd have none of it. Her friends would call every day and she'd have little tea parties in her room where her mother would serve sandwiches and Selma would lean back on her pillows, looking pale and interesting.

He didn't know what went on at the tea parties, but he noticed that the regular attendees didn't hold him in very high regard. He wasn't sure what Selma had to say about him, but he was sure it wasn't good. Even his daughters, aged five and seven, would recoil slightly when he walked into a room.

He didn't mind this as much as he might have, as the girls looked and acted more like Selma every day. Rarely did a week pass that one or both of the girls didn't stay home from school with some non-specific ailment. On those days the girl or girls would be bundled into their mother's bed where the two or three of them would be wrapped up with shawl and nightcaps, no matter what the weather.

A bad situation, but made easier by the presence of Becky Johnson. Becky had started working for him when she was only sixteen. That had been five years ago and every year she seemed to grow sweeter and lovelier. She was kind to the customers, especially the older ones, and the ones who couldn't get around very well.

She was eager, bright, and quick on her feet. He knew that she kept company with one of the Crockett boys, but he had reason to believe that it wasn't serious. Darryl was quietly convinced that Becky returned his affection, although it had never been discussed. Couldn't be discussed, not really. After all, he was a married man, at least technically, and she was an unattached young woman.

Sometimes, in the course of their day, Darryl's hand would brush against hers, or his arm would brush against her back. When things like that happened he would have to fight the urge to groan with the pleasure of it, the pleasure of her. Sometimes it would make him so crazed he'd have to go into the storeroom for a few minutes just to collect his thoughts.

Darryl hadn't given much notice to the visions and miracles until he'd seen the merchandising potential. Even then, he'd only seen the situation as an opportunity to carry a different line of goods. Until what happened to Becky.

What with the visitors in town, business was picking up, especially over in the medal and statue department. Becky had started coming in on a more or less regular basis once again and as she had an artistic bent, he'd assigned her the task of replenishing the religious goods department. He knew that she'd done a good job because he'd watched her every move.

Lots of people were making a fuss because three days after Becky was restocking the medals and statues she got that letter from the lawyers. An eight-thousand-dollar inheritance. Right out of the blue from someone she hadn't seen since she was three years old. That was more money than most people could expect to make in years and years.

It was enough to go off and start fresh. If a person had eight thousand dollars she could leave town and take anyone she wanted along with her. He'd have to find a way of mentioning that to her. If she hadn't already thought of that very thing all by herself.

'So, girls, which one of these looks the most like your lady?' He'd watched them come in and immediately head for Becky's display. In unison they pointed to a small statue toward the back of the display. She was slightly different from the others in that she had a bit of hair peeking out from her veil and her body was slightly turned toward the right.

'That one at the back, Mr Strikings. You should get a whole lot more of those because that's what she looks like the most.'

'I'll have to ask Becky if we've got any more of those in the back. Maybe we could put a sign on her that she's the real McCoy.' He smiled in the direction of the girls, but in truth he was smiling at the mention of Becky's name.

'Did Becky put her up there?' Glory Gorman reached over and took the statue in her hands.

He took the statue away from the child and replaced it in its former position. Darryl had strict rules about handling the merchandise. 'Yes, she did.'

'And then she got all that money, right?'

'I think it was a few days later.'

'You definitely need to get some more of these out, Mr Strikings. Maybe you could even take one home to your wife.' Glory looked up at him and grinned.

He checked the bill of lading against his inventory book again after he'd closed the doors for the night. He'd ordered and received sixteen of the statues and he'd sold eight of them. For the third time he counted the statues on the shelf and came to the number nine. Ten including the bloody-footed Jesus, but he was only concerned about the Madonnas. Again he checked the bill of lading and found two different sizes of statue noted; twelve and five inches. He pulled the tape measure from his pocket and measured the one that the girls had pointed out. She was seven inches tall.

He took her off the shelf and put her on his desk in the storeroom. It was all nonsense, of course, but it wouldn't do any harm to keep her separate, keep her safe.

He thought he might even find it soothing to see her standing on his desk first thing in the morning. Maybe last thing at night, just after he closed up, it would be nice to know she was there, sort of watching over him.

Even if it was nonsense, which it was, it was a nice kind of nonsense. Besides, what was the point of being a free thinker if your thoughts weren't free to think what you wanted? No one would know she was back here except him and Becky. Maybe if she asked him about it he'd tell her.

If he told her maybe she'd tell him how she really felt too. It would give them both the chance they'd been looking for. A chance to tell each other how they felt without shame or fear.

He turned and took one more look at her before he turned out the lights and let himself out the back door and headed home to Selma. She did make him feel a little better.

When he arrived home his mother-in-law told him that Selma had had a bad day and was already asleep, along with the girls.

After a bowl of soup he went to bed in the little room where he'd slept since the birth of his second daughter and dreamed all night of Becky and the little Madonna.

In the morning he was awakened by the sound of sobbing coming from Selma's room. Tying his robe hurriedly around his waist he entered her bedroom to find his mother-in-law holding a limp, white Selma in her arms. Selma's skin had a grayish-blue tinge and he could see the whites of her eyes under the half-opened lids.

'She tried to tell you, but you wouldn't listen! Didn't she always say she was sick?' The old woman rocked her long white infant back and forth as tears splashed down on the pale face.

Darryl backed out of the room slowly. Numbed, the only thought he could process was the one that told him he was finally free.

CHAPTER SEVENTEEN

'What's going on?' Glory walked into the front room and found the grown-ups acting in a very unusual fashion. Aunt Flo was crying, but she was smiling at the same time. Mama was grinning like the Cheshire Cat in the storybook and leaning over and giving Aunt Flo a hug. Uncle Hoyt and Mr Elmo were laughing like the biggest joke in the whole world had just been told.

'I said, what's going on?' Finally they turned to look at her. Four grown-ups with grins that made them look really silly like the Crocketts' middle boy who was still a boy even though everybody knew he was almost thirty. He was the one who liked to sit in front of the Mercantile for hours and play cat's cradle with people when they walked by. Glory didn't know why he liked to play cat's cradle, because he wasn't very good at it.

'We've just been having ourselves a celebration, Glory girl.' Uncle Hoyt picked her up in his arms like he hadn't done since she couldn't even remember. He put a big loud kiss on her cheek and laughed again while everybody except Glory laughed right along with him. 'Miss Glory Gorman, you have just been kissed by the foreman of the mill!'

'The mill's closed. They closed the mill when that wall fell down in New York City.' This made the grown-ups laugh some more, which was getting to be fairly irritating.

'Glory, the mill is being reopened. A man came through because he'd read about Mary and the miracles and he wanted to have a look around. He liked what he saw and decided to buy the mill and open it back up.' Mr Elmo was grinning almost as wide as Uncle Hoyt. 'I think your Uncle Hoyt should buy you five pounds of penny candy on his first payday. If it hadn't been for you and Pammy this guy never would have come to town.'

'It's true?' She turned to Mama, who actually had her hand right on Mr Elmo's arm. 'Uncle Hoyt is going to buy me that much penny candy?'

'If he does, he better make sure he's willing to stay up all night if you get a bellyache.' Aunt Flo laughed and rubbed her hand across her own belly, which was just as big as ever, but now had more of a curve to it.

'It's true, Glory girl, and I'm going to buy you and Pammy five pounds of penny candy each. I may even eat some of it myself.' He kissed her again and set her down.

'Everything has just changed for this lousy little town. Men are going to be working and women will know that they can put a decent meal on the table and keep their children in clothes and shoes. I still can't quite believe it.' Mama had stopped grinning, but it was still a real nice smile she was wearing.

She had a soft look about her and Glory climbed onto her lap without even asking because it looked so inviting. Mama rewarded her with a little hug and a kiss on the top of her head. After Mama planted that kiss, Glory looked up and saw that Mr Elmo was smiling at the two of them. That was just the kind of thing she'd been hoping to see for weeks now, but Mama hadn't been very encouraging. She'd even been treating Mr Elmo kind of mean, but he didn't seem to mind much and maybe that was the most encouraging thing of all.

'What with the mill reopening and the factory starting up, I wouldn't be surprised if you even had people moving in instead of moving out.' Mr Elmo reached over and actually touched her mama's hair. When he pulled his hand back, Glory was glad to see that he still had all his fingers. She realised that things were a lot better than she had thought.

'What factory?' Glory wiggled herself into a comfortable position. It took a little more work because Mama wasn't nearly as cushy and squishy as Aunt Flo.

'Once the mill is up and running, Mr Abaddon, he's the new owner, he's planning to start a small factory making furniture from some of the wood that the mill turns out. That's why he's putting me in as foreman. He talked to a few people and they all told him I was his man.' Uncle Hoyt put a hand on Aunt Flo's shoulder and gave her a little pat. 'He said you talk about wood in this town and the one name you hear is Hoyt Gorman.'

'Hoyt, I am just so proud of you.' Aunt Flo started crying again and laughing all at the same time.

Darryl Strikings stepped out into the back yard and pulled the collar of his coat up to partially cover his ears. The nip that had been in the air just a couple of weeks ago had graduated into a full-blown bite. Still, it was better than staying inside and listening to the carrying-on of the women. Those tea-party cronies of Selma's made it sound like she'd been Eleanor Roosevelt instead of someone who'd spent four years in bed because she was too lazy to get up. Darryl was fairly certain that her death was another indication of her lack of character and passion.

Brother Scott had gone on about her being a wonderful wife and mother who'd been so brave in the face of her illness. He couldn't help wondering why if she'd had some illness it had never been given any kind of name. Brother Scott said she was looking down from Heaven because now she was an angel who'd be praising God throughout eternity. Darryl hoped that God wasn't really counting on Selma to keep up with the other angels because she'd just want to put her harp down it would make her arms ache so.

Now, if Brother Scott wanted to know something about angels he didn't have to look much farther than Becky Johnson, who'd sat in the church during the funeral looking absolutely beautiful. Her slim back had been ramrod straight and she'd kept her hands folded in her lap like she was a princess or something.

The minute she'd heard about Selma, she'd come by the house to tell him not to worry about a thing. At first he wondered if she was proposing to marry him then and there, but she was talking about the store. Good as her word, she'd kept the Mercantile open and told him to stay away as long as he needed to. Course, he couldn't stay away, not for more than a few hours at a time. He'd come up with a million different reasons to pop in and check on things just so he could see Becky behind the counter of his store.

His mother-in-law, former mother-in-law, he reminded himself, had insisted that she wanted to take the girls to see her other daughter in Lawrence right after the funeral. She said it would help the poor motherless tots to get over their loss and he'd readily agreed. He was driving them to the station in Barlow in two hours. Didn't know how long they'd be gone.

However long, it would be long enough. That Crockett fellow was still around, even took Becky to the funeral, but he'd already started something that should get him out of the way. Since Selma had passed, he'd been able to bring up Crockett's idiot brother twice. He and Becky had a nice talk about idiocy and how it sometimes ran in families. A girl like Becky certainly wouldn't willingly marry into a family that already had one proven idiot. Not when she could marry him, a man who'd already produced two girls who were bright enough. They seemed a little poorly and pale, but that was mostly due to Selma's example. Given the positive example of a robust girl like Becky, all that would change. Or they might just stay in Lawrence. That might be the best thing of all.

A person only had to look at Becky Johnson to see that she was destined to be the mother of a brood of sturdy sons. There was something about her walk and the set of her hips. She was the kind of girl who'd give birth easily and often. Not like Selma with her narrow girlish hips and her female complaints.

A good breeder, that's what the farmers called women like Becky, women like Eva Gorman. He could still see Eva right after she'd birthed that kid. Bold as brass, she'd come into the Mercantile with the baby in a little wicker basket she'd slung onto her hip.

The baby had started crying and the front of Eva's shirt had gone all wet with the milk that started flowing from her body. He'd actually seen it pumping right through the fabric. If some genie had offered him three wishes right then, the first wish would have been to put his mouth on the big breast he could see through the wet fabric and gorge himself on all that sweetness. The second wish would have been to give Big Eva the biggest one she'd ever had and the third wish would have been to keep on doing the first and second again and again.

Not that Becky Johnson was a slut like Eva Gorman. Half the men in town said they'd been with Eva, but he thought some of that might just be talk. He'd said he'd been with her too, but in fact when he'd asked her the slut had just laughed at him. He'd asked real nice too and even told her he'd give her a discount on anything in the store, but she'd laughed even more. Still, she'd had that kid, and that said a lot.

Becky would be his and there'd never be a whisper about her. They'd have to wait some kind of decent interval because folks love to talk, but it would be worth it. There'd be all the time in the world for them. He reached in his pocket and pulled out the medal he now carried with him everywhere. The medals all looked pretty much alike, but he'd examined them all and pock-eted the one that looked the most like his little Madonna. He kissed the medal and slipped it back in his pocket.

'Darryl?' Becky stood behind him with a cup of coffee and a dazzling smile. 'I thought I might find you out here.'

Charley Little pulled his boots off and left them by the back door. He went into the kitchen and pumped some water into the sink which he used to soap his hands and arms all the way up to his elbows. On the road he'd gotten in the habit of washing every chance he could, at least for the first year or so. After that it didn't seem as important. After that he started looking and smelling like all the others.

Every last one of them. He'd jump on a freight car and see himself, half a dozen times over, sitting in that very car. Drinking, sleeping, staring out at nothing, they all looked the same. Some were older, too many were younger, but they all had the same clothes, the same eyes, and the same face.

He'd stopped washing about the same time his face became the same as the others'. He'd seen himself and the others as part of a hive that none of them could quite find or completely forget. He was one of the swarm of men who travelled the country and rode the rails. Spread over thousands of miles, they lived communally, sharing meals and bottles, stories and lies.

He would have stayed on the road if it hadn't happened. When it happened it was like a mirror had been held up to his face, his own face, not the face he shared with all the others. He'd looked at his face and he began to see what he'd lost and he'd begun to see a way to get it back. He traveled for three more months, always in a circle, always headed for home.

'Charley, come help me turn him.' His mother stood in the doorway.

'Right with you, Ma.' He followed her into the small, back bedroom where his father now lived.

'You came back just in time, Charley.' His mother poured coffee into his white mug before sitting heavily across the table from him. She held a white mug of her own in her red, big-knuckled hands.

'I wonder if he thinks I came back just in time.' He jerked his head in the direction of the back bedroom. His father had been so angry when he'd come up the path. He'd yelled and screamed and hit Charley in the jaw. His mother had been happy to see him, but his old man had stayed red in the face all day and had his fit that night. Hadn't said a word since. Just lain there, day in and day out. His mother would spoon mush into his mouth three times a day and change his diaper about the same number of times.

'I don't believe he thinks at all, son.' She leaned over and patted Charley's hand. 'As far as I'm concerned, you came back just in time. Since he's not thinking I don't think you should even try to think about what he might be thinking, if he could think, that is.' She blinked her eyes quickly as though she were suddenly confused.

'If you say so, Ma.'

'I just wish you could have seen your way to come home sooner.'

'I was never that far away. I even was less than a mile from here a few times.' Hated to admit that, knew it would hurt her. Easier for her to think of him being in California or Washington State all that time.

'And you never came to see me?'

'I wasn't me, Ma. You get lost out there. You lose track of who you are and where you're from. Does that make any sense?'

'No. Not a bit of sense. Your people have been on this land since twenty years before the Civil War. How can something like that slip your mind?'

'I had a different mind out there, Ma. I had a mind I shared with all the other men. Being just yourself isn't the way it is on the road.'

'If you weren't just yourself, how did you get yourself back?'

'It's not important.'

'It brought you home so it's important to me.'

'Something happened that made me see myself for what I'd gotten to be and I didn't like it much. Scared me so bad to see what I'd almost done.'

'Tell me, Charley.'

'It happened a few months ago, back in the summer. I was just outside of town. You know, the other side of town, in the woods?' He waited until she nodded her head. 'Somebody had passed me a bottle of some kind of rotgut that morning.'

'Drinking? In the morning?' Mrs Little was strict Temperance. Unless it was for medicinal purposes.

'Yeah, morning, night, hours didn't mean anything much.'

'Go on.'

'I guess I'd fallen asleep in the woods.'

'Sounds more like you passed out. Charley, haven't I always warned you about the evils of drink?'

'Do you want to hear this or not, Ma?'

'Go on then.'

'I was sleeping it off and when I wake up, some kids are there. This kid runs into me and I grab her. I don't know what I think I'm going to do with her, I just grab her. Next thing I know this other kid starts screaming and the one I'm holding starts scream-ing and I just ran off. I just kept running.'

'Boys or girls?'

'Does it matter?'

'Boys or girls, Charley?'

'Girls. Two little girls.'

'Strange.'

'What's strange, Ma?'

'I'm not sure. Something about your story sounds almost like something I've heard before. Like something I've read or some-thing.'

'I didn't make it up. I'm telling you the truth.'

'I'm sure you are, Charley.' She took a sip of coffee. 'I'll think about this and I'm sure it will come to me.'

CHAPTER EIGHTEEN

She moved her hand across his chest and let it rest there. Everything was so still except for the beating of his heart under her hand. Once she found that spot she didn't want to move and risk losing the rhythm of him. It had taken her months to get the rhythm of him. The rhythm of a man hadn't mattered before, but somehow it mattered in all things to do with Elmo Robinson. Not a thing she could explain even, maybe especially, to herself.

'Penny for your thoughts, Eva.' His hand stroked her back as his words rumbled from his chest. Her head to his chest, she'd felt the words an instant before she heard them.

'I don't have any thoughts, Elmo. We just worked all the thoughts out of my head for the next twelve hours.' Not true, but she didn't want to talk to him about what had just happened, not yet. She couldn't remember the words he'd used to find his way to her bed. Not that she hadn't wanted him there. Wanted him from the very first. Wanted him every time she'd tried to slake her desire for him with one of her usual no-accounts. Kept holding him back and never quite sure why. It was something more than getting Glory's hopes up, that was for sure. It had been about wanting to be a part of him. In tune, in sync, in his rhythm, or him in hers.

'There's talk of the first snow tonight. Seems a crime to send a man out of a warm bed into a blizzard in the middle of the night.'

He was probably right about the first snow, she knew that. The snow overdue and his skin felt so warm under her hand. The first snow was usually the end of October and here it was the middle of November. The snow would be the white fluff kind, it was that cold. As if she could turn him out in that. She pressed her hand ever so slightly before she spoke. Pressed into his heart.

'First snow isn't usually a blizzard, but you can stay until morning.' She lifted her head and looked at him. She could barely see him in the dim light of her bedside candle, but still she watched, not wanting to forget the way he looked propped against the head of her bed. Sex had been Eva's battleground before Elmo Robinson put his shoes under her bed. A battle-ground where she never won, but she never lost, yet always saw opportunity for victory on the horizon.

'I thought you didn't want Glory to see me.'

'Glory sees you every time you're in town, which isn't nearly often enough, I might add.' Two, three times a month at most. The town wasn't much of a story these days, although new folks were still driving in to look around. All sizes, shapes, colors, and ages. Every last one of them hoping to catch a glimpse of something they couldn't explain. Hoping for some of that magic her daughter took for granted.

'Glory doesn't see me doing this to her mama.' He kissed her as his arms tightened their grip around her. His legs entwined with hers and rolled her over until she was on her back and he was stretched on top of her. His head loomed above hers, his heart beating faster than it had moments before.

'You can leave before she gets up.' She kissed the soft skin in the hollow where his throat met his chest.

'I don't want to leave in the morning, Eva.'

'But I'll want you to leave.' A lie, but one she couldn't help telling.

'Do I always have to do what you say, Miss Eva Gorman?' She could feel him smiling down at her, felt the teasing words in his touch. His breath was warm on her hair, on her skin.

She pushed him away and sat up in bed. She didn't bother to cover herself up, but turned on the bedside lamp. 'This isn't some joke, Elmo. This isn't something I'm saying so that we can have some kind of sassy conversation that ends with a slap and a tickle.' So many things he needed to know. She knew what he saw. Saw the strength and the bravado. Didn't see the other.

'Eva, I want to take care of you, take care of Glory.'

'I can take care of both of us.' She had so far and she could forever. Not in a mewling, mealy-mouthed fashion either.

'I know you can. I've watched you for months and I know you can take care of yourselves. I guess what I'm saying is I want to be a part of your lives. I want to take care of you and I want you to take care of me.' He climbed out of bed and knelt, naked, on the braided rug by the side of her bed. 'Marry me, Eva.'

Eva leaned forward and held his head next to her heart so that he could hear her rhythms while she listened to the blood rushing through her brain, past her ears. She thought about the words she would need to say, but first she wanted just those sounds of blood and veins to be heard.

When words finally came, when she could finally speak, she didn't answer him with a yes or a no. Told him she'd need some time. They talked some more and then they'd done it again, and then again. His hands soft and slow, she'd been surprised to see that they didn't leave a trail of blue sparks across her flesh. Felt like they should have. The whole night felt like something in one of those stupid stories that Flo loved to read and sigh about.

On a quiet day at the library she'd read about the temple prostitutes in Ancient Greece and Rome. It made more sense now. The last time had felt like a worship of sorts. A hymn to each other and a prayer to the flesh. A sacred act for the two of them that reduced the size of the whole world to something that would fit in the bed.

Unable to sleep, she'd wrapped herself in a quilt and sat on the window seat to watch him sleep and think about what he'd said. A fresh start for the three of them. He'd promised her a little house with room for another baby or two. She felt her womb contract at that. Happened every time she held a newborn child. This time without the fear or the shame. A little house with him, away from the town and all the no-accounts who knew her or thought they did. A house that would be hers and not Hoyt's or Flo's. A house that didn't still smell of Joe's grief, rattle with Evangeline's loss.

Dim light poured into the window and she could see that the first snow had indeed begun. Fairly heavy, it was beginning to cover the shrubs and the sidewalks up and down the street. She yawned and closed her eyes, just to rest them for a moment. The heat they'd made was already slipping out through the old walls and the warped storm window. Cold, she pulled the quilt up around her ears and buried her nose in it. He'd only been in her bed a few hours, but the quilt smelled of him. Bay rum and talc, fried chicken and sperm.

He awoke in the soft blue dawn. Reaching for her, his hand found the empty space and he opened his eyes. Eva was curled on the window seat, swathed in a patchwork quilt, her fall of thick hair spread across her shoulders like a shawl. He blinked and blinked again, afraid to move any other muscle.

A figure, a pale figure of a woman, seemed to stroke Eva's hair and then it moved as though it was making a minute adjustment to the quilt. Eva moved slightly as the figure appeared to plant a kiss on top of her head. Eva lifted her head as the figure slowly dissolved in the soft light.

He closed his eyes to keep the tears back. He wasn't sure what he had seen and thought maybe he wasn't meant to know. He sat up as Eva opened her eyes and smiled at him. It was the same room she'd always slept in, she'd told him that the night before. Whatever he'd seen was part of Eva and part of the room. Part of what made her belong to the place.

Elmo Robinson didn't know what it meant to belong to a place. His father, Ace Robinson, had written for newspapers all over the country. Ace had seen his life as one long adventure and had never understood why his wife Irene hadn't shared his attitude.

Irene had told him again and again, but Ace wasn't one to listen, at least not to Irene. Irene had been known to say that Ace would only listen to a person if they were talking from the top of a burning building or from behind prison bars. Ace felt that people were only truly interesting when they were in the midst of a crisis.

Not that Irene hadn't been in a crisis. The daughter of a Norwegian farmer and his wife in Minnesota, Irene had felt that her whole life with Ace had been a crisis. All she'd wanted was a little excitement, a little glamor before she settled down a mile or so from her parents' farm with Carl Claussen, her childhood sweetheart. A little glamor before she moved into the little house that Carl's parents had lived in when they were first married. They'd be the fourth Claussen newlyweds to live in the little soddie, Carl had told her, pride in his voice.

She and her best friend Corinne Rasmussen had planned to spend a week in St Paul, trying on wedding dresses and seeing the shows. That's what all the girls did, if they could. Of course their mother or their aunt would make the dress. Silly to pay good money when homemade was just as good, better even. Still, they trooped into St Paul and tried on the fancy dresses and the ladies in the shops, handsome in their black gowns, didn't seem to mind. Her first stop would be Challstrom's because they had genuine imitations from Worth's in Paris. Mavis Brown had been married in a wonderful gown that looked just like one she said she'd tried on in Challstrom's.

The first thing she saw when she stepped off the train was Ace Robinson winking at her. It wasn't as though she wasn't used to men winking at her, she was, but this was different. Ace had a black derby hat cocked over one eye and he looked at her like he didn't give a damn what she did, but he knew she'd do what he wanted. He looked at her the way she'd sometimes wished Carl had, but never did. Her mother had given her a book about marriage that made her go all red and damp when she'd read about 'becoming one'. She'd tried to imagine how it would be, but Carl's face had never fit into her imagination. She blinked her eyes twice and realised that the face under the black derby would fit perfectly.

Corinne said her wedding gift to her best friend would be to keep her mouth shut if Irene wanted to talk to the dandy and before she knew it he was standing in front of Irene with his derby shoved back so that she could see his handsome face. He had slim, angular hands and she could almost hear Carl saying he wouldn't last five minutes on a hog farm. She had to agree, but she thought that was actually a very good thing.

Three days later, Corinne Rasmussen traveled home alone with two letters in her handbag. One was to Irene's parents and the second one was to Carl Claussen. Before she stepped onto the train, Corinne had stood up with Irene in front of the Justice of the Peace to witness her marriage to Ace Robinson. It had been the most beautiful, romantic moment that Corinne had ever seen. Nine months later, Corinne received a letter from Elko, Nevada, which announced the birth of a son to Mr and Mrs A. Robinson. Corinne sent a pair of bootees which she'd made, but they were never received as the little family had already moved on to Butte, Montana.

The excitement died out for Irene about the same time her morning sickness cleared up. At heart a farmer's daughter, she longed for her girlhood home and the sense of permanence that came from having an elderly grandfather in the back bedroom and fourteen first cousins that lived within a five-mile radius. In the morning she missed the sweet smell of manure blended with the sounds and smells of a farmhouse breakfast. Irene missed the chores, the chatter, the church, and even Carl. She longed to return home, but knew she'd no longer be welcome with her growing burden of unborn child and marital shame. Bad enough that she'd run out on Carl Claussen and embarrassed her family without being a failed wife returning with nothing to show for her rebellion but another mouth to feed.

She tried to make their rented rooms seem warm and homey, but her enthusiasm for housekeeping died with their sixth move in three years. Little Elmo was a diversion for his first two years, but then he clearly grew to favor his father, in appearance as well as attitude. Elmo was reading by the age of four and his choice of reading material was always the newspaper. His toys were paper and pencil, his hobbyhorse was his father's shoulders as the pair visited various haunts looking for stories. Elmo grew up on five-cent tavern lunches and newspaper talk.

Three days after Elmo's fifth birthday, Irene dropped him off at his kindergarten class and caught a train for St Paul. In spite of the cooperation of the police in three different states, she was never found. Soon, Elmo was spending the time he wasn't at school in the newsroom of whatever paper his father was working on. By the time he was eight he had to look at Irene's pictures to recall her face.

He left school on his twelfth birthday and took a job as an errand boy in the newsroom of the *Wichita Eagle* where his father was working the rural desk. By the time his father died, four years later, Elmo was a cub reporter. Because of his youth, he was assigned any story that dealt with children, animals, or school budgets. Even though Elmo Robinson had been the first to report a shortfall in the school budget that seemed to coincide with the mayor's separation from his wife and his taking up with Miss Lorelei Gasmere, he hadn't graduated too far in the newspaper office.

Elmo could have followed his father's example and moved every few months, but every time the possibility presented itself he had only to drive by the solid white houses on the edge of town to change his mind. Irene's son had inherited some of her longing for place and home. Ever since she'd gone he'd planned to replace her with another. At first he'd thought in his infant way of somehow acquiring another mother. One who wouldn't leave or be silent for days on end. As he matured he changed his dreams of acquisition to a wife who would give him children and a home of his own.

Every year he'd push his dream back another twelve months. There were a number of reasons to wait, and all of them were valid. Times were hard and the Depression had affected everything, even newspapers. He wanted to marry a woman and he only met girls. He only met frivolous girls. Nice girls from good families weren't interested in a man with no family. There were a hundred other reasons that set his dreams back, but the strongest reason was the way he felt the day that Irene left.

'You'd better get dressed. Glory is going to be up in an hour or so.' She stretched and shook her hair out as he reached for his clothes.

'Did you know she was here last night?' He put down his shirt and kissed her on the knee. Offering her himself and his information. A supplicant.

'Glory?' Eva looked toward the closed door.

'No, the lady was here. Glory's lady was here. While you were sleeping she leaned over and kissed you.' He reached over and touched the top of her head. 'Right there. I thought maybe you felt it. It was about the time you woke up. She fussed with your quilt and she kissed you.'

'You sure you were awake?'

'I'm sure.' The telling of it had brought tears to his eyes and he wiped them away, hoping she hadn't seen them. Her strength required the same from him.

She pulled his hand away from his face. 'Don't do that.'

'What?'

'Don't wipe them away. I like the way they look.' She leaned forward and licked a drop of moisture from his jaw.

'She'll hold you here, Eva. Just like she always has.'

'I haven't seen her since I was a little kid. She hasn't held me here, other things did that.'

'Then you'll come with me? You'll marry me and come to Wichita?'

She nodded and began to make tears of her own. 'I'll come.'

'Eva, you'll never regret this.'

'One thing, Elmo.' She held up her hand as he tried to hold her.

'Anything, anything in the world.'

'I can't leave until Flo has the baby. I owe her that.'

'When's the baby due?'

'Spring. March or April.' She rested her head against his shoulder.

'Then you'll marry me.'

'Then I'll marry you.'

CHAPTER NINETEEN

Glory was so excited, she thought she might wet her pants or maybe even throw up. She looked around and knew that most of the kids, even the big ones, felt the same way. They'd been working on the ornaments and the pageant for over two weeks and now it was all finally happening. Even Bubba Weston was going from foot to foot just like one of the little kids. It was a First, that's what Teacher kept saying. A First.

It started when Mrs Matthews thought it would be nice to have a community Christmas tree. She'd started talking about it months ago. Mrs Matthews talked some of the men into cutting just about the biggest fir tree in the state and covering it with a tarp at the back of Crocketts' farm. Nobody but the men who'd cut the tree had seen it, but Uncle Hoyt had assured Glory that it was huge.

Mrs Matthews and some of the other women had started a fund for some lights. She had a bake sale and even went door-to-door until they raised over fourteen dollars for three strings of electric lights. Mr Strikings had ordered the big fat ones for her and she said he'd even given her a real nice price. Folks agreed that was generous of him since everyone knew he wasn't a

Christian, even though he was said to keep a statue of Mary on his desk. That seemed like an odd thing to do for someone who claimed to be a free thinker, but then it had been a pretty odd year generally.

Mama said that odd things were all about making comparisons. She said that when nothing ever happens, even a little thing like a white cat having striped kittens can seem odd. Course, in a town where the Virgin Mary comes to make calls and people kind of get used to having miracles on a regular basis, things like a free thinker who has his own personal statue of the Madonna seemed everyday.

It had been Teacher's idea for the kids to make the ornaments for the tree. Something about the ornament project had started the wheels turning in Teacher's head because before anybody knew it, they were being measured for shepherds' costumes and angels' wings. She said it would be inspirational as well as educational.

Teacher had looked frazzled for two weeks, mostly because of having to choose a Mary for the pageant. Joseph was easy because Bubba Weston was the biggest boy by about a mile and fifty pounds. Dora Harris was the original choice, what with her being the biggest girl, but the Baptists and the Catholics thought it was unfair to choose the daughter of the Presbyterian minister for the most important theatrical role of the year.

Teacher was an Episcopalian, which Reverend Harris said was almost a Catholic, but a little better than a Catholic because most of the presidents and Founding Fathers had been Episcopalians. As the only Episcopalian in town, Teacher was in a somewhat delicate position in all matters theological, especially when it came to choosing things like who would be Mary or who should win the blue ribbon for the Easter egg decorating contest. No matter who she chose, everyone knew there was bound to be criticism.

Finally it was decided that three names would go into a hat and the part of Mary would be chosen that way. All parties were agreed, so the name of Dora went into the hat along with Pammy Reynolds representing the Catholics and Ivy Scott doing the job for the Baptists. Glory, among others, had pointed out that Pammy and Ivy were way too young to be Mary, but Teacher's face was breaking out in an angry-looking rash and, one by one, the objectors simply shut up. Which was too bad, because Glory had her own idea about who should be Mary. Personally, she felt Teacher should have chosen Aunt Flo.

True, Aunt Flo wasn't a student at the school, but it was supposed to be a community pageant. And Aunt Flo was carrying a baby like Mary was on that first Christmas. Mainly, though, she thought Aunt Flo looked the way Mary must have looked. Not that Mary was real fat, because she probably wasn't, but she must have looked real proud and important the way Aunt Flo looked. Aunt Flo looked almost like a queen. She stood up real straight and carried her big belly in front like she expected people to bow down when they got a good look at it. Not that she was acting uppity or anything. She was just so proud of that big lump under her dress.

Glory had actually mentioned Aunt Flo as a possibility for the role of Mary, but Teacher had jerked her head back and sniffed the air like she'd stepped in something nasty. She hadn't even answered Glory, but rolled her eyes like a horse does when it isn't used to wearing a saddle.

Dora's name came out of the hat although Dora pretended that she didn't care too much about the whole thing. She made a big flouncy deal about not caring, but almost everyone but the tiniest kids knew that she and Bubba were a little bit sweet on each other. Suspicion had started about them back in the fall when Bubba began acting like a human being and stopped thumping the other kids. Dora feeling the way she did about Bubba made the whole thing romantic in a way that Christmas pageants weren't usually supposed to be.

Teacher had tried to keep everybody happy by making Pammy the Angel Gabriel and assigning the parts of two of the Wise Men to the Scott girls. That seemed all right until she

announced that the third Wise Man was going to be the
youngest of the Jutes, Alfie. Alfie had been getting treatment for
the ringworm and the Scott girls' mother was worried about
the sharing of crowns, not to mention gold, frankincense and
myrrh.

Glory had lost track of things about then because it was
around that time that Teacher produced an enormous jar of glitter for the ornaments. Wonderful stuff that with the addition of
glue could turn any bit of almost anything into a thing of magic.
Glory would twirl the sparkly things above her head and be
rewarded with a shower of shimmering dust that was almost
impossible to get out of her hair, even with a hundred stokes of
the big hairbrush.

The children had gone into the woods and gathered hundreds
of pine cones, seed pods, and other interesting things which
could be brushed with glue and then dipped into the jar of glitter. It was surprising to see how really festive an empty snake skin
could look after it was dipped in glitter and hung on a piece of
ribbon. When the gigantic box of ornaments was handed over to
the men who were doing the actual decorating and stringing of
the tree, Glory felt so proud she thought she might cry. All that
beauty and some of it coming from her own hands.

Glory ran to the privy one more time, just to avoid a last-
minute rush. She carefully held her wings above the wooden
seat, which wasn't easy because they were so stiff and long.
Teacher had made her one of the regular angels, but she'd given
her the biggest wings of all, even bigger than Pammy's. She still
had a whole lot of the glitter stuck to her hands, face, and hair,
and when she looked in the mirror which hung in the school-
room's coat closet she was pleased to see that she did look like an
angel, a real one. At least until she opened her mouth where her
big front teeth hadn't grown in all the way.

Fifteen minutes left to go and then they'd all troop down to
the Town Hall at the top of Main where the tree would be set
up. First they'd do the pageant and get that over with. Teacher
said by then it would be dark and while everybody was singing

Christmas carols somebody would throw the switch and the town would have its community Christmas tree. A First.

Glory was surprised at how much applause there had been after the pageant. Almost everybody in town was watching, but she figured nobody had noticed all the things that went wrong, at least not judging by the applause.

LB wet his pants while he was walking up to the manger with the other shepherds. One of the other shepherds noticed and started whispering and giggling about it. Ivy Scott, who was supposed to be really serious because she was bringing gold to the Baby Jesus, got silly and made the hand sign for donkey ears behind Mary-Dora's head. This made Joseph-Bubba, who was very nervous anyway, start laughing and trying to stop laughing, which just gave him the hiccups. He was trying to laugh and hold his breath all at the same time, which meant about every fourth breath he'd make a huge hiccup that could be heard all the way to the back of the hall.

Alfie Jute started scratching at the ringworm and ended up dropping his jar of frankincense right on top of the head of the Baby Jesus, who was in fact a big flashlight wrapped in a baby blanket. That big jar of frankincense broke the top of the Jesus-flashlight and made the light go out. Mary-Dora picked up the baby-flashlight and tried to put it back together while everybody was looking at her and singing 'Silent Night'.

Still, everybody applauded and said it was the best pageant they'd ever seen. Teacher's face looked splotchy, but she was smiling and Glory was just glad that they had two weeks of Christmas vacation so Teacher would have a chance to forget all the mistakes they'd made.

It was even prettier than she thought it would be. The lights wrapped all around the tree in a criss-cross pattern that reminded her of the way Mama sometimes braided ribbons through her own hair. The ornaments danced and bobbed in the light, cold air, catching and reflecting the colors of the lights. Even the snow beneath the tree seemed to be alive with the lights and colors of the tree.

Mr Virgil was up in the front, standing on a box in front of the tree so that everybody could see him. He was in charge of the Choral Sing-Along and doing a real good job. He was smiling and swinging his arms and blowing on his little pitch pipe. It sounded wonderful, all those voices on the cold air.

Glory looked around and saw that most folks were smiling and some were even linking arms with each other and swaying. The whole town sounded as good as something you could hear on the radio. It was almost another miracle because last Christmas Eve there hadn't been anything at all like this.

Last Christmas Eve had seemed almost sad, what with most kids knowing that Santa wasn't going to be able to put much beyond a few nuts and maybe an apple in their stockings. Even in church most people had understood that Christmas was just another time to get through.

But now the mill was open and twenty men had jobs they didn't have before. Not just the mill, but people were still coming into town to look in at the diner and see the Lady. Mr Strikings was so busy he'd even convinced Becky Johnson to stay around and work full-time even though she was an heiress. Two days ago the Mercantile had two full boxes of oranges and now they were all gone. Same with the ribbon candy and the peppermint sticks. Even the china dolls and the tin toys had left the shelves. Combine that with the funny grins on the faces of the grown-ups and even Bubba Weston could figure out that it was going to be a pretty good Christmas morning for most of the kids.

Glory turned and smiled at her mama and Mr Elmo. Mr Elmo winked at her and pulled her mama a little closer to him. When they had told her they were getting married after Aunt Flo had the baby she had tried to act surprised, but she wasn't. It didn't matter that some people thought the miracles were over or never had been miracles at all because she had the proof. She turned back toward Mr Osburne and caught a whiff of smoky air which smelled real sweet.

They were in the middle of 'O Come All Ye Faithful' when some people stopped singing and started shouting. Glory looked around and saw a red glow off to the north and realised that the sweet smoke smell was coming from that direction. It only took a second or two for the shouting to get more specific about what was on fire. She heard the word 'mill' shouted again and again and watched as every able-bodied man started running in the direction of the glowing sky.

Norville Tucker hesitated for a moment before he shouted something to Glory's mama and handed her his two little kids. Glory watched as her mama shouted something to Aunt Flo and handed the two little kids over to her sister-in-law before running off into the dark to join the men. About half a dozen of the other young women did the same, leaving a confused and crying mob of women, children, and old men standing under the light of the community Christmas tree.

Glory was about to say something to Aunt Flo, but stopped when she saw the look on the woman's face. Aunt Flo looked like she wasn't going to be in the mood to talk.

Eva reached behind her, taking the full bucket from Bubba Weston and passing it up to Darryl Strikings. Someone had called for a fire truck, but the damn thing was burning so fast they all knew it would be too late arriving to do any kind of good. The bucket brigade was pointless too, but at least it was something. Something better than standing around while that whole bright new future they'd all been looking at turned to cinders.

She kept peering ahead as far as she could. Elmo and Hoyt had run up there with blankets and sacks hoping to beat the thing into submission. Damn fools, but she knew how they felt. If she hadn't known they would stop her, she'd be up there too. She couldn't tell who was who in the crazy light the fire was throwing. Against the flames everybody was just so many black silhouettes dancing around with buckets and horse blankets.

Eva watched as the roof finally gave way, sending flames and sparks high into the night. A horrible scream was followed by the yelling of a dozen panicked men. She dropped her bucket and ran to the front of the line, certain she'd find one or both of her men dead. Her tears were already falling and a horrible noise was in her ears. It took her a few seconds to realise that the high-pitched sound was her own screaming.

Elmo was lying face down in the blackened snow next to the body of a man that was still smoldering. Eva felt faint with relief as she dropped beside him and he turned his face toward her. He coughed and smiled weakly, his teeth white against the smudged black of his face.

Eva looked to the body beside them, recognising Norville Tucker, at least what had been Norville Tucker, the man who'd handed her his babies. Virgil Osburne was kneeling beside him, wiping away the blood and muttering something she couldn't hear even though she was right next to him.

She helped Elmo stand, but he fell back down, vomiting up something black against the dirty snow.

CHAPTER TWENTY

The life of Norville Tucker had attracted less attention in the town than his death. He'd arrived two years before with a newborn daughter and a slim, lively wife named Rosie. Their arrival in town hadn't been unplanned, Norville had marked it on his map as somewhere that looked like a good place to camp for a few days. What had been unplanned was their staying instead of driving through, all the way to California.

It wasn't just their car breaking down, although that had started them thinking. Rosie was all for fixing the car up somehow and driving on West, but Norville had never seen himself as a Californian. He'd seen the state enough in the movies and had never been able quite to picture himself sitting under palm trees being neighbors with Chinese and Mexicans. His people, and Rosie's too, had always lived in the sweet green hollows of the Ozarks. They would have stayed, but when his brother started feeling the way he did toward Rosie, going seemed to be the thing to do.

It wasn't that he hadn't trusted Rosie, because he had. He'd trusted her, but his brother was pretty hard to resist. He had a natural way with women, everybody said so. Maybe if there had still been good jobs in the mines it would have made a difference, but times had gotten pretty bad in the mines so that was no reason to stay.

Things hadn't exactly been booming in the town when their car broke down, but he'd knocked on a few doors and met Miss Weesie Cartwright and her mother. Miss Weesie needed a few odd jobs done around the house, what with there not being any sort of Mr Cartwright for about fifty years. That was the start, and then old Mrs Cartwright took a shine to Rosie and liked to have her around as much as possible. Miss Weesie was so grateful for the free time and the improved attitude of her mama, she let them stay in the three empty rooms at the back of the newspaper.

Miss Weesie brought over a few things and so did a few other people. Pretty soon, Rosie had things fixed up pretty nice and the little family was content and happy except for Thursdays when the paper was printed. After the first Thursday Rosie always made sure that she and Baby June were over visiting with Mrs Cartwright because of the awful noise the old printing press would make.

Things went along fine until about six weeks after Rosie gave birth to a baby boy they named Baxter. Norville came home one day after working the harvest out at the Crocketts' to find a note stuck on top of a ham sandwich that Rosie had left on the table for his supper. She'd decided that California was the place for her after all.

Since her intention was to become a movie or radio star she'd decided the children should stay with Norville rather than be exposed to some of the immorality that the movie magazines hinted at. Rosie assured Norville, in case he was worried, that she could handle all the immorality Hollywood could dish up and then some.

Norville spent two days in utter despair until Brother Scott heard about the situation and a gaggle of good Baptist women descended on him with food and offers of babysitting. One of the most helpful was Miss Jewel Hampson, who was almost pretty if you didn't look at her straight on. Miss Jewel handled those babies like they were her own until she found out that Norville had been out two nights in a row sniffing around one of the Jute girls.

Miss Jewel had looked at his nocturnal wanderings in the Jute girl's direction in entirely the wrong light. He had been in the process of getting right beside her at the Christmas-tree lighting to tell her that very thing when word of the fire had started. He'd tried to hand the babies to Miss Jewel, but she was busy gathering up her various nieces and nephews. Instead he'd shoved them off on Eva whom he'd met only once or twice.

Norville rushed to the mill along with every other man in town under the age of seventy-three. Young and fit, he was put to work at the front after a wet square of sacking had been shoved in his hands. A fiery timber brought him down when the roof collapsed, crushing his legs beneath him and setting his clothes alight. His last thought was that Miss Jewel would now be more sympathetic toward him.

It was the noisiest night Glory could remember. It had been almost midnight before she and the babies had been put to bed, but that hadn't stopped the noise. Mr Elmo had been put into the bed in the big bedroom and he was coughing like he didn't have any intention of stopping soon. Baby June had been put in a cot next to Glory's own bed and little Baxter had been put in the room that Aunt Flo and Uncle Hoyt shared.

Glory had not been planning to sleep much anyway, not with it being Christmas Eve and all. All month she'd been planning to sit up most of the night and wait for Santa and maybe even have a little talk with him, but now she was pretty sure he wouldn't be coming. Everybody knew that one of the rules about Santa was that he had to at least think that everyone was asleep, and clearly almost everyone was awake.

Ever since they got home, different men had been coming to the door asking Uncle Hoyt what he thought would happen next. Uncle Hoyt just kept telling anybody who asked that he'd have to talk to the owner and he'd let everybody know as soon as he did. Mama was stomping around like the old days, except her face was still smudged with black and she didn't have much to say to anyone.

Baby June was quiet, but Baxter was crying and crying, even though Aunt Flo kept rocking him back and forth in the rocking chair. That was the thing that made Glory go to bed, watching Aunt Flo. She'd been looking so happy and good and everything, but now she was just rocking back and forth with that little baby while tears ran down her cheeks. She didn't even bother to wipe the tears away.

The second man who'd come to the door told Uncle Hoyt that Charley Little had died in the fire too. Part of the roof had fallen on him like it had on Baby June and Baxter's daddy. Somebody, she wasn't sure who, had said that was even sadder than Norville because Charley was one of their own. When Aunt Flo heard that she just pulled Baxter a little closer to her and rocked a little faster.

In the morning Glory ran downstairs to check and see if there was anything in the stocking she'd hung by the fireplace the day before. She'd hung it right after breakfast when just about everything was real nice. Glory felt almost ashamed of wanting to look in her stocking, but she'd been looking forward to it for days and days and then a little more time on top of that. Even though she was pretty sure that Santa wouldn't have come because there had been people around all night long, she was looking forward to seeing her stocking in a 'maybe it could still happen' sort of way.

Aunt Flo was still in the rocker, but now she was asleep, her head off to the side and her mouth slightly open. Her mama was walking back and forth across the floor with Baxter over her shoulder. She was rubbing his back and very softly humming the song about the dead goose that Glory had loved when she was little.

'Mama?'

'Merry Christmas, Glory.' Her mama smiled, at least with her mouth. Her eyes looked dark and smudged.

'Did he come?' She whispered so that she wouldn't wake up Aunt Flo.

'Find out for yourself, sugar.'

Glory rushed to the fireplace to find a stuffed stocking and a china doll in a green dress wearing the tiniest white shoes she'd ever seen. 'He came, Mama, even with the fire he came.' She put her hand into the stocking and pulled out an orange, some nuts, a candy cane, and a clicker that was painted like a bullfrog.

'I don't think Santa would be stopped by something like an old fire, do you?'

'I guess not.' She grinned at her mama and clicked the clicker a few times. Mama smiled a little more with her eyes then, Glory was pleased to see.

'Is Baby June still asleep?'

'Yeah. She slept all night, but I think she wet her diaper because it smells like pee up in my room.'

'I'm afraid we're going to have to get used to that pee smell in your room until we find these babies' mother or someone else who can take care of them.'

'This baby won't pee and that's a good thing.' She kissed her new doll and smoothed out her dress. 'I think I'll call her Holly because she's my Christmas surprise.' She made the doll dance in the air for a moment or two while she looked at her mama. It was easy to see from the look on Mama's face that she didn't have much Christmas spirit.

'I'm going to cook it because I'm not going to let a perfectly good ham go to waste just because nobody is hungry.' Flo shoved the ham into the oven and slammed the door shut.

'I didn't say you shouldn't cook it, Flo, I just said I wasn't sure if you should cook it today.' Eva was pouring hot water into a teapot to take up to Elmo.

'It's Christmas, isn't it?'

'It is definitely Christmas, Flo.' Eva felt weary down to the ends of her hair, but hadn't been able to find the time to sleep. Between checking on Elmo, walking the baby, minding the little girl and answering the front door to half the town, she'd barely had a chance to sit down in twenty-four hours.

'Then I'm going to cook the darned ham because Christmas was when Mary had Jesus. We have to celebrate Christmas so we don't make her mad. Christmas is all about Mary, isn't it? Maybe she's already mad and maybe that's why this happened.' She put her face in her hands and started crying. 'Maybe she's forsaken us. Maybe because some folks made fun of her coming, maybe because some folks said it was a ghost and not Mary. If things don't change she could take my baby. Already two men are dead.' Flo sat down in a kitchen chair and grabbed the edge of the table to stop her hands from shaking right off the ends of her arms. 'Maybe she wants my baby, Eva. Maybe she's going to take my baby the way she took those men.'

Eva took her sister-in-law's hand in one of hers and smoothed the hair away from her face with the other. 'Listen to me, Flo. Are you listening to me?'

Flo nodded her head. 'Umm.'

'We don't have to do anything today except get through to tonight. If you want to fix a big old Christmas dinner with all the trimmings, that's okay by me. I'll help you do it to keep you off your feet. If you don't want to do a thing but go up to bed and finally get some real sleep, that's okay too. The mill burning down was bad, it was real bad, but I don't think Mary had anything to do with it. Mary didn't kill those men and she's not going to kill your baby. Your baby is going to be fine, just fine. Look at Glory. Look at Hoyt and me and you and all your family. We're made for having big healthy babies, women like us.' She gave Flo's hand a kiss before squatting next to her chair.

'Now your baby is going to be fine, but only if you're fine. As upset as you are, I think we should have the doctor out to take a look at you and the baby.'

'No, Eva, that's one thing I will not do.' Flo sat up straight and glared at Eva. 'The doctor didn't do any good when I was trying to catch. When I knew this baby was coming I promised myself that no doctor was coming near it until after it was born. There are enough women in this town who never used doctors for birthing and I'm going to be one of them.'

'Listen, Flo. I'm just asking you to be sure that you and the baby get the best care possible.'

'And you listen to me. I am having the best care possible. I'm using the same person who brought me into this world. Mrs Crenshaw brought me and my sister into this world and half the town besides. She delivered just as many babies as your daddy ever did, more even.'

'I know that, Flo.' Mrs Crenshaw *had* delivered as many babies as her father had, but now she was over seventy and her once nimble fingers were crippled with arthritis.

'My child is a gift from Mary. That's what Father Greene said. He said my child was a gift from the mother of God Himself.' Flo slumped down again, her face in her hands. 'I'm just so scared that something else is going to go wrong. I'm so scared. The mill is gone and two men are dead. I walked in on Hoyt this morning and he had tears in his eyes, Eva. Your brother was crying like a little boy. I don't know what's going to happen to this town now that the mill is gone.'

'We'll get by, just like we did before.' She patted her sister-in-law on the shoulder. 'Besides, we still don't know what the insurance was on the mill. Maybe it will be rebuilt. Maybe this will make even more jobs. Let's just get through today the best we can.'

'I wonder if you'd mind if I went and lay down for a little while?' Flo pulled herself up from the chair.

'Do you feel all right, Flo? You don't look too good.'

'Just tired, and my back hurts from sleeping in that rocking chair half the night.'

'You go up and try to get some sleep.'

'Call me if you need help with the babies or anything.'

'Glory and I can take care of the babies, you go take care of yourself.'

'Thanks, Eva.' Flo headed toward the stairs, her hands rubbing at the small of her back.

Hoyt removed his hat and brushed the fresh snow off his shoulders before he knocked on the door. He knew he should have come by earlier in the day, but it had taken him this long to get all the callers out of his house. Everyone had the same question and he always gave the same answer and everyone left unsatisfied. He'd tried to call Abaddon, the mill owner, but there hadn't been any answer. Several people had seen him the day before, himself included, but apparently he hadn't returned to his home. Course it was Christmas, he reminded himself, even if it didn't feel like Christmas apart from the snow. Mr Abaddon must have gone to see relatives or friends. Hoyt rapped his knuckles on the door.

A small elderly woman answered and peered at him. 'Did you come to see him?'

'I came to see the Littles, Miss Ruth.' Hoyt nodded at Ruth Childs, Mr Little's sister who lived down the road.

'Hoyt? Hoyt Gorman?' She squinted slightly and opened the door to let him in. 'You want to come look at Charley? We've got him all cleaned up and laid out.'

'I'll see him after I've had a word with his parents.'

'You'll see him now then, because his mama won't leave his side. Says she's only got a day or two before he goes in the ground and she loses him forever.' The small woman wiped at her face. 'We're all going to lose him, Hoyt. All over again, but this time we know he won't be coming back.'

'I know, Miss Ruth.'

'Well, come with me.' She walked through the kitchen, into the adjoining room where a dark-suited Charley was laid out in a pine coffin atop two sawhorses. His mother sat next to him wearing a faded black dress.

'Miss Helen.' He nodded and looked at Charley for a second. More to be polite than anything, because most of Charley's head was thickly bandaged. Hoyt couldn't help thinking that the body could have been just about anybody's.

'Hello, Hoyt.'

'I came over as soon as I could to extend my condolences to you and Bill.'

'You're kind of late. Almost the last one to come, you are. We've had two dozen callers today, but you're the last. You should have been the first, Hoyt Gorman. You and your family should have been the first ones because you're the reason that this happened. If it wasn't for the Gormans my boy never would have come back when he did. He came home when he did because of her.'

'I'm sorry I'm late, ma'am, I truly am. I know I was in charge of the mill and I should have been here sooner, but this has been the first chance I've had to get away. I came as fast as I could.'

'I'm not talking about the mill, you fool.'

'You're not?'

'I'm talking about your niece, Hoyt. This is her fault.'

'Glory? What does Glory have to do with Charley?'

'That hobo she and the other girl saw in the woods was my Charley. Wasn't a hobo at all. It was just my boy trying to come back home after too long. But they scared him off and he stayed away even longer. Some folks are saying that those little girls are having miracles and seeing angels and such, but it isn't so.' Her lower lip trembled and she put a wadded-up handkerchief to her mouth.

'It was just Charley trying to get home and then the mill opened and folks said it was so wonderful, but then it burned down and it took my boy with it. He's the only child I ever had and now he's going away for good. He's going away for good, Hoyt Gorman.'

CHAPTER TWENTY-ONE

Virgil Osburne and his sister, Miss Alma, had debated about whether or not to open the cafe the day after Christmas. They always had before, but Miss Alma thought it would show respect to Charley and Norville if they just kept it closed for a few days. Finally they'd agreed that Virgil would go ahead and open up an hour late and just serve coffee. That way Miss Alma could stay home and not compromise her convictions and Virgil would feel that things were being conducted in a business-like fashion.

His hand went to his chest as soon as he opened the door to the cafe. A pipe in the ceiling had burst, leaving an inch of icy water on the floor and nothing more than a wet, dirty-looking wall where the Mary/Evangeline image had been. He closed the door behind him and walked back to tell his sister what had happened.

As he walked home he passed by Father Greene, who was headed in the opposite direction. Father Greene was almost running, his overcoat flapping around him like the wings of a black bird.

'Father.' Virgil tipped his hat, not intending to stop. The

sooner Alma knew, the better. The plumbing could be fixed and the water mopped up, but Alma had become awfully attached to the image on the wall and it had been wonderful for business. Alma had even been talking about adding some things to the menu to make it more appealing to the out-of-town visitors. Just last night she'd been talking turkey croquettes and marshmallow dainties.

'Virgil, have you heard? Terrible news.' Father Greene stopped, skidding slightly on the tightly packed snow.

He nodded. 'Shame about those two boys. A real tragedy.' For a second, no longer, he'd thought that Father Greene had been referring to the wall of the cafe. Virgil was grateful that Father Greene had reminded him about the dead boys. Reminded him that there were worse things then a burst pipe, a smudged wall and a probable reduction in business.

'Yes, but there's been another death. Raymond Reynolds died.'

'Raymond?' It took Virgil a few seconds to conjure an image of Raymond Reynolds in his head. He couldn't recall if Raymond had ever been in the cafe. He didn't think he had been, but that would make sense as Raymond Reynolds had spent his weeks on the road. A life like that would make a man want to stay home and eat at his own table. 'Raymond died in the fire, too?' Virgil couldn't imagine Raymond with his double-breasted suit and pencil mustache joining in to fight the fire. After all, he had stayed out of it himself because he knew he could be of more service by keeping the women and children calm around the Christmas tree.

'No, it wasn't the fire at all. It seems that Raymond choked on his Christmas dinner. I don't know the whole story yet because I didn't get here until this morning. My housekeeper Judith told me about poor Raymond and those tragic young men. I don't suppose you know whether or not that Norville fellow was a Catholic, do you?'

'Miss Weesie would know if anyone does.'

'Yes, of course. I'll check with her later. Well, yes.' Father

Greene turned away abruptly and hurried in the direction of the Reynolds home.

Lucille Reynolds sat in front of her dressing-table mirror and tried to adjust her face. Three people had already told her that she must be in shock. She'd lowered her head and her eyes and hadn't said anything to that, although she knew better.

She was in realisation. As soon as she'd seen Raymond turn blue after shoveling the third wad of cornbread stuffing into his mouth she realised that she was going to enjoy being a widow.

Things would have to settle down first, of course. The children had been terribly upset, but she figured that was mostly because he'd looked so damned unattractive in those last minutes. It wasn't as though either of them were that fond of him, after all. Or even saw that much of him, for that matter.

As soon as the Catholic undertaker from Deleur had picked him up, she'd sat the children down and explained to them how life insurance worked. She had explained that Raymond had had quite a bit of it and that money wasn't going to be any kind of problem, not at all. She told them that their father would keep loving them and providing for them, even if he was going to be in Heaven. Personally, she felt he wouldn't get too far past the Sacred Heart Cemetery in Deleur. Raymond had never seemed the type to even want to go to Heaven.

Still, she told herself, she would miss him. Wouldn't she? Everyone who'd come by had said that she would. Every widow who had come through the door had said how hard it was going to be, but they seemed to be doing just fine, every last one of them.

The doorbell rang and she listened as Pammy opened it. She heard Father Greene's voice and smoothed her black dress before she left her room to greet him. She composed her features into what she thought must be a suitable expression of grief and shock.

Glory took her new doll and went to play in the corner of the basement where her mama used to keep the paintings. She had to really, just to keep away from Baby June. Baby June had already tried to eat one of her doll's little white shoes and she'd peed right in the middle of the kitchen before breakfast.

She'd tried to talk to Mama, but her mama was upset because Elmo had to go back to Wichita even though he was still coughing and didn't feel very good. Besides that, Aunt Flo felt sick and was staying in bed so Mama had that Baxter fussing on her shoulder most of the time. Uncle Hoyt wasn't around because he was down at the burned-out mill along with some policemen and firemen who'd come in before eight in the morning.

She'd offered to go down to Pammy's house, just to get out from underfoot, where her mama had said she was, but then her mama had gotten even more upset and said she'd talk to her about it later. She'd almost just snuck off to Pammy's house, but decided against it because all the grown-ups were in such a bad mood. If things were this bad at her house, they were probably just as bad, if not worse, at Pammy's, what with her daddy being home and Miss Lucille being so high-strung and all.

She sat in the middle of the basement floor and closed her eyes. She started praying to Evangeline and asking her to come help find some place for the babies to stay that was far away from her. She sat and listened with all her might, but all she could hear was the old boiler wheezing in the corner. She opened her eyes and looked around as much as she could without moving her head, but she didn't see anything that made her think that Evangeline or Mary was anywhere around.

Glory looked into Pammy's room to make sure the coast was clear before she opened the window. She knew she was supposed to stay home, but she needed to know if Pammy had seen Mary or anything else worth mentioning. She'd heard Aunt Flo talking yesterday in the kitchen about Mary and it had sounded scary, in a crazy sort of way. Mama had said that Aunt Flo was just tired, but Glory thought she had sounded crazy. She pushed the window open and climbed onto Pammy's bed.

She tiptoed to the closed door and pressed her ear to the

wood. She could hear Miss Lucille and she thought the man's voice she was hearing was Father Greene's. She slowly twisted the doorknob and opened the door a crack so that she could see across the hallway into the front room. She could see Pammy and LB sitting on the big couch and it looked like they were praying. At least Pammy had her eyes closed and LB had his squeezed shut real tight. She kept listening and it was definitely Father Greene talking.

After a minute or two the children opened their eyes and Glory waved her hand, just outside the door. It didn't take long for Pammy to glance up and then say something before she walked toward the bedroom door. Her eyes were down and her face was all pink and splotchy.

'Why didn't you come in the front door?' Pammy was wearing her very best dress in the whole world. It was such a good dress that Glory had never actually seen her wear it before. It was dark blue, almost black velvet with a Battenberg lace collar. Glory knew it was Battenberg lace because Pammy had told her about a million times that it was Battenberg lace. It was so nice it wasn't even kept in Pammy's room, but hung in her mother's closet.

'I'm not supposed to be here, that's why. Why are you dressed up and why are you praying with your brother?'

'Didn't you hear about our daddy?'

'What about him?'

'He choked to death yesterday. The Lord works in mysterious ways.' Pammy shrugged and looked in the direction of the front room.

'How did he choke to death?'

'He was real drunk, but Mama says we're not allowed to mention that because that would be speaking ill of the dead and we're above such things.'

'Is he still here?' Glory craned her neck to see into the front room.

'No, the undertaker picked him up right away because Mama said she'd swoon if she had to touch him.'

'That's real sad, Pammy.'

'Mama is always saying that she's going to swoon, but I've never seen her swoon, not even once.'

'I mean it's sad that he's dead. I know he was gone most of the time, but at least you had a daddy and I always thought that was kind of nice. I guess because I don't have one, I thought it was nice that you had one.'

'Mama says we're all in shock. She's not crying because she's in shock.'

'Did you cry?'

'At first I did. I cried so much I almost forgot why I was crying, but I haven't cried today. I might cry some later, but Father Greene said it was better to pray than to cry. He said we should look to the Holy Virgin and use her as an example because she suffered too.'

'Maybe she's suffered so much she's finally got good and mad the way a person does when they're just plain fed up. Maybe she's just fed up with this town.'

'What are you talking about?'

'The Lady did all these nice things for people. She got rid of the hobo, and she got the mill opened and she brought Charley Little back and lots of other things. She showed herself to practically the whole world down at the diner, but still lots of people said it wasn't anything. Maybe she got good and mad and burned down the mill and killed your daddy. Aunt Flo is in bed right now because she's afraid whatever is going on will kill her baby.'

'That's crazy because Mary doesn't kill anybody.'

'Maybe Evangeline does. She's my mama's mama and my mama has a bad temper and so does Uncle Hoyt sometimes. Maybe they got their bad tempers from Evangeline.'

'I'm going back in the front room and I think you'd better go home.' Pammy left the room and shut the door behind her.

'They think it was all some big fraud thing, Eva.' Hoyt sat hunched on the sofa with his head in his hands.

'I don't understand what you're talking about. What do you

mean it was a big fraud thing?' It was almost nine at night and she'd finally got the little girls to bed, but Baxter seemed determined to be the first baby ever to stay awake for twenty-four hours straight. Every time she tried to put him down, he'd start crying hard enough to break her heart. Right now she was standing and swaying back and forth while Baxter was lying, belly down, across her forearm.

'Mr Abaddon insured the mill for a lot more than it was worth. That's all they know for sure right now.'

'Has anybody talked to him?'

'Yeah, they caught up with him this morning at his office. Says he had all the insurance because he was planning to build the mill and the factory up this coming year.'

'That sounds reasonable enough.'

'It does, except some of us saw him driving out of town like his butt was on fire. Just before the pageant he was at the mill. He leaves and the thing is on fire.'

'Who all saw him?'

'Me, Darryl over at the Mercantile, and Will Heath. He almost knocked Will over he was driving so fast.'

'What happens now?'

'It looks like I'll have to testify myself right out of a job. Not that I guess he ever had any intention of working the mill, not really. I guess all I've lost is a lie.'

'None of this is your fault, Hoyt.'

'I was the one who got people excited. They listened to me and they trusted me. That police inspector says guys like Abaddon use guys like me to get the trust of the other folks in the town. I was his stooge.'

'For a few weeks, a few men had jobs and that's not all bad.' She sat down in the rocker and put Baxter in her lap.

'I thought things had really turned for us, Eva, for all of us. After all the things that started this summer, I really thought things had turned.'

'Maybe things aren't made to turn that fast, Hoyt. Things don't turn overnight, at least not most of the time.'

'They did for you. Look at you and Elmo. You and Glory will go off with him and start a whole new life.'

'Not until your baby is born and we figure out what to do with this one and his sister.'

'My baby. I wonder what my baby is going to think about his old man.'

'He's going to think you're a good man who works hard to take care of his own.'

'Watch out, Eva. If anybody heard you talking that way they might think you didn't hate me the way you do.'

'I hate you a little bit because you're a thick-headed ass, but mostly I love you.'

'I guess I feel the same way about you, you mean-tempered bitch.'

'I'm going to miss you, Hoyt. I'm going to miss living here and fighting with you.'

'It won't be the same, that's for sure.'

'Life goes on, or doesn't, as the case may be.'

'What do you mean?'

'I was just thinking about Raymond Reynolds.'

'What about him?'

'Didn't you hear? He died right in the middle of eating his Christmas dinner yesterday.'

'Poor bastard. Another victim of the miracles, I guess.'

'What are you talking about?'

'I forgot to tell you what Charley's mother told me yesterday. She told me that the hobo the girls saw in the woods this summer was just Charley trying to screw up his courage to come on home. He got scared and ran off. That's all that happened.'

'I always figured it was just one hobo or another turning tail. I never thought it had anything to do with a miracle. What does that have to do with Raymond dying, anyway?'

'Didn't Raymond get some fancy promotion after the girls asked for it?'

'Yeah, I guess, but a lot of people have had a lot of things happen, good and bad. I don't think you can take one person and one incident and start talking about anybody being a victim of the miracles.'

'Maybe not, Eva, but things sure as Hell seem to be falling apart on us right now. All the good things are falling apart.'

'Not all of them, Hoyt. Your wife has never been happier and you're about to have the baby you two have wanted for so long. I'm going to be moving out and you'll have the house to yourselves. And don't forget that there is still a nice greasy-looking image of the mystery lady on the wall of the cafe.' Eva chuckled, causing Baxter to startle and squeak.

'I forgot to tell you about that. Virgil stopped by the mill and said that a pipe burst in the ceiling of the cafe. He's got an inch of water on the floor and nothing on his wall but a wet spot.'

'Nothing but a coincidence. It was cold enough to freeze the balls off a brass monkey so I'm not surprised that a few pipes burst. Besides, I was never convinced that Virgil's wall had anything to do with anything else. Glory thought it looked like Evangeline, but I didn't.'

'Not even a little?'

'Well, I guess it looked like her, but did anybody expect that smudge to stay up there forever?'

'I don't know.'

'Well, I think I do know. Some good things happened and people started feeling better about themselves because they figured something holy was happening to them. Nothing changed then and nothing has changed now. Things can be as good or as bad as we want them to be.'

'I hope to God you're right, Eva.'

'I hope I am, too, Hoyt. I really hate being wrong.'

'I know that much is true.' He yawned and stretched. 'I'm beat half to death. I think I'll crawl in bed next to my wife and see if I can get some sleep.'

'First take this scrap off of me so I can spend five minutes in the bathroom without an interruption.' Eva slid the baby from her lap into Hoyt's arms.

'I remember when Glory was a baby it didn't bother you to

let her just fuss herself to sleep. Why don't you do that with this one?'

'I feel like I, we, have to take extra good care of him just in case he's figured out that his mama is gone and his daddy is dead. Just give me five minutes.'

CHAPTER TWENTY-TWO

School was the last place in the whole world she wanted to be, but her mama wouldn't listen even though she told her about a million and a half times that she wanted to stay home so she could be there when her cousin was born. She pulled out her exercise book and copied out what Teacher had put on the board.

Something had started in the middle of the night, but she hadn't been sure what it was. She'd heard some voices, but she'd been so tired that she just rolled over and fell asleep again. Of course, she'd figured out what was going on when she came down for breakfast and found Mrs Crenshaw drinking coffee and wearing a clean blue apron. Her mama had already told her that Mrs Crenshaw was the lady who helped other ladies get the babies out through the secret passage that all grown-up ladies had.

She'd snuck a peek into the big bedroom when she went back upstairs and Aunt Flo was indeed sitting up in the big bed. The fancy cradle that her mama and Uncle Hoyt had made for the new baby stood empty at the side of the bed. Aunt Flo was smiling at two of her friends who were sitting with her and all three of the women were knitting tiny little things on skinny needles. Her mama shooed her out and gave her the tiniest smack on the bottom, but she was still glad she'd had a chance to get a look at what was going on.

She'd looked into her mama's bedroom and found one of the Jute girls, she wasn't sure which one because they all looked alike, and she was minding Baxter and stupid Baby June who was always in the way and not even the least little bit cute.

When the babies had first come to stay with them it had been kind of exciting and Glory thought it would be like playing dolls only the dolls would actually swallow the food that you mashed into their mouths. The only thing that was true was they did indeed swallow the food, but then they would just poop it out the other end.

Baxter wasn't too bad because he couldn't do anything but stay where you stuck him. He couldn't even sit up by himself and Mama said it would be another month or two before he'd even try to learn. Now that they knew that cow's milk gave him gas and made him cry, they only gave him goat's milk and he was pretty happy most of the time. He had a nice gummy smile that he used quite a bit and made a funny little sound that Aunt Flo said was a laugh.

Baby June was a mess because she wanted to do things for herself, but she couldn't do anything at all because she was an idiot and would probably always be an idiot. She was always yelling 'mine, mine' and 'dis, dis'. It had been cute for the first day or so, but Baby June didn't have the brains to know that Glory's things weren't 'mine' or 'dis'. Because she wanted to do things for herself she wanted to use the toilet and not wear a diaper, but she didn't really know how to use the toilet. Usually she'd just mess her pants and then try to flush the pants down the toilet. The whole time she was flushing, she'd be yelling 'mine, mine'. Poor Uncle Hoyt had already taken the toilet apart twice this week.

Mama had tried to find some kind of family members to take them, but she said it seemed almost like Norville and Rosie

6 Joyce Mandeville

didn't even exist until that day that their car broke down in town. Father Greene was trying to get them into a Catholic orphanage, but it wasn't easy because there was a long waiting list. Mama said they'd just have to be patient and take care of the babies the best they could because it was the only decent thing to do. There was a county orphanage, but Uncle Hoyt said he wouldn't take a cat there so that wasn't going to help.

She finished copying the words off the board and closed her book after she'd checked that Pammy was also closing her book. After they'd spent so much time thinking about not being best friends anymore, they'd become best friends again. Partly because they liked each other and partly because some of the other kids said they'd been telling fibs and making things up all along. The Baptist kids were the very worst and Glory was glad that she hadn't decided to make that Ivy Scott her new best girlfriend.

Miss Lucille said the Baptists were always the worst and Glory couldn't help wondering if she was right. For one thing the Baptist kids were always saying to Pammy and LB that their daddy died because he was a drunk. Pammy would just put her head up, but LB had gotten in a couple of fights over this and had the only broken nose in the whole school on a boy under eight years of age.

Some of the kids even said Charley and Norville were dead because of what the girls had started. Teacher always shushed the kids up if they said anything like that, but Glory had found out that if something is said often enough, you can start believing it, even if you're almost positive it isn't true.

Even Darryl Strikings, who wasn't even a Baptist, although his wife was one before she died, told the girls he should send them a bill for the thirty-five dollars' worth of stock he couldn't sell because nobody cared about any of that stuff anymore. That made Miss Lucille so mad she went in and threw, actually threw, thirty-five dollars across his counter and told him she didn't want to hear another word about it. Now that Miss Lucille was kind of rich with that insurance money she was a lot freer with what she had to say for herself.

Uncle Hoyt said they were practically Catholic now, but that wasn't true. It was just that the Catholics were the only ones that didn't think she and Pammy had just been making up stories to make themselves look important. Father Greene had even been invited into the school to talk about times in history when other people saw Mary, but Brother Scott heard about it and made a lot of trouble. He wrote to everyone he could and said it was Anti-American and Teacher almost got fired, which would have been bad because she was so tall and skinny Glory was pretty sure that Teacher would never have a husband to take care of her.

Uncle Hoyt was sort of right about Aunt Flo being almost a Catholic. She even had a string of rosary beads that Father Greene had given her. She wanted to name the new baby either Mary or Joseph and she was even talking about having the baby baptised by Father Greene. Uncle Hoyt said it was crazy, but Glory could tell that he didn't care much one way or the other. Since the mill had burned, he didn't care one way or another about anything at all except how Aunt Flo was feeling and how the baby was moving.

Since it was free time she pulled out a fresh piece of paper and her crayons to make a picture for Aunt Flo. Aunt Flo had always loved her pictures and hung them all over the kitchen. Glory drew the fancy cradle that her mama had painted with all kinds of animals and wild-looking plants. She drew in the pretty yellow blanket that Aunt Flo had knit up for the baby, but she couldn't quite imagine what the baby's face should look like. She shut her eyes and tried to draw the picture in her head, but no matter how hard she tried, she couldn't see a face.

She watched him for a few minutes before she walked up to him. An hour earlier Eva had sent him out to chop wood, just to get him out of the house. Every time somebody walked down the stairs he'd look up like a scared deer. It didn't make any difference that ten different women told him that the first ones took the longest.

'Hoyt?' She watched him turn toward her. Sweat was pouring from his face even though the air was still February cold and blustery in March.

'Has anything happened?' He whacked the ax into a stump before he turned to his sister.

'Things are starting to move a little faster.' But only a little. Eva felt she should have been farther along, but Hilda Crenshaw said there was nothing to worry about.

'Is she okay? Is she in a lot of pain?'

'You try squeezing a roast chicken out your right nostril, Hoyt, and then ask me if she's in pain.' She smiled to soften her words and put her arm around his shoulders. 'Flo's doing fine, just fine. It hurts like Hell, but she'll forget about it by the time you start thinking you'd like to have another one.'

'I don't think I could go through this again, Eva.'

'You don't thing you could go through it?' She raised her eyebrow and looked at her brother.

'You know what I mean.'

'I know, Hoyt. I just like to tease you a little bit. Why don't you come in and I'll fix you something to eat? You're going to need the energy for rocking that cradle.'

'I don't think I can eat anything, Eva. Not with her upstairs, not until we know how things are going to go.'

'Things are going to go fine, Hoyt. Just like I told Flo. A girl like Flo was made for making babies. She was just a little bit of a late starter, that's all.'

'I wish she would have gone to see the doctor. Maybe if we called a doctor now it would speed things up and the baby would be born sooner.'

'Babies take their own time, Hoyt.'

'Glory practically fell out of you. I remember Flo saying that.'

'I was a lot younger than Flo when Glory was born and that helps a lot.' And she'd walked for miles and miles every day as soon as she suspected that she'd caught. She'd walked and she'd run, hoping to shake the thing loose. The doctor told her she'd actually speeded up delivery by giving herself the life of an athlete those months. She remembered telling him that it was the longest delivery in history as she'd been trying to shed herself of the pregnancy for what felt like years.

'I just hope that Flo is right and her Virgin Mary is watching over her like she thinks she is.'

'Well, Hoyt, even if Flo's Virgin has left town she's still got Hilda Crenshaw and half a dozen other women who know how to scoop up a baby when it comes out.'

'I still wish she had the doctor in.'

'And I wish you'd stop talking and come inside with me. It's freezing out here.' She took his hand and led him toward the kitchen door.

It was the scream that woke him up. He'd fallen asleep on the couch downstairs to the sounds of the women talking and moving about. He'd heard Flo, too. Strange, animal sounds that he couldn't imagine coming from a little pink mouth like hers, but Eva said it was Flo. Panting and grunting to bring his child into the world. He'd tried to stay awake, but he'd been awake since four the previous morning when her waters had broken and flooded his side of the mattress.

Hoyt jumped to his feet before he was fully awake. The scream came again, died for a moment and then repeated itself. He'd stayed downstairs ever since the women had arrived, but now he found himself on the stairs, running toward the big bedroom.

Flo lay curled on her side, blood-stained hands held up to her face. Even through the mask she'd made with her hands he could hear her screams. Wild, animal-like sounds that had never come out of his wife's or any human's mouth.

Hilda Crenshaw held a blanket-wrapped bundle and Mrs Matthews was vomiting into a basin by the window. Other women, their faces blurring into one, milled around his wife and the room. Eva spun him around and pushed him out of the door. He could feel her damp breath on the back of his shirt as she followed him out.

'Flo?' He wanted to ask, but could only get the one word out.

'Flo is going to be all right. It's over now, Hoyt.' She put her arms around him.

Her mouth was next to his ear and he heard and felt the words at the same time. 'It was still, Hoyt. It was a stillborn.'

He felt Eva trembling and then realised that the trembling was from inside of him. Eva was holding him up. 'Boy or girl?' It seemed to matter. He needed to know what it was that he would never see grow up. He needed to know what it was that wouldn't make him proud or break his heart.

'Come sit down, Hoyt. You're shaking all over.' She released her grip on him for a second before clasping his arm and leading him into the bedroom he shared with Flo. She sat him on the edge of the bed and sat beside him, her arm across his shoulders, holding him tight.

'Boy or girl?' She'd painted the cradle for either a boy or a girl. Even the yellow blanket. Flo used yellow so that it would be good for a boy or a girl. Either one, they'd agreed, either one would be fine.

'It wasn't formed right, Hoyt. That happens sometimes. Usually it ends early, but this went full term.'

'Not formed right?'

'That's right.'

'What's not formed right?'

'I think we need to think about Flo right now. We need to think about you and Flo.' She patted him on the hand.

'What's not formed right?'

'Hoyt, it doesn't matter, not now.'

'It matters to me, Eva.' He had to see it and hold it.

'You need to trust me, Hoyt. You need to believe me when I tell you that you don't need to see it, or know anything more about it.'

'It? Won't you at least tell me if it's a boy or a girl?' Flo's screams had died down to an exhausted sob.

'I don't know which it is. I didn't look that close.'

'I need to see Flo and I need to see our baby.'

'Let's go see Flo first. The other can wait.' Eva stood, took his hand and led him into the big bedroom.

He waited downstairs for Eva. The dawn was coming through the windows and all the women had left once Flo had fallen asleep. Not so much fell, he told himself, but sobbed herself into a stupor and finally unconsciousness. She hadn't spoken a word and he'd had few to offer. Every breath he took seemed to be a decision as to whether he would choose to live or allow himself to die.

'Hoyt?' Eva walked into the room holding the bundle of yellow knit blanket.

'Let me see.' He held out his arms, but she held the bundle close to her breast.

'It won't make anything easier, Hoyt.'

'It can't make it harder either, can it?'

'I guess not.' She handed the bundle over and turned away.

He unwrapped the bundle slowly, afraid to see what it held. As more of it was revealed, he unwrapped faster, looking for anything that resembled the picture of the baby he'd kept in his mind all those months. He wrapped it back up and put it on his shoulder the same way he did with Baxter when he was fussy. 'It doesn't even look like a baby.' Bits of hair or fur, some skin, some sacs of fluid and something that had looked like a mouth, but nothing that looked like a head. But still he wanted to hold it and offer it, himself, some comfort.

'Nature makes mistakes too, I guess.' Eva gently took the bundle away from him.

'Remember that time we broke the front window at the Mercantile?' They had been about seven then. Wild and unsupervised, they'd thrown a pop bottle through the biggest window they could find, just to see how it would look when it broke.

'I remember.'

'It was so much fun and then it went all wrong when old Mr Strikings caught us. I remember wishing then that I could have taken those minutes back.'

'What brought that up?'

'I feel that way right now. If I could just take the time back from Christmas Eve to now. If I could just lose these last few months. I want to go back to when the mill was open and my wife was carrying my baby.'

'I know it doesn't seem like it now, but there are going to be good times again. Things aren't going to stay as bad as they are right now.'

'I'm not so sure, not anymore.' He took the bundle from her and cradled it in his arms.

CHAPTER TWENTY-THREE

Glory had tried to tell Mama and Uncle Hoyt, but they wouldn't listen. She reckoned it had started with Aunt Flo because she was the first one who stopped listening and talking. Somehow, by one grown-up doing something, or not doing something, they all fell into line. Uncle Hoyt and Mama pretended to talk and they pretended to listen, but they didn't, not really.

She'd even tried to tell Father Greene, but he just told her that they could talk things over later. He stopped by nearly every day. He'd go up and sit with Aunt Flo and talk to her and pray for her. He'd make signs above her head and sprinkle water around her. Sometimes she'd touch the water and look up at the ceiling like she was trying to see if the roof was leaking, but it wasn't. She still held on to the rosary he'd given her, but it was getting smaller, just like Aunt Flo.

Aunt Flo had given up eating after the baby that wasn't quite a baby had been born. Mama would take a tray up to her three times a day, but she didn't eat anything. Except for the beads. Glory had never actually seen her eat one of the rosary beads, but the rosary was getting smaller and there didn't seem to be any other explanation. Glory was pretty certain that every other day or so, Aunt Flo would put one of the glossy blue beads in her mouth and swallow it down. Swallow it down so it could rest where the not quite a baby had rested and then died.

Glory had told Pammy about what she'd seen, but Pammy thought they should just keep their mouths shut about the whole thing. Glory had to admit that Pammy had a pretty good point. Hardly anybody even half believed in what had happened anymore.

It was almost like it had never happened, at least not the good things. The bad things had happened and she only had to look around her own house to see that. It looked like it was going to take forever to get Baby June and Baxter into the Catholic home and Mama had a million reasons why Elmo wasn't coming to town anymore.

Eva sat down at the kitchen table and looked at the empty piece of paper. She picked up the pen and wrote the date and 'Dear Elmo' in the left-hand corner before putting the pen back down.

She'd known how it was going to be the second she'd seen that thing come out of Flo. Even before she'd taken a good look at it she'd known it was going to be the end of everything she'd been wanting.

Elmo kept planning her move to Wichita and she hadn't had the heart to tell him that it would never happen. Eva still wrote to him twice a week and tried to make things sound like they were getting better, but she knew things were only getting worse. Maybe Hoyt could take care of two little kids or a crazy wife, but he couldn't do both, nobody could. Eva knew she was as tied to the house as the wisteria that wrapped itself around the porch.

Eva picked the pen back up and wrote as quickly as she could. She wrote quickly because she didn't need to think too much about what she was writing. She'd been writing the letter for over a month. She just hadn't put it to paper yet.

My life is here and always has been. Hoyt and Flo were willing to give my daughter a home even while I was hoping she'd die inside of me. I owe them a debt and right now it looks like I'll be spending the next few years paying that debt off.

I think this would seem tragic except I know you'll be fine. I'll be fine too. We just won't be fine in the same life like we thought we would. Part of me will always love you. Please don't try to make me change my mind because I can't.

Eva

She folded the single sheet into the envelope and hurriedly scrawled Elmo's name and address. She could hear Baxter crying upstairs.

Darryl Strikings closed and locked the door of the Mercantile behind him. He took one last look in the big front window before adjusting the bundle under his arm and heading toward his house. He decided to take his usual route even though it meant he would have to walk right by Becky Johnson's place.

He knew he'd probably catch a glimpse of her because he usually did. That was the reason why he always stayed about half an hour at work after Becky left. Gave her a chance to be sitting down for dinner when he was walking by. She always sat in same spot, facing her father, her mother to her left. She'd sit there with her perfect face framed in the window.

He paused three doors from her house, as he usually did. He took a deep breath and resumed walking toward her front window and her perfect profile. He'd kept smiling the whole time she told him. She was so excited and happy and he just kept smiling and nodding like this was information he'd been hoping to receive.

She said it was going to be in June and she wanted him to be there. June, less than three months away, and she would become Mrs Crockett. She'd said Mrs Crockett like it was a rare and wonderful thing, although there were already two other women walking around with the same name. Plain women with lives that revolved around the farm. To think that Becky Johnson would become a plain Mrs Crockett and spend her days out there with that ordinary boy and his sunburned neck. No doubt she would bear him a herd of grubby children and be worn and spent by the time she was thirty.

He'd decided what to do when he thought of Becky having that herd of Crockett children. He could almost see her coming into the Mercantile with a sticky paw in each hand and her dress swollen with another result of coupling with the sunburned Crockett. She'd get heavy all except for her face, which would get lean and scrawny. As her hips widened, her neck would become ropy until her big belly would appear to hang from the cords on her neck. She'd look like one of those old milch cows that folks kept tied up in their back yards.

He took one last look at her perfect profile and her smooth neck before ducking his head into his collar and heading home.

He went down into the basement and out of habit looked around for leaks and other potential problems. Everything looked all right and normal. The floor of the basement was hard-packed earth that always smelled damp and moldy, but it looked dry. He knelt down and patted at the floor, just to be sure.

Finally he looked up and checked the beams. He wanted to make sure that he'd be seen as soon as somebody walked into the basement. Darryl had thought this through and the last thing he wanted was to be there for days and nobody knowing about it. He found the right beam and tossed the rope over it.

He tied one end of the rope to a beam and made a noose on the other side. He turned a pickling crock over and shoved it under the noose. Quickly, before he had time to think about it, he climbed on the crock and slipped the noose over his neck. He shoved his hands deep into his pockets so that he wouldn't be tempted to grab at the rope and give himself a second chance.

Darryl was a third-generation free thinker and had never felt that his life was poorer for his lack of belief in God. He'd always felt that a belief in God was more a lack of self-confidence than anything and he'd never lacked for self-confidence. Even when he was a little boy he'd known that he would someday own the Mercantile, which would make him one of the most important men in town.

But now, with his hands shoved down his pockets, a rope around his neck, and his feet on an upturned pickling crock, he felt a need for something else. He closed his eyes and thought about Becky, but that just brought tears to his eyes. He tried to think of his daughters, but their faces seemed smudged and blurred inside his brain. Just as he stepped off the crock the faces of his daughters and Becky swirled up into the face of the little statue he'd kept on his desk at the Mercantile.

He felt his feet swing, his throat gag, and then his butt hit the packed earth. Confused, he looked up and saw the broken beam above his head. He yanked his hands out of his pockets and scrambled to his feet.

'Termites.' He ran his hand across the edge of the shattered beam. 'Jesus H. Christ, I've got termites.' He grinned and raked his hand through his hair. For a moment he considered whether or not it was worth a second try, but he kept seeing the face of the little Madonna.

Lucille Reynolds hadn't even mentioned what she'd been thinking about to Father Greene although she knew he would have listened. It was a shame, she thought, the men who were really good at listening were the same men who would never get married. If there were more sense to the world it would have been the other way around. But then, she reasoned, there wouldn't be that many men who would be getting married and that might or might not be a good thing.

She hadn't mentioned it to him mainly because she knew he had other ideas about how her money should be invested and spent. Just two days ago he'd been going on and on about how she should be casting her bread upon the waters, which she was pretty sure meant that she should be giving hunks of her cash to a Catholic charity of his choosing.

She paused for a moment at the Johnsons' door to straighten her hat before knocking. As she rapped her knuckles on the wood, she watched the little medallion on her wristwatch swing in the light from their front window.

'Why, Miss Lucille.' Becky Johnson opened the door, wearing the same friendly smile she used from behind the Mercantile's counter.

'Good evening, Becky. Forgive me if I've interrupted your meal.'

'We just finished. Come on in.' She opened the door wider and stepped aside to let Lucille in.

'If we do what I'm suggesting we can get the mill reopened. I've already spoken to a bank that's willing to loan us the rest of what we'll need if we put in fourteen thousand.' It had come to her in a dream two nights before. She'd seen herself behind a desk at the mill. She'd had to talk to four different banks, but the fourth one had been interested.

'It would take almost my whole inheritance. I, well, we had been talking about using part of that money to buy some land.' She'd practically promised Teddy that they would do that very thing. He hated being just one of the Crocketts and had always wanted his own land.

'Becky, you have to do what you think is right. If you've already promised your future husband that you'll buy him that land then that's what you better do. I was a wife for over ten years and I know better than anyone that you have to do what your husband wants you to do. I should know because I never did what I wanted until Raymond, God rest his soul, passed on.' She watched Becky's face pale as she spoke.

'I want the land, too. We'll work it together.' Becky licked her lips and clasped her hands in her lap.

'That's right, you will. You'll work right alongside of him through thick and through thin. You'll be as much a part of the farm as all the Crockett women are.' Lucille thought of Sukie Crockett with her saggy bosoms and willed Becky to do the same. In her mind she saw Becky's future sister-in-law Tina, the one with the hairy moles on her face. It was hard to imagine the fresh-faced Becky ending up like either of those two, but she knew she would.

The Crocketts had a good farm and they all worked hard. The farm was the best-looking one for miles, everyone said so. The Crocketts always used the most modern methods and poured every cent they could back into the farm. Every cent that could have been diverted to face cream, magazines, new furniture, pretty fabric, a tortoiseshell hair clip, a lipstick, or a store-bought dress was spent on the farm. It was the Crockett way and there wasn't a soul in town who didn't know it.

'It's a good life, Miss Lucille.' Becky smoothed the fabric of her skirt over her knees. 'The Crocketts are good people.'

'The Crocketts are wonderful people and your Teddy is the pick of the litter. I know one of his brothers is real slow, but that happens sometimes. No need to think that any of your young-sters will be slow. Just look at poor Flo Gorman. Who would have thought that the Gormans would have the problems they've had? Little Glory is as cute as a bug and as smart as they come. Hoyt and Eva are such handsome people and Flo's got a lovely face, but still they had that tragic thing happen to them. So many things can go wrong with childbirth.'

'I'm not really planning to have a family straight off. I thought I might wait a while, get the farm going real good and all.'

'That's smart, Becky. Of course you can't wait too long, but then you probably know that. A woman can't be sure she'll have healthy children much beyond thirty. Oh, some do, but you can't count on that.' She smiled sweetly at Becky and decided not to say another word.

Becky sat quietly, but she'd moved her hand up to her throat. She kept stroking it like she had a piece of food stuck there that she was trying to massage down to where it belonged. When she tired of massaging she moved the hand to her mouth where she tapped the fingernail of her index finger against her front teeth.

'I'd need to put in seven thousand dollars?'

'You or somebody else. I could probably find two or three other investors, but I came to you first. I liked the idea of two women running a mill so I thought I should talk to you.'

'I don't know anything about running a mill.'

'Neither do I, Becky. I thought we could hire Hoyt Gorman to be the day-to-day manager. He's back to picking up what he can in the way of carpentry since the fire.'

'What would we do?'

'You know something about keeping books from working at the Mercantile, don't you?'

Becky nodded. 'Darryl has been having me do some of that the last year or so.'

'Good. I know something about it too. I spent three months at commercial college studying bookkeeping before I married Raymond. I'll tell you something, Becky. I wish now I'd finished that course.'

'It won't take two of us to keep the books, at least not at first.'

'I was thinking you could go out and get the orders for us.'

'Me?'

'I've been watching you, Becky Johnson, and you're a natural at selling. You make folks enjoy being parted from their money and you could do that with lumber if you put your mind to it.'

'I don't know anything about selling lumber.'

'Lumber, buttons, eggs, what's the difference?'

'Who would I sell it to?'

'Stores, building companies, lumber yards. All over the state.'

'I'd travel all over the state?'

'Not at first, but it wouldn't be long before you were away more than you were home. I can see you now with your brief-case, getting off the train in Wichita.'

'I can see it, too. I can really see it.' She nodded her head and looked at Lucille. 'Count me in. Teddy is going to kill me, but count me in.'

CHAPTER TWENTY-FOUR

The thing that woke her was Baby June's whimpering. She did that a lot. Even when she was asleep she couldn't just be completely quiet and lie there like other people. She would whine and whimper and make sounds like a puppy that had been locked outside.

The other thing she did that was enough to drive Glory crazy was the way she'd bang her little bed back and forth while she was falling asleep. Thump, thump, thump she'd go for ten or fifteen minutes before her stupid eyes would finally close. She seemed to be one of those kids who took what was theirs and half of everybody else's.

After the whimpering stopped, Glory lay on her back and tried to get back to sleep. It didn't help that spring was more than halfway gone and the birds were making a racket even though it was so early she had at least two hours before she needed to get up and go to school. Her mama called it the 'dawn chorus', but she thought it was just another reason to be mad.

Not that she needed another reason. She had to share her room and her mama with the two dumb babies and the kids at school were being really awful to her and the two Reynolds kids. She thought by now she'd be living in Wichita with her mama and her new daddy, but every time she brought that into the conversation her mama would get this sad look and find some excuse for leaving the room or getting too busy to talk.

She used her fingers to keep track of all the reasons that she should be mad. Aunt Flo always said, or used to say before she stopped talking, that folks should just count their blessings. Glory wondered if Aunt Flo was still counting her blessings or if she'd taken to counting all the reasons she had to be sad and angry. She counted off the kids at school, not living in Wichita, the two dumb babies, one finger for each dumb baby, and not seeing Elmo Robinson for weeks and weeks.

Glory shoved her angry hand in the air and wiggled her thumb in circles. Her thumb was fatter than her fingers so that was what she used to count her biggest angry-thing of all. This angry-thing of having the lady gone that was all hers and that made her the angriest of all. Even her mama and Pammy weren't willing to listen.

For almost two weeks now she'd known and tried to tell about the lady being gone but nobody would listen. Every last person had so much on their minds that whenever she said any-thing at all it seemed like she was like one of those people in the movies but not one of the new talkies. She would move her mouth, but it didn't seem to matter if she made a noise or not because nobody was listening, at least not to her.

Just when she got so angry that she thought she might start crying, she felt the air around her change and she began to relax. It felt almost like being in a warm bathtub except it was dry. Her room was filled with air that felt thick, soft, and warm. It reminded Glory of the way a piece of white-bread toast felt inside; warm and thick, and so soft. She sighed and rolled over on her side. She closed her eyes and thought she felt the covers being tucked around her ears. She was back. Whoever she was, she was back.

★

'Darryl, can I talk to you?'

He looked up from his desk. He hadn't even heard her come in. 'Sure, Becky. Come have a seat.' He hadn't seen her for the last two days. Not since she told him about her decision to marry Teddy Crockett. Not since the night he discovered that he had termites in his basement. Not since he found them the hard way.

'Do you recall what I said last week, about quitting work and getting married in June?'

'Yeah. I remember you saying something about that.' The rope burn around his neck seemed to throb at his casual words. Darryl was glad that his high collar covered the angry-looking welt.

'I had thought, I had intended to work until the first part of June, but something has come up to change that. I'm going to have to stop working for you real soon.' Becky was looking at her hands, which were clasped in her lap.

'I see.' Teddy Crockett had knocked her up. The filthy scum with his freckles and cocky ways had already put her in the family way. Already trapped the prettiest girl in town into a life of farming and breeding. Turned her into just another piece of livestock on that farm. Taken all that sweetness and beauty and dashed it for his own use.

'You do?'

'Of course I do.'

'Who told you?'

'Nobody needed to tell me, Becky. I've seen it all before.' He looked at her and smiled sadly. 'I don't blame you. Crockett was the one who should have known better.'

'Known better about what?'

'About these things. I've got half a mind to horsewhip him myself.' He felt better then. Maybe he could cheer her a little if she felt that she had a champion. Not that a champion was going to do her much good, not now. A champion wouldn't save her from a life of drudgery and boredom with Teddy Crockett and his big, hard-working family. The family with the idiot strain, he reminded himself. Why, even now, Becky's sweet, flat belly could be holding not the seed of a healthy, normal child, but an idiot like that big Crockett boy. Such a miserable fate for such a lovely girl.

'Why would you want to horsewhip Teddy?' She frowned and tilted her head. The wrinkling of her brows only made her more attractive than ever to Darryl.

'For putting you in this position, Becky. Others might disagree with me, but I maintain that it takes two for this to happen.' Part of being a free thinker, after all. Darryl prided himself on being willing to look at issues without having his vision clouded by stupid, Church-imposed morality. Sheer nonsense in this day and age to think that all women were the inheritors of Eve's bad judgment.

She nodded. 'That's why Lucille Reynolds and I are going to do it together.'

'Lucille Reynolds?' It was Darryl's turn to wrinkle his eyebrows. He'd read something once, but he hadn't believed it could really happen. It had been about women pleasuring each other in that way, but it hadn't made any sense then and it didn't make any sense now. Everybody knew what a woman needed in that department, and it surely wasn't anything that Lucille Reynolds or any other woman could provide.

'Lucille and I are buying the mill.'

'So Teddy didn't, you know?' He made a churning motion with his hands. He wasn't sure what he was trying to indicate so he kept his movements fairly loose. Free thinker or not, there were certain words that couldn't be said to a woman unless you were married to her. Selma hadn't allowed them even then. She had felt that even the term 'it' was racy and refused to make any verbal reference to the act whatsoever.

'What are you talking about, Darryl?'

'So, you and Lucille are buying the mill.' He nodded his head and leaned back in his chair. He hoped these two things combined would give every appearance that he knew what he was talking about, although he didn't. He was still thinking about the forbidden words and how they would sound if he whispered them into Becky's ear. He thought about what she might be wearing, or not wearing, when he whispered those words.

'I was going to use my inheritance to buy some land, but Lucille had this other idea. I don't know, but there's something about being a career girl that sounds pretty good.'

He thought maybe she'd look wonderful in some silk stockings when she said those words. Maybe just the stockings and nothing else. He scratched thoughtfully at his chin while he tried to formulate a question or statement which made some kind of sense. 'What does Teddy think?'

'He's not talking to me right now, but Lucille says that's to be expected. She says he'll either get over it or he won't. She says if he doesn't get over it, then he wasn't the man for me.' Becky rapidly blinked her eyes and made a slight sniffing sound. 'I know she's right, but I've been sort of assuming for a long time that I'd be Teddy's wife someday. It's fine for Lucille, she's been married, but my mother says that men aren't interested in girls who want to be career girls. She says I'll end up an old maid like my Aunt Lottie.'

'I think it's fine to be a career girl, if that's what you want. You've been a career girl here with me for a long time.' Darryl took a deep breath and forged ahead. He suddenly felt a little taller and somewhat brave. He felt like one of those soldiers he'd read about who fought during the Great War. 'You being a career girl has never kept me from being interested in you, Becky. I think you are just about the most interesting girl I've ever met.' In his mind she unrolled those stockings and slipped them off her long legs. In his mind she was sitting there wearing nothing but lacy white garters and an expression of extreme sexual passion.

'Really?'

'I've been thinking that when a few months have passed . . .' He didn't want to bring up Selma. Not now. Not with his heart swelling with love and other emotions, noble and base. Not when in his mind she was brushing her hand across her chest, across the blushing skin that went from her neck to her little rosebud nipples. He wasn't sure how to bring a dead wife into the conversation without sounding somewhat unromantic. He would have liked to never mention her again, but if he and Becky were to have any future in town, they'd have to do things the right way. If she was ever going to be in his bed for real they'd have to do things the way folks expected them to be done.

Maybe in New York or Chicago a fellow could just take what he wanted and needed, but not around here. Even if in his mind's eye the most beautiful girl in the world was licking her lips and pulling her knees just a little ways apart so that he could catch a glimmer of moist, pearly pink. Even then, folks expected certain things.

'Maybe we could talk again.' She lowered her eyes.

'I'd like that, Becky.' He fought the urge to reach across the desk and pull her into his arms the way those guys in the pictures always did. He wanted to see her throw her head back in abandon, exposing her white neck and her heaving breasts. He wanted to ravish her on top of the notions counter. He wanted to paint her body with maple syrup and lick it off while she groaned in ecstasy. He felt almost dizzy thinking about the things he wanted to do. Amazing things that no two people had ever done. Certainly not if one of them had been married to Selma for several years.

'Good. Then we'll talk once in a while.' She smiled at him, her tears gone. 'It's nice to talk to a man who understands me, like you do, Darryl.'

'Yeah, we'll talk.' He nodded pleasantly and hoped she hadn't noticed the beads of sweat on his face or the tremor in his voice.

For the first time in his life Elmo Robinson knew how his father Ace must have felt. As he loaded his last suitcase into the car he felt a kinship with his father and his father's need to move away, to move on.

Some of the old-timers at the paper had remembered Ace and

joshed around with Elmo. They'd done it for years. This one or that one asking when he was going to start acting like his father's son and hit the road. Of course, now that he was actually leaving they were the ones who were most surprised of all.

Good friends, every last one of them. Not a single question about Eva or the marriage he'd been talking about for weeks. Even Mick Flanagan who he'd been planning to rent a house from didn't say boo about the change in plans. Elmo hadn't looked for it in the mirror, but he could only assume that his face had changed to the point where it could clearly be read that he was a jilted man.

As if it wasn't bad enough to be jilted, it was even worse to be put aside for a couple of orphaned brats and a fat woman who'd forgotten how to speak. Actually shoved aside by a life she said she'd hated. He climbed into the driver's seat and started the engine. Elmo let it warm up a minute or two before he pointed the car toward New York.

New York had been the best choice, the only choice really. New York was a town for newspapers. Had more than any other place in the whole country. He had a few contacts there, or at least his editor at the *Eagle* had a few contacts and had made a few phone calls for him. Another thing about New York was the size of the damn place. Not like Wichita or any of the other lousy prairie towns he'd been reporting on for the last few years.

When a place was the size of New York a man had a chance to spread himself out. Meet a lot of different people, date a lot of different women. People who could see the world for what it was. Women who didn't see themselves tied down out of guilt or misplaced loyalty. People with drive and ambition. People with talent and moxie, that's who he needed to meet.

He'd never loved Eva, he could see that now. Hindsight was always twenty-twenty, he knew that. He didn't blame her, not for a minute, not really. He'd allowed himself to be seduced by his idea of her. Elmo had thought about things a lot since he received Eva's letter. He'd thought a lot about Eva and who he thought she was.

It helped that he hadn't seen her for a few weeks. Part of Eva's appeal, he knew, was the way he felt when he was close to her, or knew he would be close to her soon. Something about her skin. Maybe it was her coloring that he'd found so hard to resist. Whatever it was it had almost blinded him to the reality of the situation.

Nothing more than another girl in a hick town. He hadn't been able to see that until a day or so ago, but once he saw it it was all he could see. Sure, she was smart enough and had read more than anyone he knew, but she was still just a hick. And she did paint, but it was that modern stuff and who could tell if that kind of thing was any good or not? Combine being a small-town hick with having an illegitimate child and he wondered what he'd ever seen in her.

Not that Glory wasn't a great little girl, because she was. Sweet and sassy and she would be cute as a button once her front teeth grew in. He'd asked Eva about the child's father, but Eva had given him a look that practically made his scrotum shrink up to his belly button. Told him he was never to mention it again.

As though a man didn't have a right to know. What kind of woman was as bold as brass to have the child like that and keep the father a secret? Unless she hadn't known herself. It sounded like the kind of thing that Eva would do. Have more than one lover at a time. Not that he hadn't done similar things, as had most of the guys he knew, at least those who could, but she wasn't some guy.

He was best out of it. Not that he wouldn't miss her, but missing someone and loving someone were two completely different things. As different as night and day. Whether or not she knew that might be something else entirely. He didn't like the idea of her having the last word. Eva needed to know that he'd be fine without her. Better than fine. She'd done him a favor.

He drove past the farms and fields and composed the letter he'd send her once he got to New York. He wanted to give her something to think about. Maybe something that could help her and make her life better. Give her some guidance and some wisdom from a man's perspective. She needed that. He owed her that much.

Elmo thought he'd write the letter on hotel stationery, which meant he'd have to stay in a pretty fancy hotel if he was going to impress Miss Eva Gorman. Not that she was used to fancy hotels. Not by a long shot. But Eva was the sort of woman who always made a fellow feel like she was just a little smarter, just a little classier than she really was. Even though she was fairly smart and classy for a small-town hick.

By the time he was in New York another five days would have passed. Add to that the four days the letter would take and Eva wouldn't get his letter for another nine or maybe even ten days. In nine or ten days quite a bit could happen. In nine or ten days she could change her mind. Not necessarily about him, but about something. She could take up with someone new. The mother of those babies could finally show up. Miss Florence could get better. Hundreds of things could change in nine or ten days.

Elmo knew for a fact that his hands never left the steering wheel. He also knew for a fact that he never intended to turn off the road headed east, but two and a half hours later he found his car parked in front of the big house with the wraparound porch. He paused for a moment to admire the fresh paint. Bright yellow, trimmed in white. The white trim had been his idea. Easing the car into gear, he drove away.

CHAPTER TWENTY-FIVE

The morning promised to be warm, almost warm at least. The cold had lasted into May and for the last three days Eva had found herself sniffing the air and hating the smells around her. It happened in almost every house in town and it happened every year. It always happened about the time when people started thinking they might go crazy if it didn't warm up and stay that way. Thought they might start killing each other if they didn't see a little more green grass or see a few bugs flying around in the air.

The months of storm windows, coal heaters, and hearty meals would be weighing down the air this late in the spring. Up and down the street, storm windows would be propped open and the clotheslines would start fluttering with throw rugs and bedspreads. Buckets of sloppy, soapy water were carried through rooms and folks started going out to the mailboxes without their coats.

She'd picked up a few things at the Mercantile yesterday and noted that there seemed to have been a run on cleaning supplies, just like the years before. Eva bought some floor wax along with her weekly box of laundry powder after she'd enquired after Darryl's happiness. She knew he was miserable about Becky being over at the mill and she just couldn't keep herself from reminding him that Becky wasn't in the back room of the Mercantile and most likely never would be again.

It wasn't so much animosity as keeping her hand in. She could hardly tease Hoyt these days. In spite of the mill opening up again, his misery was something that could almost be tasted when he walked into a room. He'd spend every free moment he had trying to pull his wife back to where she had been before the birth. In the evenings the last thing she heard as she fell asleep was Hoyt in the next room talking to his quiet wife while she fell asleep on the bed they no longer shared.

Once the breakfast dishes were done and she'd settled Baxter and Baby June in the playpen for a few minutes, she rolled up her sleeves and started in on the laundry. She'd done the usual laundry the day before, but this was the spring-cleaning laundry. The satisfying stuff that she knew she wouldn't have to do again next week. It was the week-after-week that was the thing she couldn't bear to look at.

Eva glanced at the clock to see how much longer it would be until one of several Jute girls would come by and let her get to the library where she could be alone and get something done without the constant interruptions of one child or another.

She hurried out to the back yard with an armful of braided rugs she had gathered up earlier in the morning. As she hung them on the line the light breeze threw the dust from the rugs back in her face. The grit stung her eyes, but she wiped the tears away without losing the rhythm of the work. Tears didn't slow her down, not anymore. She didn't even try to hide them from Glory, hadn't done that for weeks. Tears were a part of their lives now, like laundry on Monday and summer in July.

She ignored the sounds coming from the open window as long as she could, but finally she had to throw the last three rugs onto the porch and hurry into the house. The sounds were wet and wet was the worst kind of mess to clean up.

Baby June had climbed out of the playpen in the front room and was leaning over into the tub of warm soapy water and trying to pull a sodden bedspread onto the floor. Eva scooped her up without a word and carried her back into the front room and imprisonment. She was lifting the child over the wooden bars when Baxter held his arms up and whimpered for attention. His face was screwed up like a bread roll that needed proofing.

'That's it. This morning I'm delegating a little authority whether she likes it or not.' She picked up Baxter and slung him on her other hip and hurried upstairs with both the babies. 'You two are going to spend some time with Miss Florence and you two little darlings are going to enjoy it.'

She'd done this before, at least half a dozen times. She'd dump one or both of the kids in Florence's room in hopes of getting some sort of reaction out of her, but it hadn't worked. Eva hadn't really expected it to work, not after the first time, but it was enough of a change of scene that it would keep the babies quiet for a few minutes. Even Baby June hadn't managed to get into any kind of trouble in Flo's room.

It was just Flo's room now. Hoyt slept on the sofa down in the living room because he couldn't bear to share a bed with his silent wife. What with Flo never leaving the bed, the room stayed as tidy as could be. Completely safe for babies, even the big ones that decided they wanted to go back to being babies, Eva thought ruefully. Eva had lost some of the considerable sympathy she'd felt for Flo on the same day she'd sent that letter to Elmo.

'Flo, I'm leaving the babies up here with you.' She placed the children on the floor and walked over to Flo's bed. 'I've got to get through the laundry before the Jute girl comes and I can't do that if I'm having to watch these two.' Flo stared back at her and then blinked her eyes. To her own surprise, Eva leaned over and kissed her sister-in-law on the top of her sour-smelling head. Being mad at Flo was as pointless as being mad at Baxter or a bowl of goldfish. 'I won't be long, sugar.'

'Elmo. Are you ever a sight for sore eyes.' Virgil Osburne left his corner booth and hurried over as soon as Elmo opened the door. 'Your ears must have been burning, Elmo. Alma and I were talking about our favorite boarder just last night.'

'Virgil.' He put out his hand and shook Virgil's vigorously. He knew how much Virgil admired a good handshake. Virgil had told him he didn't trust a man who shook hands for anything less than fifteen seconds. During those fifteen seconds Virgil expected both hands to go up and down as rapidly as factory pistons. 'How are you and Miss Alma?'

'We're fine. We're better than fine. Come sit down.' He led Elmo to the booth and sat down once he'd assured himself that Elmo was comfortable. 'Are you staying with us tonight?'

'I'm afraid not, Virgil. I wanted to take one last look around, that's all.'

'Last look?' Virgil's eyebrows knit across his furrowed brow like a graying caterpillar. 'But you and Miss Eva, what about you and Miss Eva?'

'She doesn't want to marry me anymore. What with the trouble that Hoyt and Florence have had, she doesn't feel like she can leave.'

'Do you still love her?'

'I am so mad at her I could wring her neck, but yeah, I still love her. I think I've loved Eva Gorman since the first time I saw her.' He looked away from Virgil, not quite ashamed of what he'd said. He'd noticed before that he could say things to Virgil that he couldn't say to other men. He'd noticed that about a guy who'd worked at the *Eagle*. He'd been another queer like Virgil. They were good to talk to. Like talking to a nice woman only easier because they were still men, mostly.

'And what are you going to do about it?'

'There's nothing I can do about it, Virgil. She sent me a letter and made it very clear that she had to be where she was, doing what she was doing.'

'So you're going to do what? Go back to Wichita and be by yourself for the rest of your life? Find someone new who's never going to be Eva? Marry somebody else who isn't Eva and spend the rest of your life half-hating her because she'll never be Eva?'

'I'm going to New York. I've got my bags in the car.'

'Eva Gorman isn't in New York, Elmo.'

'No, but the best newspapers in the country are in New York and a couple of million other women are there, too.'

'Elmo, this isn't about newspapers and you know it.'

'I know that, Virgil. This is about my whole life, not just Eva and not just newspapers.'

'Elmo, I'm going to tell you a story and I want you to listen.'

'I'm listening.'

'Good, because it's about my life, so I think it's about the most interesting story I've ever told, even though I've never told the story to anyone but my sister Alma.

'Back when I was in my twenties, we're going way back here, I met the most amazing person. I was in St Louis for a church music convention and he was one of the speakers. He was like me, only about ten times better. I had known him less than twenty-four hours before we were so close that we were finishing each other's sentences. He made me understand that I was different from most men, but I wasn't different from him. My world was so much better because he was in it. I was better and happier with him then I'd ever been in my entire life. Before or since.

'He lived in Maryland. Taught at a college there. He asked me to join him. He wanted me to pick up and move all that way to be with him.'

'You didn't do it?'

'No, I didn't do it. I wanted to, but I kept worrying about what would happen to my mother and what would happen to Alma. I worried about what would happen to me if he stopped loving me. I think that was the real reason that I didn't go. I was so scared that he would stop loving me. I regretted my decision almost immediately.'

'Why didn't you let him know you'd changed your mind?'

'I didn't change my mind, I just regretted my decision. You see, Elmo, I lacked courage. I lacked the courage to live the life I really and truly wanted and deserved. By the time I realised what I'd done, it was too late to turn back. We were both a few years older and he'd found someone that wasn't afraid to live. Bless him.' He reached across the table and covered Elmo's hand with his own. 'Eva and I have always had a special bond. I understand her. I see myself when I look at Eva and I don't want Eva to live with my regrets.'

'She won't come with me, Virgil.'

'Then come to her. Make a life with her here.'

'Even if I wanted to live here, I couldn't make a living.'

'Can't make a living here, in the town of visions and miracles?' He smiled and removed his hand from Elmo's.

'A fat lot of good miracles and visions did this town.'

'I like to think that miracles and visions are all a matter of perspective. I was saying that to Miss Weesie just the other day. She was saying that she'd like to sell the newspaper now that her mother has finally gone to her reward.'

'Mrs Cartwright died?'

'About a month ago. Just finally got tired of being the third oldest person in the state, I guess. Anyway, Miss Weesie is ready to retire. Problem is she still needs a tiny bit of income from the paper. I had the feeling she'd let it go with almost nothing down and even carry the loan on it. Good opportunity, at least it would be a good opportunity for someone who could see it from the right perspective.'

Her daddy had always said it was the best thing to do, but she'd always hated it anyway. She'd never actually seen him do it, seen him put them in the weighted sack, but she'd seen what happened when Old Cat figured out that something was wrong.

She'd walk around mewing and crying. She'd look and look and move things around. She'd keep that up for a day or two just like she was now. The thing was, Flo couldn't remember seeing Old Cat for years and years. Still, she could hear her crying. She closed her eyes and tried to sleep a little more, but the mewing and crying wouldn't stop.

Other sounds, too. Like Old Cat was worrying a mouse or

something. Rustling and sniffling on the floor. Breathing sounds, too, like she made when another litter was making its way out of her.

Flo opened her eyes, but the room was wrong. She'd expected it to be the room she shared with her sister because of the Old Cat sounds. Course that room was a long time ago. Before Hoyt and all the years. Old Cat mewed again and she lifted her head to look over the edge of the bed at it.

The baby was on his back with a toe pulled into his mouth. His eyes met hers and he grinned and wiggled at her before making another Old Cat sound. The other one, the girl, was lying on the floor and moving her arms and legs like she was swimming on the floorboards. One of her swimming legs shot out and kicked at the baby, making his eyes go round and his mouth stop grinning.

His arms went down slack and then he curled them back up and started wailing in protest at the kick which had landed on the side of his head. Flo watched him and found herself thinking that somebody should do something. After a minute or two of thinking that somebody should do something, she started thinking that maybe she should do something for the child. Once she had come to the realisation that she should do something it seemed the most natural thing in the world to throw her legs over the side of the bed, lean over, and take Baxter into her arms.

Baxter looked up at her, made a few minor adjustments to his position, and smiled at her. Baby June saw this attention that her brother was receiving and took it on herself to climb onto the bed to get her fair share of whatever was being handed out. Flo put her hand on the child's soft hair and started singing the song about the dead goose that Glory had always loved.

After she'd sung about the dead goose, she sang the one about the birds and butterflies pecking out the eyes and it didn't even seem too sad. Not as sad as it had always sounded before. Or maybe it was just because nothing could make her sadder than she'd already been.

★

Teacher had her back to the blackboard when Glory snuck out of the door. She'd never done it before, but something, some feeling in the back of her legs, made her feel like she had to go home and see what was going on. She knelt down as she passed by the schoolhouse windows and then she slipped behind the big Dutch elm in the playground. She took a look behind to make sure she wasn't followed and then ran as fast as she could toward home.

Eva mopped up the mess that Baby June had made with the laundry tub before heading to the back yard to finish hanging up the rugs. She hummed under her breath as she pushed the pegs against the line and slapped at the rugs. She stopped humming as she stepped back, away from the line.

Eva turned her head at the sound that seemed to be coming from the upstairs window of the house. When she recognised the sound, the voice, she sat down on the cold, damp earth and just listened to Flo singing the same songs she used to sing when Glory was a baby.

CHAPTER TWENTY-SIX

Glory saw the fancy car turn the corner and head toward her house. Now she understood why she could no more have stayed in her classroom than flown to the moon. Mama had said he was never coming back, but he was back.

Just like she knew he would be. She never believed he was gone for good, not really. Whatever good things had happened had been all knit up with him and Mama and her having a daddy of her own. That was the thing she'd wanted most of all. Even more than the wonderful red shoes, which she'd almost grown out of.

Miracles were about belonging and being in the right place. Even if Mr Elmo didn't know it, he belonged with them and they belonged with him.

She turned the corner and ran up the alley toward her house.

Eva was shaking and half afraid that she might throw up. Everything was jumbled up in a mess of relief that Flo was talking, fear that she would stop, and anger that she hadn't started talking weeks before. The two women sat on the bed together with the babies. They clung to each other and the babies, afraid to let go and maybe let things run backwards to the way they'd been just a few hours ago.

'How long, Eva? How long has it been since, you know?' Flo's voice was a sharp whisper. Not having been used for weeks and weeks it was hard-edged and scratchy.

'Just a while now.'

'Where is it now? What did you do with it?'

'We had a little funeral, just the three of us. Father Greene said a few words and we put the baby with Evangeline and Joseph. Hoyt built a little coffin and I painted it white.'

'Just plain white?'

'Yeah.'

'I sort of wished you would have painted something pretty on it, like you did the cradle. I guess that cradle is never going to be used.'

'You can try again, Flo. You and Hoyt are still young.'

'Not that young anymore, Eva. I've had my baby.'

'Suddenly we seem to have a surfeit of babies.'

'What's that mean?'

'We have an excess of babies.'

'No, no excess. Mine is always going to be missing.'

Hoyt sat cross-legged on the bed with Flo in his arms. Cradled by him, her head rested against his chest as he stroked her head and wept into her hair.

'I think the time for that is gone, Hoyt.' She put her hand to his face and wiped at his wet cheeks.

'I thought you were gone. First the mill and then the baby, and finally you. I felt like my whole life, our whole lives were being sawed away.'

'I'm back now. I don't know where I went, but I'm back.'

'I had days where I was afraid to look at you. I was so scared that I would walk in and find that you were completely gone.'

Flo sat up and faced him. 'I'm back and I'm staying.' She leaned forward and kissed him gently on his lips. 'It's all going to come back to us.'

'Except the baby, but I guess we can try again.'

'We've got two babies.'

'They're not ours.'

'They could be. They're too young to remember anything else but here, anything but us.'

'Everyone would know they weren't ours. I don't think we could keep a thing like that secret, not in this town.'

'It doesn't have to be a secret, Hoyt. We tell them the truth when they're old enough to understand it.'

'You don't think you'll look at those children and think about our baby every time you see them? I think I would. That doesn't seem fair to them or us.'

'Then we won't think that way. We'll just think about how they're little children who need a home and that we have a home that needs little children.'

'It's going to be a pretty full house around here.'

'Not for long. Eva and Glory will be moving out to Wichita before long.' Flo curled back into his arms.

'Not now, hon. She told Elmo her place was here.'

'We'll have to fix that, won't we?'

'What makes you think we can fix it?'

'Hoyt Gorman, I've just come back from Hell. An experience like that gives a person faith in the future.'

Elmo Robinson's hands were shaking as he signed the agreement with Miss Weesie. As Virgil Osburne had predicted, she was eager to sell the paper and had offered attractive terms. He left her front parlor with the taste of gingerbread in his mouth, agreement papers in his pocket, and the keys to the office of *The Guide*.

Forgoing his car, he ran the three blocks to the library. In front of the library he took a moment to compose himself and get his breath back. He turned toward the street and tidied his hair with his hands. He thought about going back to Miss Weesie and seeing if she'd change her mind. No money had changed hands, after all. Maybe if he left her a note along with the papers he could just climb into his car and drive on to New York.

New York had millions of people. He could blend in there, he knew he could. A job with a steady paycheck wouldn't be that hard to come by, not with the references he had. He could get a nice little apartment and date pretty girls and handsome women. He could go out every night and buy a new suit once a year, maybe twice.

If he didn't leave, the best he could look forward to was living in the town the rest of his life, running a two-bit newspaper. He'd be living with Eva and her temper and raising another man's child. A night out would be a sandwich at the cafe and all his clothes would come from the Mercantile. If he was lucky enough to afford any new clothes. *The Guide* didn't make much, although it had some potential.

Of course if he stayed he could start doing some real writing, he told himself. The kind of thing that Steinbeck and Fitzgerald were doing. He'd be with Eva and her beautiful skin that smelled of perfume although she didn't even own a bottle of the stuff. And her temper wasn't that bad, not really, not when they were together.

And Glory was a great kid, a really great kid. They could always have more. He could almost see a dining-room table with two or three younger versions of himself sitting down to a meal. He could see Eva with her beautiful hair, grown a little silvery and pale, but still beautiful. He took a deep breath and thought he could almost smell her skin. He turned around to face the library door and found himself looking into Eva's eyes.

'Are you coming in or should I just plant some petunias in your shoes so that you at least serve some purpose by standing out here?'

'Eva.' It was all he could think to say.

'Who were you expecting, Elmo?'

'You, I came to see you.'

'Well, I guess you'd better come in then.' She held the door open for him.

'I've just come from seeing Miss Weesie. Miss Weesie Cartwright?'

'We've only got one Miss Weesie in town. Weesie isn't a very common name.'

'Her real name is Louise. I don't know if you knew that or not.'

'Did you drive all the way down here from Wichita to find out what Miss Weesie's Christian name is?'

'I don't live in Wichita anymore, Eva. I quit my job. I was headed to New York, but there was something I had to do down here.'

'What was that?'

'What was what?' He licked his lips and felt his hand begin to shake again. He tried to smile, but a tick started on the left of his mouth and he could feel the whole side of his face moving around. He put his hand to his mouth to stop it.

'Why did you come here?' She stared at him for a moment. 'Have you been drinking? You look awful.'

'No, I wish I had been drinking. That would have helped.'

'Helped what, Elmo?'

'I just bought *The Guide* from Miss Weesie.' He pulled the key out of his pocket. 'It's all mine. Actually, she's holding the papers on it, but I'm the new owner.'

'I thought you were going to New York.'

'I was. I was until I realised something.'

'What, that you'd always wanted to own a weekly newspaper in a small town?'

'No. I realised that I've always wanted to belong. I've always wanted to belong to a place and a person.' He felt tears forming in his eyes and he didn't bother to blink them away. 'Eva, when I wake up in the morning I want to roll over and see your hair spread across my pillow. When I'm happy, or angry, or excited, or sad, I want to tell you about it. On the day I die, I want to be holding your hand.'

'Is this what you really want?'

He nodded and swallowed hard. 'Yes.'

'Have you read Thomas Hardy?' She watched as he nodded. 'I think it's in *Far from the Madding Crowd*. He says to her, "When you look up, you'll see me." Something like that.' She wiped the tears from her own face. 'That's what I want. When I look up, I'll see you.'

He pulled her to him and they both began to weep in earnest, but it didn't take long for their bodies to respond in a fashion more typical of two healthy young people who are in love.

Mr Heath found Mrs Clay on his front porch with a box of seedling petunias and marigolds that she'd thinned from her own garden. Normally her would have grumbled his thanks and later thrown them away, but not now.

He thought about that thing, that so-called vision that had taken place in Mrs Clay's flowerbed. Almost as though she could read his mind, she assured him that these plants had been grown from the seeds of last year's flowers. He took them and planted them right away. It was silly, he knew that, but a vision wouldn't be a bad thing.

'Hi, Darryl.' Becky marched behind the counter of the Mercantile and helped herself to a bottle of aspirin.

'Hi, Becky. Something wrong?' She looked pale and pinched around her mouth.

'Headache. My head is about to split wide open thanks to that Teddy Crockett.'

'Lovers' quarrel?' He tried to sound jaunty and carefree, but even he could hear the jealous whine in his words.

'I told him I have to be away for two days next week and he makes it sound like I'm going off to the Belgian Congo for the next ten years.'

'I guess he's going to miss you. Can't blame a guy for that.' Darryl could understand Teddy missing her. He certainly missed her. He often walked into walls he missed her so much. He'd even taken to writing poetry and composing short songs as a means of expressing his sadness. He always destroyed the poetry and the songs as soon as they were written because even Darryl knew they were awful. But they helped. For an hour or two they would help.

'I don't think he's going to miss me at all. I think he's just gotten in the habit of being mad at me. He's been mad at me ever since I told him about buying into the mill.'

'Well, he had a dream about buying his own land and living there with you. Dreams die hard, Becky.' His did. He still dreamed of Becky.

'What about my dreams? He's never even asked me about my dreams.'

'What are your dreams?'

'My dream is to have a man in my life who loves me because I'm me and not something he thinks I am.'

'Oh, Becky.' Darryl didn't think about it for even a second. If he'd thought about it, he wouldn't have done it. Certainly not with Mrs Matthews and Hilda Crenshaw standing over there looking at fabric but listening to every word. Just as Mrs Harris walked in the front door he grabbed Becky's hand and led her to the back room. Quick as cats, the three women scuttled to the doorway to watch.

'Darryl, what are you doing?' Becky looked at him, her beautiful mouth slightly open in surprise.

'This.' Darryl kissed her like he'd never kissed a woman before. He was fairly certain that he was in fact inventing a new way to kiss. It must have been because this kiss was so soft and gentle, but at the same time so demanding and sweetly expressive. Darryl Strikings put so much of himself into that kiss that he almost passed out. He may have indeed passed out and not even noticed because Becky Johnson was hanging on to him so tight.

One of the ladies in the front cleared her throat, which made the couple come more or less to their senses. As they composed their faces and left the back room, neither of them even noticed that the little Madonna was back on Darryl's desk. Had they noticed, they would have seen that she appeared to be smiling.

★

Glory ran around to the front of her house, but Elmo Robinson's car wasn't there. She ran toward the library, all the time hoping and praying that he'd be inside. Halfway there she stopped and tore the red shoes off of her feet. They'd been too tight for over a month now, but she hated not to wear them. It had seemed ungrateful somehow, like tossing away a gift or the ability to saw a woman in half. But now they were just slowing her down and she couldn't let that happen because the rest of her felt as fast as lightning.

As she turned the last corner she saw them coming out of the library with their arms around each other. Elmo, even though it was the middle of the day and he didn't even know who might be watching, kissed her mama right on the mouth and ran his hands up inside her hair, which for some reason was no longer in a braid. Something about that hair being down made her one-hundred-percent, 'A'-plus-with-a-star certain that she finally was getting a daddy.

She squinted up at the sun. She wasn't sure, but she thought she saw it dancing.

EPILOGUE

Eva and Elmo were married in June of that year. Eva left the library and returned to painting. Elmo, in addition to publishing *The Guide*, started a small literary magazine, *Prairie Wind*, to which he was the major contributor. The magazine launched several careers, including his own.

In 1940 Elmo sold the magazine and the newspaper to devote more of his time to writing. Eva continued to paint and after the war they bought the old Jute place and opened it as an artists' colony. Soon, Eva's rather erotic-looking florals were being reprinted on posters and cards around the country. Elmo became a successful novelist as well as being a regular contributor to *The New Yorker* and *Vanity Fair*.

They died seventeen years later en route to Paris where they'd been planning to visit their daughter Glory. When their bodies were recovered from the wreckage of the plane, their fingers were found to be entwined.

Florence raised her two children, Baxter and June, in the Catholic faith. Hoyt became a vice-president of Reynolds Enterprises. They remained in the big house until their deaths.

Florence died in 1967 from heart disease and Hoyt died a year later. Most folks assumed that he had died of a broken heart.

Lucille Reynolds bought out Becky (Johnson) Strikings' share of the mill in 1938. When war was declared, lumber prices rose and Lucille was well placed to hear opportunity knocking. She grew the one mill into four and went on to build the largest furniture factory in the Midwest. Lucille died in 1991 in spite of most people thinking she'd never die because she couldn't take Reynolds Enterprises with her.

Becky Johnson married Darryl Strikings one week after Eva wed Elmo. After selling her share of the mill, she and Darryl ran the Mercantile until their retirement in 1967. Their son, Darryl Junior, runs it today, although he now specialises in antiques and Country Decor. The Mercantile still sells buttonhooks, but now they are priced at twenty dollars.

Father Greene never returned to drink and became a leading force behind the mystical Cursillo movement in America. In spite of lack of interest within the Catholic hierarchy, he never doubted that he and others had been touched by the miraculous. He died in 1968.

Baxter Gorman was drafted by the Army three weeks after he graduated from high school. He was sent to Korea where he lost part of his right foot to a land mine.

On his return, he went to college, earned a law degree and lives in Orlando, Florida, where he works for the Disney Corporation.

He is married and has three grown children. An avid golfer, last year he scored a hole in one.

Baby June started working in real estate after dropping out of her second year in college. She eventually became the president of a small savings and loan in Arizona. There was something of a scandal when the savings and loan failed, owing more than fifteen million dollars. There was an extensive investigation which resulted in charges, but she was never convicted. Today she lives back at the big house on a small trust fund which Florence and Hoyt had set up for their children.

Little Beau enlisted in the Marines on his eighteenth birthday. He died on Omaha Beach.

Pammy Reynolds became Sister Marie. She taught at St Dominic's School in New Orleans for forty years. Today she is retired and lives in the convent next door to St Dominic's. She sends a Christmas card to Glory every year and sometimes receives one in return. She never mentions the events of that year, but is often heard to say that she has been greatly blessed in her life.

Glory graduated from Sarah Lawrence with a degree in English Literature. Her parents wanted her to get a teaching degree so she sold her mother's car and fled to Paris. She spent the next five years painting, writing, waiting tables, and begging her family to wire her money.

In 1951 she met, and moved in with, Jack Phillips, the award-winning war correspondent. They moved to London in 1959 where they married four hours before their son was born. Jack died of self-inflicted gunshot wounds in 1962.

Glory moved herself and her son, Michael, to the old Jute place in 1963. In 1964 she published a novel which became an immediate bestseller and was later seen as one of the most influential books of the decade. She has written several other books, but none has been as well received as the first.

Today she is still living in the artists' colony at the old Jute place. She vividly recalls seeing the visions and communing with Evangeline, but readily admits that she has suffered from delusions in the past and in the present.

Warner Books now offers an exciting range of quality titles by both established and new authors. All of the books in this series are available from:

Little, Brown and Company (UK),
P.O. Box 11,
Falmouth,
Cornwall TR10 9EN.

Fax No: 01326 317444.
Telephone No: 01326 372400
E-mail: books@barni.avel.co.uk

Payments can be made as follows: cheque, postal order (payable to Little, Brown and Company) or by credit cards, Visa/Access. Do not send cash or currency. UK customers and B.F.P.O. please allow £1.00 for postage and packing for the first book, plus 50p for the second book, plus 30p for each additional book up to a maximum charge of £3.00 (7 books plus).

Overseas customers including Ireland, please allow £2.00 for the first book plus £1.00 for the second book, plus 50p for each additional book.

NAME (Block Letters) ....

....

ADDRESS ....

....

....

☐ I enclose my remittance for ....

☐ I wish to pay by Access/Visa Card

Number ☐☐☐☐☐☐☐☐☐☐☐☐☐☐☐☐

Card Expiry Date ☐☐☐☐